THE WORKS OF
BENJAMIN DISRAELI
EARL OF BEACONSFIELD

VOLUME
6

AMS PRESS
NEW YORK

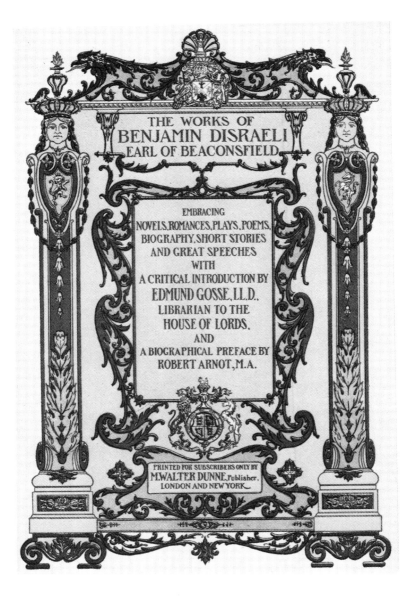

THE WORKS OF
BENJAMIN DISRAELI
EARL OF BEACONSFIELD

EMBRACING
NOVELS, ROMANCES, PLAYS, POEMS,
BIOGRAPHY, SHORT STORIES
AND GREAT SPEECHES
WITH
A CRITICAL INTRODUCTION BY
EDMUND GOSSE, LL.D.,
LIBRARIAN TO THE
HOUSE OF LORDS,
AND
A BIOGRAPHICAL PREFACE BY
ROBERT ARNOT, M.A.

PRINTED FOR SUBSCRIBERS ONLY BY
M. WALTER DUNNE, Publisher,
LONDON AND NEW YORK

Copyright, 1903, by M. Walter Dunne.

AFTER AN ORIGINAL DRAWING BY CLARE VICTOR
DWIGGINS.

'My first, my only, my enduring love!'

(See page 27, *Tragedy of Count Alarcos.*)

CONTARINI FLEMING

A PSYCHOLOGICAL ROMANCE

BY

BENJAMIN DISRAELI

EARL OF BEACONSFIELD

VOLUME II.

M. WALTER DUNNE
NEW YORK AND LONDON

Library of Congress Cataloging in Publication Data

Beaconsfield, Benjamin Disraeli, 1st Earl of, 1804-1881.
    Contarini Fleming: a psychological romance.

    (The Works of Benjamin Disraeli, Earl of Beaconsfield;
v. 5-6)
    Vol. 2 also includes the author's Count Alarcos and
Popanilla.
    Reprint of the 1904 ed. published by M. W. Dunne,
New York.
    I. Title.
PR4080.F76 vol. 5-6   [PR4081.5]   828'.8'09s   [823'.8]
ISBN 0-404-08800-7 (set)   76-12449

HOUSTON PUBLIC LIBRARY

Reprinted from the edition of 1904, New York and London
First AMS edition published in 1976
Manufactured in the United States of America

International Standard Book Number:
Complete Set: 0-404-08800-7
Volume 6: 0-404-08806-6

AMS PRESS INC.
NEW YORK, N.Y.

CONTENTS

CONTARINI FLEMING

PART THE FIFTH
(*Continued.*)

CONTENTS

PART THE SIXTH

PART THE SEVENTH

POPANILLA

CONTENTS

ILLUSTRATIONS

———

PART THE FIFTH.

[*CONTINUED*]

CHAPTER IV.

SEVILLE.

THERE is not a more beautiful and solemn temple in the world than the great Cathedral of Seville. When you enter from the glare of a Spanish sky, so deep is the staining of the glass, and so small and few the windows, that, for a moment, you feel in darkness. Gradually, the vast design of the Gothic artist unfolds itself to your vision: gradually rises up before you the profuse sumptuousness of the high altar, with its tall images, and velvet and gold hangings, its gigantic railings of brass and massy candlesticks of silver, all revealed by the dim and perpetual light of the sacred and costly lamps.

You steal with a subdued spirit over the marble pavement. All is still, save the hushed muttering of the gliding priests. Around you are groups of kneeling worshippers, some prostrate on the ground, some gazing upwards, with their arms crossed in mute devotion, some beating their breasts, and counting their consoling beads. Lo! the tinkling of a bell. The mighty organ bursts forth. Involuntarily you fall upon your knees, and listen to the rising chanting of the solemn choir. A procession moves from an adjoining chapel. A band of crimson acolytes advance waving censers, and the melody of their distant voices responds to the deep-toned invocations of the nearer canons. There are a vast number of chapels in this Cathedral on each side of the principal nave. Most of them are adorned with masterpieces of the Spanish school. Let us approach one. The light is good, and let us gaze through this iron railing upon the picture it encloses.

I see a saint falling upon his knees, and extending his enraptured arm to receive an infant God. What mingled love, enthusiasm, devotion, reverence, blend in the countenance of the holy man! But, oh! that glowing group of seraphim, sailing and smiling in the sunny splendour of that radiant sky, who has before gazed upon such grace, such ineffable and charming beauty! And in the background is an altar, whereon is a vase holding some lilies, that seem as if they were just gathered. There is but one artist who could have designed this picture; there is but one man who could have thus combined ideal grace with natural simplicity; there is but one man who could have painted that diaphanous heaven, and those fresh lilies. Inimitable Murillo!

AFTER AN ORIGINAL DRAWING BY FREDERICK MORGAN.

*A Spanish bull-fight taught me fully to comprehend
the rapturous exclamation of Panem et Circenses.*

(See page 3, *Contarini Fleming.*)

CHAPTER V.

A Spanish Bull-Fight.

SPANISH bull-fight taught me fully to comprehend the rapturous exclamation of 'Panem et Circenses!' The amusement apart, there is something magnificent in the assembled thousands of an amphitheatre. It is the trait in modern manners which most effectually recalls the nobility of antique pastimes.

The poetry of a bull-fight is much destroyed by the appearance of the cavaliers. Instead of gay, gallant knights bounding on caracoling steeds, three or four shapeless, unwieldy beings, cased in armour of stuffed leather, and looking more like Dutch burgomasters than Spanish chivalry, enter the lists on limping rips. The bull is, in fact, the executioner for the dogs; and an approaching bull-fight is a respite for any doomed steed throughout all Seville.

The tauridors, in their varying, fanciful, costly, and splendid dresses, compensate in a great measure for your disappointment. It is difficult to conceive a more brilliant band. These are ten or a dozen footmen, who engage the bull unarmed, distract him as he rushes at one of the cavaliers by unfolding and dashing before his eyes a glittering scarf, and saving themselves from an occasional chase by practised agility, which elicits great applause. The performance of these tauridors is, without doubt, the most graceful, the most exciting, and the most surprising portion of the entertainment.

The ample theatre is nearly full. Be careful to sit on the shady side. There is the suspense experienced at all public entertainments, only here upon a great scale. Men are gliding about selling fans and refreshments; the governor and his suite enter their box; a trumpet sounds! all is silent.

The knights advance, poising their spears, and for a moment trying to look graceful. The tauridors walk behind them, two by two. They proceed around and across the lists; they bow to the vice-regal party, and commend themselves to the Virgin, whose portrait is suspended above.

Another trumpet! A second and a third blast! The governor throws the signal; the den opens, and the bull bounds in. That first spring is very fine. The animal stands for a moment still, staring, stupefied. Gradually his hoof moves; he paws the ground; he dashes about the sand. The knights face him with their extended lances at due distance. The tauridors are still. One flies across him, and waves his scarf. The enraged bull makes at the nearest horseman; he is frustrated in his attack. Again he plants himself, lashes his tail, and rolls his eye. He makes another charge, and this time the glance of a spear does not drive him back. He gores the horse: rips up its body: the steed staggers and falls. The bull rushes at the rider, and his armour will not now preserve him; but, just as his awful horn is about to avenge his future fate, a skilful tauridor skims before him, and flaps his nostrils with his scarf. He flies after his new assailant, and immediately finds another. Now you are delighted by all the evolutions of this consummate band; occasionally they can save themselves only by leaping the barrier. The knight, in the meantime, rises, escapes, and mounts another steed.

The bull now makes a rush at another horseman; the horse dexterously veers aside. The bull rushes on, but the knight wounds him severely in the flank with his lance. The tauridors now appear, armed with darts. They rush with extraordinary swiftness and dexterity at the infuriated animal, plant their galling weapons in different parts of his body, and scud away. To some of their darts are affixed fireworks, which ignite by the pressure of the stab. The animal is then as bewildered as infuriate; the amphitheatre echoes to his roaring, and witnesses the greatest efforts of his rage. He flies at all, staggering and streaming with blood; at length, breathless and exhausted, he stands at bay, his black, swollen tongue hanging out, and his mouth covered with foam.

'Tis horrible! Throughout, a stranger's feelings are for the bull, although this even the fairest Spaniard cannot comprehend. As it is now evident that the noble victim can only amuse them by his death, there is a universal cry for the matador; and the matador, gaily dressed, appears amid a loud cheer. The matador is a great artist. Strong nerves must combine with great quickness and great experience to form an accomplished matador. It is a rare character, highly prized; their fame exists after their death, and different cities pride themselves on producing or possessing the eminent.

The matador plants himself before the bull, and shakes a red cloak suspended over a drawn sword. This last insult excites the lingering energy of the dying hero. He makes a violent charge: the mantle falls over his face, the sword enters his spine, and he falls amid thundering shouts. The death is instantaneous, without a struggle and without a groan. A car, decorated with flowers and ribbons, and drawn by oxen, now appears, and bears off the body in triumph.

I have seen eighteen horses killed in a bull-fight, and eight bulls; but the sport is not always in proportion to the slaughter. Sometimes the bull is a craven, and then, if, after recourse has been had to every mode of excitement, he will not charge, he is kicked out of the arena amid the jeers and hisses of the audience. Every act of skill on the part of the tauridors elicits applause; nor do the spectators hesitate, if necessary, to mark their temper by a contrary method. On the whole, it is a magnificent but barbarous spectacle; and, however disgusting the principal object, the accessories of the entertainment are so brilliant and interesting that, whatever may be their abstract disapprobation, those who have witnessed a Spanish bull-fight will not be surprised at the passionate attachment of the Spanish people to their national pastime.

CHAPTER VI.

A Day in Spain.

HERE is a calm voluptuousness about Spanish life that wonderfully accorded with the disposition in which I then found myself; so that, had my intellect been at command, I do not know any land where I would more willingly have indulged it. The imagination in such a country is ever at work, and beauty and grace are not scared away by those sounds and sights, those constant cares and changing feelings that are the proud possession of lands which consider themselves more blessed.

You rise early, and should breakfast lightly, although a table covered with all fruits renders that rather difficult to those who have a passion for the most delightful productions of nature, and would willingly linger over a medley of grape, and melon, and gourd, and prickly pear. In the morning you never quit the house; and these are hours which might be delightfully employed, under the inspiration of a climate which is itself poetry; for it sheds over everything a golden hue which does not exist in the illuminated objects themselves. I could then indulge

(7)

only in a calm reverie, for I found the least exertion
of mind instantly aggravate all my symptoms. To
exist, and to feel existence more tolerable, to observe
and to remember to record a thought that suddenly
starts up, or to catch a new image which glances over
the surface of the mind, this was still left me.
But the moment that I attempted to meditate or combine, to ascertain a question that was doubtful, or in
any way to call the higher powers of intellect into
play, that moment I found myself a lost man; my
brain seemed to palpitate with frenzy; an indescribable
feeling of idiocy came over me, and for hours I was
plunged in a state of the darkest despair. When the
curse had subsided to its usual dull degree of horror,
my sanguine temper called me again to life and hope.
My general health had never been better, and this
supported me under the hardships of Spanish travelling. I never for a moment gave way to my real
feelings, unless under a paroxysm, and then I fled to
solitude. But I resolved to pursue this life only for
a year, and if at the end of that period I found no
relief, the convent and the cloister should at least
afford me repose.

But 'tis three o'clock, and at this time we should
be at dinner. The Spanish kitchen is not much to
my taste, being rich and rather gross; and yet, for a
pleasant as well as a picturesque dish, commend me
to an olla podrida! After dinner comes the famed
siesta. I generally slept for two hours. I think this
practice conducive to health in hot climes; the aged,
however, are apt to carry it to excess. By the time
you have risen and made your toilet, it is the hour
to steal forth, and call upon any agreeable family
whose tertulla you may choose to honour, which you

do, after the first time, uninvited, and with them you take your chocolate. This is often in the air, under the colonnade of the patio, or interior quadrangle of the mansion. Here you while away the time with music and easy talk, until it is cool enough for the Alameda, or public promenade. At Cadiz and Malaga, and even at Seville, up the Guadalquivir, you are sure of a delightful breeze from the water. The sea-breeze comes like a spirit; the effect is quite magical. As you are lolling in listless languor in the hot and perfumed air, an invisible guest comes dancing into the party, and touches all with an enchanting wand. All start; all smile. It has come; it is the sea-breeze. There is much discussion whether it be as strong as the night before or whether weaker. The ladies furl their fans and seize their mantillas; the cavaliers stretch their legs and give signs of life. All arise. You offer your arm to Dolores or Catalina, and in ten minutes you are on the Alameda. What a change! All is now life and animation. Such bowing, such kissing, such fluttering of fans, such gentle criticisms of gentle friends! But the fan is the most wonderful part of the whole scene. A Spanish lady, with her fan, might shame the tactics of a troop of horse. Now she unfurls it with the slow pomp and conscious elegance of the bird of Juno; now she flutters it with all the languor of a listless beauty, now with all the liveliness of a vivacious one. Now, in the midst of a very tornado, she closes it with a whirr, which makes you start. In the midst of your confusion Dolores taps you on your elbow; you turn round to listen, and Catalina pokes you in your side. Magical instrument! In this land it speaks a particular language, and gallantry requires no other mode to express its most subtle conceits or its most unreasonable demands than this delicate machine. Yet we should remember that here, as in the north, it is not confined to the delightful sex. The cavalier also has his fan; and, that the habit may not be considered an indication of effeminacy, learn that in this scorching clime the soldier will not mount guard without this solace.

But night wears on. We seat ourselves, we take a final, a fanciful refreshment, which also, like the confectionery of Venice, I have since discovered to be oriental. Again we stroll. Midnight clears the public walk, but few Spanish families retire until a much later hour. A solitary bachelor, like myself, still wanders, lingering where the dancers softly move in the warm moonlight, and indicate, by the grace of their eager gestures and the fulness of their languid eyes, the fierceness of their passion. At length the castanet is silent, the tinkling of the last · guitar dies away, and the Cathedral clock breaks up your reverie. You, too, seek your couch, and, amid a sweet flow of loveliness, and light, and music, and fresh air, thus dies a day in Spain!

CHAPTER VII.

SPANISH WOMEN.

T HE Spanish women are very interesting. What we associate with the idea of female beauty is not perhaps very common in this country. There are seldom those seraphic countenances which strike you dumb, 'or blind; but faces in abundance, which will never pass without commanding admiration. Their charms consist in their sensibility. Each incident, every person, every word, touches the fancy of a Spanish lady, and her expressive features are constantly confuting the creed of the Moslemim. But there is nothing quick, harsh, or forced about her. She is unaffected, and not at all French. Her eyes gleam rather than sparkle; she speaks with vivacity, but in sweet tones, and there is in all her carriage, particularly when she walks, a certain dignified grace, which never deserts her, and which is remarkable.

The general female dress in Spain is of black silk, a *basquina,* and a black silk shawl, a *mantilla,* with which they usually envelop their heads. As they walk along in this costume in an evening, with their soft dark eyes dangerously conspicuous, you willingly believe in their universal charms. They are remarkable for the beauty of their hair. Of this they are proud, and indeed its luxuriance is equalled only by the attention which they lavish on its culture. I have seen a young girl of fourteen, whose hair reached her feet, and was as glossy as the curl of a Contessa. All day long even the lowest order are brushing, curling, and arranging it. A fruit-woman has her hair dressed with as much care as the Duchess of Ossuna. In the summer they do not wear their mantillas over their heads, but show their combs, which are of great size. The fashion of these combs varies constantly. Every two or three months you may observe a new form. It is the part of the costume of which a Spanish woman is most proud. The moment that a new comb appears, even a servant wench will run to the melter's with her old one, and thus, at the cost of a dollar or two, appear the next holiday in the newest style. These combs are worn at the back of the head. They are of tortoise-shell, and with the fashionable they are white. I sat next to a lady of high distinction at a bull-fight at Seville. She was the daughter-in-law of the captain-general of the province, and the most beautiful Spaniard I ever met with. Her comb was white, and she wore a mantilla of blonde, without doubt extremely valuable, for it was very dirty. The effect, however, was charming. Her hair was glossy black, her eyes like an antelope's, and all her other features deliciously soft. She was further adorned, which is rare in Spain, with a rosy cheek, for in Spain our heroines are rather sallow. But they counteract this slight defect by never appearing until twilight, which calls them from their bowers, fresh, though languid, from the late siesta.

The only fault of the Spanish beauty is, that she too soon indulges in the magnificence of *embonpoint*. There are, however, many exceptions. At seventeen, a Spanish beauty is poetical. Tall, lithe, and clear, and graceful as a jennet, who can withstand the summer lightning of her soft and languid glance! As she advances, if she do not lose her shape, she resembles Juno rather than Venus. Majestic she ever is; and if her feet be less twinkling than in her first bolero, look on her hand, and you'll forgive them all.

CHAPTER VIII.

THE SANTIAGOS AGAIN.

T MALAGA, I again met the Santiagos, and, through their medium, became acquainted with a young French nobleman, who had served in the expedition against Algiers, and retired from the army in consequence of the recent revolution in his native country. The rapturous tone in which he spoke of the delights of oriental life, and of his intention to settle permanently in Egypt, or some other part of the Ottoman Empire, excited in me a great desire to visit those countries for which my residence in a Grecian isle had somewhat prepared me. And on inquiry at the quay, finding that there was a vessel then in harbour, bound for the Ionian Isles, and about to sail, I secured our passage, and in a few days quitted the Iberian Peninsula.

CHAPTER IX.

MODERN CORFU.

N SIGHT of the ancient Corcyra, I could not forget that the island I beheld had given rise to one of the longest, most celebrated, and most fatal of ancient wars. The immortal struggle of the Peloponnesus was precipitated, if not occasioned, by a feeling of colonial jealousy. There is a great difference between ancient and modern colonies. A modern colony is a commercial enterprise, an ancient colony was a political settlement. In the emigration of our citizens, hitherto, we have merely sought the means of acquiring wealth; the ancients, when their brethren quitted their native shores, wept and sacrificed, and were reconciled to the loss of their fellow-citizens solely by the constraint of stern necessity, and the hope that they were about to find easier subsistence, and to lead a more cheerful and commodious life. I believe that a great revolution is at hand in our system of colonisation, and that Europe will recur to the principles of the ancient polity.

Old Corcyra is now the modern Corfu; a lovely isle, with all that you hope to meet with in a Grecian sea, gleamy waters, woody bays, the cypress, the

olive, and the vine, a clear sky and a warm sun. I
learnt here that a civil war raged in Albania and the
neighbouring provinces of European Turkey; and, in
spite of all advice, I determined, instead of advancing
into Greece, to attempt to penetrate to the Turkish
camp, and witness, if possible, a campaign. With
these views, I engaged a vessel to carry me to
Prevesa.

CHAPTER X.

I WAS now in the Ambracian Gulf, those famous waters where the soft Triumvir gained greater glory by defeat than attends the victory of harsher warriors. The site is not unworthy of the beauty of Cleopatra. From the sinuosity of the land, this gulf appears like a vast lake, walled in on all sides by mountains more or less distant. The dying glory of a Grecian eve bathed with warm light a thousand promontories and gentle bays, and infinite undulations of purple outline. Before me was Olympus, whose austere peak yet glittered in the sun; a bend of the shore concealed from me the islands of Ulysses and of Sappho.

As I gazed upon this scene, I thought almost with disgust of the savage splendour and turbulent existence in which, perhaps, I was about to mingle. I recurred to the feelings in the indulgence of which I could alone find felicity, and from which an inexorable destiny seemed resolved to shut me out.

Hark! the clang of the barbaric horn, and the wild clash of the cymbal! A body of Turkish infantry marched along the shore. I landed, and heard for the

first time of the massacre of the principal rebel Beys
at Monastir, at a banquet given by the Grand Vizir,
on pretence of arranging all differences. My host, a
Frank experienced in the Turkish character, checked
me as I poured forth my indignation at this savage
treachery. 'Live a little longer in these countries before you hazard an opinion as to their conduct. Do
you indeed think that the rebel Beys of Albania were
so simple as to place the slightest trust in the Vizir's
pledge? The practice of politics in the East may be
defined by one word, dissimulation. The most wary
dissembler is the consummate statesman. The Albanian chiefs went up to the divan in full array, and
accompanied by a select body of their best troops.
They resolved to overawe the Vizir; perhaps they even
meditated, with regard to him, the very stroke which
he put in execution against themselves. He was the
most skilful dissembler, that is all. His manner threw
them off their guard. With their troops bivouacking
in the court-yard, they did not calculate that his
highness could contrive to massacre the troops by an
ambush, and would dare, at the same moment, to
attack the leaders by their very attendants at the
banquet. There is no feeling of indignation in the
country at the treachery of the conqueror, though a
very strong sentiment of rage, and mortification, and
revenge.'

I learnt that the Grand Vizir had rejoined the main
army, and was supposed to have advanced to Yanina,
the capital; that, in the meantime, the country between this city and the coast was overrun with
prowling bands, the remnants of the rebel army, who,
infuriate and flying, massacred, burnt, and destroyed,
all persons and all property. This was an agreeable

prospect. My friend dissuaded me from my plans; but, as I was unwilling to relinquish them, he recommended me to sail up to Salora, and thence journey to Arta, where I might seek assistance from Kalio Bey, a Moslem chief, one of the most powerful and wealthy of the Albanian nobles, and ever faithful to the Porte.

To Salora I consequently repaired, and the next day succeeded in reaching Arta: a town once as beautiful as its site, and famous for its gardens, but now a mass of ruins. The whole place was razed to the ground, the minaret of the principal mosque alone untouched; and I shall never forget the effect of the Muezzin, with his rich, and solemn, and sonorous voice, calling us to adore God in the midst of all this human havoc.

I found the Bey of Arta, keeping his state, which, notwithstanding the surrounding desolation, was not contemptible, in a tenement which was not much better than a large shed. He was a handsome, stately man, grave but not dull, and remarkably mild and bland in his manner. His polished courtesy might perhaps be ascribed to his recent imprisonment in Russia, where he was treated with so much consideration that he mentioned it to me. I had lived in such complete solitude in Candia, and had there been so absorbed by passion, that I really was much less acquainted with Turkish manners than I ought to have been. I must confess that it was with some awe that, for the first time in my life, I entered the divan of a great Turk, and found myself sitting cross-legged on the right hand of a Bey, smoking an amber-mouthed chiboque, sipping coffee, and paying him compliments through an interpreter.

There were several guests in the room, chiefly his officers. They were, as the Albanians in general, finely-shaped men, with expressive countenances and spare forms. Their picturesque dress is celebrated; though, to view it with full effect, it should be seen upon an Albanian. The long hair, and the small cap, the crimson velvet vest and jacket, embroidered and embossed with golden patterns of the most elegant and flowing forms, the white and ample kilt, the ornamented buskins, and the belt full of silver-sheathed arms: it is difficult to find humanity in better plight.

There was a considerable appearance of affairs and of patriarchal solicitude in the divan of Kalio Bey. It is possible that it was not always as busy, and that he was not uninfluenced by the pardonable vanity of impressing a stranger with his importance and beneficence. Many persons entered; and, casting off their slippers at the door, advanced and parleyed. To some was given money, to all directions; and the worthy Bey doled out his piastres and his instructions with equal solemnity. At length I succeeded in calling my host's attention to the purport of my visit, and he readily granted me an escort of twenty of his Albanians. He was even careful that they should be picked men; and calculating that I might reach the capital in two days, he drew his writing materials from his belt, and gave me a letter to a Turkish bimbashee, or colonel, who was posted with his force in the mountains I was about to pass, and under the only roof which probably remained between Arta and Yanina. He pressed me to remain his guest, though there was little, he confessed, to interest me; but I was anxious to advance, and so, after many thanks, I parted from the kind Kalio Bey.

CHAPTER XI.

BY DAYBREAK we departed, and journeyed for many hours over a wild range of the Ancient Pindus, stopping only once for a short rest at a beautiful fountain of marble. Here we all dismounted and lighted a fire, boiled the coffee, and smoked our pipes. There were many fine groups; but little Spiro was not so much delighted as I expected, at finding himself once more among his countrymen.

An hour before sunset we found ourselves at a vast but dilapidated khan, as big as a Gothic castle, situate on a high range, and built, for the accommodation of travellers from the capital to the coast, by the great Ali Pacha, when his long and unmolested reign permitted that sagacious ruler to develop, in a country which combines the excellences of Western Asia and Southern Europe, some of the intended purposes of a beneficent Nature. This khan had now been converted into a military post; and here we found the Turkish commander, to whom Kalio Bey had given me a letter. He was a young man of elegant and pleasing exterior, but unluckily could not understand a word of Greek, and we had no interpreter. What was to be done? Proceed we could not, for there was not an inhabited place before Yanina; and here was I sitting before sunset on the same divan with my host, who had entered the place to receive me, and would not leave the room while I was there, without the power of communicating an idea. I was in despair, and also very hungry, and could not, therefore, in the course of an hour or two, plead fatigue as an excuse for sleep; for I was ravenous, and anxious to know what prospect of food existed in this wild and desolate mansion. So we smoked. It is a great resource. But this wore out; and it was so ludicrous, smoking and looking at each other, and dying to talk, and then exchanging pipes by way of compliment, and then pressing our hands to our hearts by way of thanks. At last it occurred to me that I had some brandy, and that I would offer my host a glass, which might serve as a hint for what should follow so vehement a schnapps. Mashallah! the effect was, indeed, miraculous. My mild friend smacked his lips, and instantly asked for another cup. We drank it in coffee-cups. A bottle of brandy was despatched in quicker time and fairer proportions than had ever solemnised the decease of the same portion of Burgundy. We were extremely gay. The bimbashee ordered some dried figs, talking all the time, and indulging in graceful pantomime, examining my pistols, inquiring about percussion locks, which greatly surprised him, handing his own, more ornamented although less effective weapons for my inspection; and finally making out Greek enough to misunderstand most ridiculously every observation communicated. But all was taken in good part, and I never met with such a jolly fellow.

In the meantime I became painfully ravenous; for the dry, round, unsugary fig of Albania is a great whetter. At last I asked for bread. The bimbashee gravely bowed, and said, 'Leave it to me, take no thought,' and nothing more occurred. I prepared myself for hungry dreams, when, to my great astonishment and delight, a capital supper was brought in, accompanied, to my equal horror, by wine. We ate with our fingers. It was the first time I had performed such an operation. You soon get used to it, and dash, but in turn, at the choice morsels with perfect coolness. One with a basin and ewer is in attendance, and the whole process is by no means so terrible as it would at first appear to European habits. For drinking, we really drank with a rapidity which, with me, was unprecedented: the wine was not bad; but had it been poison, the forbidden juice was such a compliment from a Moslem that I must quaff it all. We quaffed it in rivers. The bimbashee called for brandy. Unfortunately there was another bottle. We drank it all. The room turned round; the wild attendants, who sat at our feet, seemed dancing in strange whirls; the bimbashee shook hands with me: he shouted Italian, I Turkish. 'Buono, buono,' he had caught up; 'Pecche, pecche,' was my rejoinder,' which, let me inform the reader, although I do not even now know much more, is very good Turkish. He shouted; he would shake hands again. I remember no more.

In the middle of the night I awoke. I found myself sleeping on the divan, rolled up in its sacred carpet. The bimbashee had wisely reeled to the fire. The thirst I felt was like that of Dives. All were sleeping except two, who kept up during the night the great wood fire. I rose, lightly stepping over my sleeping companions, and the shining arms which here and there informed me that the dark mass wrapped up in a capote was a human being. I found Abraham's bosom in a flagon of water. I think I must have drunk a gallon at a draught. I looked at the wood fire, and thought of the blazing blocks in the hall of Jonsterna; asked myself whether I were indeed in the mountain fastness of a Turkish chief; and, shrugging my shoulders, went to sleep, and woke without a headache.

CHAPTER XII.

A Caravan.

PARTED from my jovial host the next morning very cordially, and gave him my pipe, as a memorial of our having got tipsy together.

After crossing one more range of steep mountains we descended into a vast plain, over which we journeyed for some hours, the country presenting the same mournful aspect which I had too long observed; villages in ruins, and perfectly desolate; khans deserted, and fortresses razed to the ground; olive woods burnt up, and fruit trees cut down. So complete had been the work of destruction, that I often unexpectedly found my horse stumbling amid the foundations of ⸱ village, and what at first appeared the dry bed of a torrent often turned out to be the backbone of the skeleton of a ravaged town. At the end of the plain, immediately backed by lofty mountains, and jutting into the beautiful lake that bears its name, we suddenly came upon the city of Yanina; suddenly, for a long tract of gradually rising ground had hitherto concealed it from our sight. At the distance from which I first beheld it, this city, once, if

(25)

not the largest, one of the most thriving and brilliant
in the Turkish dominions, was still imposing; but
when I entered, I soon found that all preceding desolation had been only preparative to the vast scene of
destruction now before me. We proceeded through a
street winding in its course, but of great length.
Ruined houses, mosques with their towers only standing, streets utterly razed: these are nothing. We met
with great patches of ruin a mile square, as if an
army of locusts had had the power of desolating the
works of man, as well as those of God. The great
heart of the city was a sea of ruins: arches and pillars, isolated and shattered, still here and there jutting
forth, breaking the uniformity of the annihilation, and
turning the horrible into the picturesque. The great
bazaar, itself a little town, had been burnt down only
a few days before my arrival by an infuriate band of
Albanian warriors, who heard of the destruction of
their chiefs by the Grand Vizir. They revenged themselves on tyranny by destroying civilisation.

But while the city itself presented this mournful
appearance, its other characteristics were anything
but sad. At this moment a swarming population,
arrayed in every possible and fanciful costume, buzzed
and bustled in all directions. As I passed on, and myself of course not unobserved, where a Frank had not
penetrated for nine years, a thousand objects attracted
my restless attention and roving eye. Everything
was so strange and splendid, that for a moment I
forgot that this was an extraordinary scene even for
the East, and gave up my fancy to a full credulity in
the now almost obsolete magnificence of oriental life.
I longed to write an Eastern tale. Military chieftains,
clothed in brilliant colours and sumptuous furs, and

attended by a cortège of officers equally splendid, continually passed us. Now, for the first time, a dervish saluted me: and now a delhi, with his high cap, reined in his desperate steed, as the suite of some pacha blocked up some turning of the street. It seemed to me that my first day in a Turkish city brought before me all the popular characteristics of which I had read, and which I expected occasionally to observe during a prolonged residence. I remember, as I rode on this day, I observed a Turkish sheikh, in his entirely green vestments; a scribe, with his writing materials in his girdle; an ambulatory physician and his boy. I gazed about me with a mingled feeling of delight and wonder.

Suddenly a strange, wild, unearthly drum is heard, and at the end of the street a huge camel, with a slave sitting cross-legged on its neck, and beating a huge kettledrum, appears, and is the first of an apparently interminable procession of his Arabian brethren. The camels were large; they moved slowly, and were many in number. There were not fewer than one hundred moving on one by one. To me, who had till then never seen a caravan, it was a novel and impressive spectacle. All immediately hustled out of the way of the procession, and seemed to shrink under the sound of the wild drum. The camels bore corn for the Vizir's troops encamped without the walls.

At length I reached the house of a Greek physician, to whom I carried letters. My escort repaired to the quarters of their chieftain's son, who was in the city in attendance on the Grand Vizir, and for myself I was glad enough once more to stretch my wearied limbs under a Christian roof.

CHAPTER XIII.

THE PACHA OF YANINA.

HE next day I signified my arrival to the Kehaya Bey of his highness, and delivered, according to custom, a letter, with which I had been kindly provided by an eminent foreign functionary. The ensuing morning was fixed for my audience. I repaired at the appointed hour to the celebrated fortress palace of Ali Pacha, which, although greatly battered by successive sieges, is still habitable, and still affords a fair idea of its pristine magnificence. Having passed through the gates of the fortress, I found myself in a number of small dingy streets, like those in the liberties of a royal castle. These were all full of life, stirring and excited. At length I reached a grand square, in which, on an ascent, stands the palace. I was hurried through courts and corridors, full of guards, and pages, and attendant chiefs, and, in short, every variety of Turkish population: for among the Orientals all depends upon one brain; and we, with our subdivisions of duty, and intelligent and responsible deputies, can form no idea of the labour of a Turkish premier. At length I came to a vast irregu-

(28)

lar apartment, serving as the immediate antechamber of the hall of audience. This was the finest thing of the kind I had ever yet seen. I had never mingled in so picturesque an assembly. Conceive a chamber of great dimensions, full of the choicest groups of an oriental population, each individual waiting by appointment for an audience, and probably about to wait forever. It was a sea of turbans, and crimson shawls, and golden scarfs, and ornamented arms. I marked with curiosity the haughty Turk, stroking his beard, and waving his beads; the proud Albanian, strutting with his tarragan, or cloak, dependent on one shoulder, and touching, with impatient fingers, his silver-sheathed arms; the olive-visaged Asiatic, with his enormous turban and flowing robes, gazing, half with wonder and half with contempt, at some scarlet colonel of the newly disciplined troops, in his gorgeous but awkward imitation of Frank uniforms; the Greek still servile, though no more a slave; the Nubian eunuch, and the Georgian page.

In this chamber, attended by the drogueman, who presented me, I remained about ten minutes; too short a time. I never thought I could have lived to wish to kick my heels in a ministerial ante-chamber. Suddenly I was summoned to the awful presence of the pillar of the Turkish Empire, the man who has the reputation of being the mainspring of the new system of regeneration, the renowned Redschid, an approved warrior, a consummate politician, unrivalled as a dissembler in a country where dissimulation is the principal portion of moral culture. The hall was vast, entirely covered with gilding and arabesques, inlaid with tortoise-shell and mother-of-pearl. Here I beheld, squatted in a corner of the large divan, a little, ferocious-looking, shrivelled, care-worn man, plainly dressed, with a brow covered with wrinkles, and a countenance clouded with anxiety and thought. I entered the shed-like divan of the kind and comparatively insignificant Kalio Bey with a feeling of awe; I seated myself on the divan of the Grand Vizir of the Ottoman Empire, who, as my attendant informed me, had destroyed in the course of the last three months, *not* in war, 'upwards of four thousand of my acquaintance,' with the self-possession of a morning visit. At a distance from us, in a group on his left hand, were his secretary and his immediate suite. The end of the saloon was lined with tchawooshes, or lackeys in waiting, in crimson dresses, with long silver canes.

Some compliments passed between us. I congratulated his highness on the pacification of Albania; and he rejoined that the peace of the world was his only object, and the happiness of his fellow-creatures his only wish. Pipes and coffee were brought, and then his highness waved his hand, and in an instant the chamber was cleared.

He then told me that he had read the letter: that the writer was one whom he much loved, and that I should join the army, although of course I was aware that, as a Frank, I could hold no command. I told him that such was not my desire, but that, as I intended to proceed to Stamboul, it would be gratifying to me to feel that I had co-operated, however humbly, in the cause of a sovereign whom I greatly admired. A Tartar now arrived with despatches, and I rose to retire, for I could perceive that the Vizir was overwhelmed with business, and, although courteous, moody and anxious. He did not press me to remain,

AFTER AN ORIGINAL DRAWING BY FREDERICK MORGAN.

A little ferocious-looking, careworn man.
(See page 30, *Contarini Fleming*.)

but desired that I would go and visit his son, Amin Pacha, to whose care he consigned me.

Amin, Pacha of Yanina, was a youth of eighteen, but apparently ten years older. He was the reverse of his father: incapable in affairs, refined in manners, plunged in debauchery, and magnificent in dress. I found him surrounded by his favourites and flatterers, reclining on his divan in a fanciful hussar uniform of blue cloth, covered with gold and diamonds, and worn under a Damascus pelisse of thick maroon silk, lined with white fox furs. I have seldom met with a man of more easy address and more polished breeding. He paid many compliments to the Franks, and expressed his wish to make a visit to the English at Corfu. As I was dressed in regimentals, he offered to show me his collection of military costumes, which had been made for him principally at Vienna. He also ordered one of his attendants to bring his manuscript book of cavalry tactics, which were unfortunately all explained to me. I mention these slight traits to show how eagerly the modern Turks pique themselves on European civilisation. After smoking and eating sweetmeats, a custom indicative of friendship, he proposed that I should accompany him to the camp, where he was about to review a division of the forces. I assented. We descended together, and I found a boy, with a barb magnificently caparisoned, waiting at the portal: of both these Amin begged my acceptance. Mounting, we proceeded to the camp; nor do I think that the cortège of the young pacha consisted of fewer than a hundred persons, who were all officers, either of his household or of the cavalry regiment which he commanded.

CHAPTER XIV.

A TURKISH DINNER.

GLADLY believe that the increased efficiency of the Turkish troops compensates for their shorn splendour and sorry appearance. A shaven head, covered with a tight red cloth cap, a small blue jacket of coarse cloth, huge trousers of the same material, puckered out to the very stretch of art, yet sitting tight to the knee and calf, mean accoutrements, and a pair of dingy slippers, behold the successor of the superb janissary! Yet they perform their manœuvres with precision, and have struggled even with the Russian infantry with success. The officer makes a better appearance. His dress, although of the same fashion, is of scarlet, and of fine cloth. It is richly embroidered, and the colonel wears upon his breast a star and crescent of diamonds. At the camp of Yanina, however, I witnessed a charge of delhis with their scimitars, and a more effective cavalry I never wish to lead.

We returned to the city, and I found that apartments were allotted to me in the palace, whither Lausanne and the rest had already repaired. In the evening the Vizir sent to me the first singer in Turkey, with several musicians. The singer chanted for an hour, in a wild, piercing voice, devoid both of harmony and melody, a triumphant ballad on the recent massacre of Veli Bey and his rebel coadjutors. Nothing appears to me more frightful than Turkish music; yet it produces on those who are accustomed to it a great effect, and my room was filled with strangers, who hastened to listen to the enchanting and exciting strain. The Turkish music is peculiar, and different from that of other Eastern nations. I have seldom listened to more simple and affecting melodies than those with which the boatmen on the Nile are wont to soothe their labours.

The dancing girls followed, and were more amusing; but I had not then seen the Almeh of Egypt.

A week flew away at Yanina in receiving and returning visits from pachas, agas, and selictars, in smoking pipes, sipping coffee, and tasting sweetmeats. Each day the Vizir, or his son, sent me provisions ready prepared from their table, and indicated by some attention their considerate kindness. There is no character in the world higher bred than a Turk of rank. Some of these men, too, I found intelligent, deeply interested in the political amelioration of their country, and warm admirers of Peter the Great. I remember with pleasure the agreeable hours I have spent in the society of Mehemet Aga, selictar of the Pacha of Lepanto, a warrior to whom the obstinate resistance of Varna is mainly to be attributed, and a remarkably enlightened man. Yet even he could not emancipate himself from their fatalism. For I remember, when once conversing with him on the equipments of the cavalry, a subject in which he was much interested, I suggested to him the propriety of a corps of cuirassiers. 'A cuirass cannot stop the ball that bears your fate,' he replied, shrugging his shoulders and exclaiming 'Mashallah!'

While I was leading this novel and agreeable life, news arrived that the Pacha of Scutari, who had placed himself at the head of the insurgent janissaries, and was the champion of the old party, had entered Albania at the head of sixty thousand men to avenge the massacre of the Beys.

CHAPTER XV.

A LIVELY SCRIMMAGE.

HE Grand Vizir set off the same night with ten thousand men, reached Ochrida, by forced marches, attacked and routed a division of the rebel troops before they supposed him to be apprised of their movements, and again encamped at Monastir, sending urgent commands to Yanina for his son to advance with the rest of the army. We met his Tartar on our march, and the divisions soon joined. After a day's rest, we advanced, and entered the Pachalik of Scutari.

The enemy, to our surprise, avoided an engagement. The fierce undisciplined warriors were frightened at our bayonets. They destroyed all before us, and hung with their vigilant cavalry on our exhausted rear. We had advanced on one side to Scutari; on the other we had penetrated into Romelia. We carried everything before us, but we were in want of supplies, our soldiers were without food, and a skilful general and disciplined troops might have cut off all our communications.

Suddenly, the order was given to retreat. We retreated slowly and in excellent order. Two regiments of the newly-organised cavalry, with whom I had the honour to act, covered the rear, and were engaged in almost constant skirmishing with the enemy. This skirmishing is exciting. We concentrated, and again encamped at Ochrida.

We were in hopes of now drawing the enemy into an engagement, but he was wary. In this situation, the Vizir directed that in the night a powerful division under the command of Mehemet Pacha of Lepanto (he who stabbed Ali Pacha) should fall back to Monastir with the artillery, and take up a position in the mountains. The ensuing night, his highness, after having previously spiked some useless guns, scattered about some tents and baggage wagons, and given a general appearance of a hurried and disorderly retreat, withdrew in the same direction. The enemy instantly pursued, rushed on, and attacked us full of confidence. We contented ourselves by protecting our rear, but still retreated, and appeared anxious to avoid an engagement. In the evening, having entered the mountain passes, and reached the post of the Pacha of Lepanto, we drew up in battle array.

It was a cloudy morning among the mountains, and some time before the mist cleared away. The enemy appeared to be in great force, filling the gorge through which we had retreated, and encamped on all the neighbouring eminences. When they perceived us, a large body instantly charged with the famous janissary shout, the terror of which I confess. I was cold, somewhat exhausted, for I had scarcely tasted food for two days, and for a moment my heart sank.

They were received, to their surprise, by a well-directed discharge of artillery from our concealed batteries. They seemed checked. Our ranks opened, and a body of five thousand fresh troops instantly charged them with the bayonet. This advance was sublime, and so exciting that, what with the shouts and cannonading, I grew mad, and longed to rush forward. The enemy gave way. Their great force was in cavalry, which could not act among the mountains. They were evidently astonished and perplexed. In a few minutes they were routed. The Vizir gave orders for a general charge and pursuit, and in a few minutes I was dashing over the hills in rapid chase of all I could catch, cutting, firing, shouting, and quite persuaded that a battle was, after all, the most delightful pastime in the world.

The masses still charging, the groups demanding quarter, the single horseman bounding over the hills, the wild, scared steeds without a rider, snorting and plunging, the dense smoke clearing away, the bright arms and figures flashing ever and anon in the moving obscurity, the wild shouts, the strange and horrible spectacles, the solitary shots and shrieks now heard in the decreasing uproar and the general feeling of energy, and peril, and triumph, it was all wonderful, and was a glorious moment in existence.

The enemy was scattered like chaff. To rally them was impossible; and the chiefs, in despair, were foremost in flight. They offered no resistance, and the very men who, in the morning, would have been the first to attack a battery, sabre in hand, now yielded in numbers, without a struggle, to an individual. There was a great slaughter, a vast number of prisoners, and plunder without end. My tent was filled with rich arms, and shawls, and stuffs, and embroidered saddles. Lausanne and Tita were the next day both clothed in splendid Albanian dresses, and little Spiro plundered the dead as became a modern Greek.

I reached my tent, dismounted from my horse, and leant upon it from exhaustion. An Albanian came forward, and offered a flask of Zitza wine. I drank it at a draught, and assuredly experienced the highest sensual pleasure. I took up two Cachemire shawls, and a gun mounted in silver, and gave them to the Albanian. Lucky is he who is courteous in the hour of plunder.

The Vizir I understood to be at Ochrida, and I repaired to that post over the field of battle. The moon had risen, and tinged with its white light all the prominent objects of the scene of destruction; groups of bodies, and now and then a pallid face, distinct and fierce; steeds and standards, and arms, and shattered wagons. Here and there a moving light showed that the plunderer was still at his work; and, occasionally, seated on the carcass of a horse, and sometimes on the corpse of a human being, were some of the fortunate survivors, smoking with admirable coolness, as if there were not on earth such a fearful mystery as death.

I found the victorious Redschid seated on a carpet in the moonlight in a cypress grove, and surrounded by attendants, to whom he was delivering instructions and distributing rewards. He appeared as calm and grave as usual. Perceiving him thus engaged I mingled with the crowd, and stood aside, leaning on my sword; but, observing me, he beckoned to me to advance, and pointing to his carpet, he gave me the pipe of honour from his own lips. As I seated myself by his side, I could not help viewing this extraordinary man with great interest and curiosity. A short time back, at this very place, he had perpetrated an act which would have rendered him infamous in a civilised land; the avengers meet him, as if by fate, on the very scene of his bloody treachery, and — he is victorious.   What is life?

So much for the battle of Bitoglia or Monastir, a very pretty fray, although not as much talked of as Austerlitz or Waterloo, and which probably would have remained unknown to the great mass of European readers, had not a young Frank gentleman mingled, from a silly fancy, in its lively business.

CHAPTER XVI.

OFF FOR GREECE.

THE effect of the battle of Bitoglia was the complete pacification of Albania, and the temporary suppression of the conspiracies in the adjoining provinces. Had it been in the power of the Porte to reinforce at this moment its able and faithful servant, it is probable that the authority of the Sultan would have been permanently consolidated in these countries. As it is, the finest regions in Europe are still the prey of civil war, in too many instances excited by foreign powers for their miserable purposes against a prince who is only inferior to Peter the Great because he has profited by his example.

For myself, perceiving that there was no immediate prospect of active service, I determined to visit Greece, and I parted from his highness with the hope that I might congratulate him at Stamboul.

CHAPTER XVII.

HELLAS.

COUNTRY of promontories, and gulfs, and islands clustering in an azure sea; a country of wooded vales and purple mountains, wherein the cities are built on plains covered with olive woods, and at the base of an Acropolis, crowned with a temple or a tower. And there are quarries of white marble, and vines, and much wild honey. And wherever you move is some fair and elegant memorial of the poetic past; a lone pillar on the green and silent plain, once echoing with the triumphant shouts of sacred games, the tomb of a hero, or the fane of a god. Clear is the sky and fragrant is the air, and at all seasons the magical scenery of this land is coloured with that mellow tint, and invested with that pensive character, which in other countries we conceive to be peculiar to autumn, and which beautifully associate with the recollections of the past. Enchanting Greece!

CHAPTER XVIII.

A VISIT TO ATHENS.

IN THE Argolic Gulf I found myself in the very heart of the Greek tragedy: Nauplia and Sparta, the pleasant Argos and the rich mycene, the tomb of Agamemnon and the palace of Clytemnestra. The fortunes of the house of Atreus form the noblest of all legends. I believe in that Destiny before which the ancients bowed. Modern philosophy, with its superficial discoveries, has infused into the breast of man a spirit of scepticism; but I think that, ere long, science will again become imaginative, and that, as we become more profound, we may become also more credulous. Destiny is our will, and our will is our nature. The son who inherits the organisation of the father will be doomed to the same fortunes as his sire; and again the mysterious matter in which his ancestors were moulded may, in other forms, by a necessary attraction, act upon his fate. All is mystery; but he is a slave who will not struggle to penetrate the dark veil.

I quitted the Morea without regret. It is covered with Venetian memorials, no more to me a source of joy, and bringing back to my memory a country on which I no longer love to dwell. I cast anchor in a small but secure harbour, and landed. I climbed a hill, from which I looked over a plain, covered with olive woods, and skirted by mountains. Some isolated hills, of picturesque form, rose in the plain at a distance from the terminating range. On one of these I beheld a magnificent temple bathed in the sunset. At the foot of the craggy steep on which it rested was a walled city of considerable dimensions, in front of which rose a Doric fane of exquisite proportion, and apparently uninjured. The violet sunset threw over this scene a colouring becoming its loveliness, and if possible increasing its refined character. Independently of all associations, it was the most beautiful spectacle that had ever passed before a vision always musing on sweet sights; yet I could not forget that it was the bright capital of my youthful dreams, the fragrant city of the Violet Crown, the fair, the sparkling, the delicate ATHENS!

CHAPTER XIX.

THE FORTUNE OF WAR.

THE illusion vanished when I entered Athens. I found it in scarcely a less shattered condition than the towns of Albania: ruined streets, and roofless houses, and a scanty population. The women were at Egina in security: a few males remained behind to watch the fortune of war. The Acropolis had not been visited by travellers for nine years, and was open to inspection for the first time the very day I entered. It was still in the possession of the Turks, but the Greek commission had arrived to receive the keys of the fortress. The ancient remains have escaped better than we could hope. The Parthenon and the other temples on the Acropolis have necessarily suffered in the sieges, but the injury is only in the detail; the general effect is not marred, although I observed many hundred shells and cannon-balls lying about.

The Theseum has not been touched, and looks, at a short distance, as if it were just finished by Cimon. The sumptuous columns of the Olympium still rise from their stately platform, but the Choragic monument is sadly maimed, as I was assured, by English sailors and not Eastern barbarians; probably the same marine monsters who have commemorated their fatal visit to Egypt and the name of the fell craft that bore them thither, by covering the granite pillar of Pompey with gigantic characters in black paint.

The durability of the Parthenon is wonderful. So far as I could observe, had it not been for the repeated ravages of man, it might at this day have been in as perfect condition as in the age of Pericles. Abstract time it has defied. Gilt and painted, with its pictures and votive statues, it must have been one of the most brilliant creations of human genius. Yet we err if we consider this famous building as an unparalleled effort of Grecian architecture. Compared with the temples of Ionia and the Sicilian fanes, compared even with the Olympium at its feet, the Parthenon could only rank as a church with a cathedral.

In art the Greeks were the children of the Egyptians. The day may yet come when we shall do justice to the high powers of that mysterious and imaginative people. The origin of Doric and Ionic invention must be traced amid the palaces of Carnac and the temples of Luxoor. For myself, I confess I ever gaze upon the marvels of art with a feeling of despair. With horror I remember that, through some mysterious necessity, civilisation seems to have deserted the most favoured regions and the choicest intellects. The Persian whose very being is poetry, the Arab whose subtle mind could penetrate into the very secret shrine of Nature, the Greek whose acute perceptions seemed granted only for the creation of the beautiful, these are now unlettered slaves in barbarous lands. The arts are yielded to the flat-nosed

Franks.   And they toil, and study, and invent theories to account for their own incompetence.   Now it is the climate, now the religion, now the government; everything but the truth, everything but the mortifying suspicion that their organisation may be different, and that they may be as distinct a race from their models as they undoubtedly are from the Kalmuck and the Negro.

CHAPTER XX.

ANCIENT GOVERNMENTS.

HATEVER may have been the faults of the ancient govèrnments, they were in closer relation to the times, to the countries and to the governed, than ours. The ancients invented their governments according to their wants; the moderns have adopted foreign policies, and then modelled their conduct upon this borrowed regulation. This circumstance has occasioned our manners and our customs to be so confused, and absurd, and unphilosophical. What business had we, for instance, to adopt the Roman law, a law foreign to our manners, and consequeptly disadvantageous? He who profoundly meditates upon the situation of Modern Europe will also discover how productive of misery has been the senseless adoption of oriental customs by northern people. Whence came that divine right of kings, which has deluged so many countries with blood? that pastoral and Syrian law of tithes, which may yet shake the foundation of so many ancient institutions?

CHAPTER XXI.

FOREIGN LITERATURES.

EVEN as a child, I was struck by the absurdity of modern education. The duty of education is to give ideas. When our limited intelligence was confined to the literature of two dead languages, it was necessary to acquire those languages, in order to obtain the knowledge which they embalmed. But now each nation has its literature, each nation possesses, written in its own tongue, a record of all knowledge, and specimens of every modification of invention. Let education then be confined to that national literature, and we should soon perceive the beneficial effects of this revolution upon the mind of the student. Study would then be a profitable delight. I pity the poor Gothic victim of the grammar and the lexicon. The Greeks, who were masters of composition, were ignorant of all languages but their own. They concentrated their study of the genius of expression upon one tongue. To this they owe that blended simplicity and strength of style which the imitative Romans, with all their splendour, never attained.

To the few, however, who have leisure or inclination to study foreign literatures, I will not recommend to them the English, the Italian, the German, since they may rightly answer, that all these have been in great part founded upon the classic tongues, and therefore it is wise to ascend to the fountainhead; but I will ask them for what reason they would limit their experience to the immortal languages of Greece and Rome? Why not study the oriental? Surely in the pages of the Persians and the Arabs we might discover new sources of emotion, new modes of expression, new trains of ideas, new principles of invention, and new bursts of fancy.

These are a few of my meditations amid the ruins of Athens. They will disappoint those who might justly expect an ebullition of classic rapture from one who has gazed upon Marathon by moonlight and sailed upon the free waters of Salamis. I regret their disappointment, but I have arrived at an age when I can think only of the future. A mighty era, prepared by the blunders of long centuries, is at hand. Ardently I hope that the necessary change in human existence may be effected by the voice of philosophy alone: but I tremble, and I am silent. There is no bigotry so terrible as the bigotry of a country that flatters itself that it is philosophical.

CHAPTER XXII.

The Golden Horn.

NDERSTANDING that the Turkish squadron I left at Prevesa had arrived at Negropont, I passed over, and paid a visit to its commander, Halil Pacha, with whom I was acquainted. Halil informed me that all remained quiet in Albania, but that Redschid did not venture to return. He added that he himself was about to sail for Stamboul immediately, and proposed that I should accompany him. His offer suited me, and, as the wind was fair, in a few hours we were all on board.

I had a splendid view of Sunium; its columns against a dark cloud looked like undriven snow, and we were soon among the Cyclades. Sixteen islands were in sight, and we were now making our course in the heart of them. An archipelago by sunset is lovely: small isles of purple and gold studding the glowing waters. The wind served well through the night, but we were becalmed the next day off Mitylene. In the afternoon a fresh breeze sprang up and carried us to the Dardanelles.

We were yet, I believe, upwards of a hundred miles from Constantinople. What a road to a great city! narrower and much longer than the strait of Gibraltar, but not with such sublime shores. Asia and Europe looked more kindly on each other than Europe and her more sultry sister. I found myself the next morning becalmed off Troy: a vast, hilly, uncultivated plain; a scanty rill, a huge tumulus, some shepherds and their flocks; behold the kingdom of Priam, and the successors of Paris!

A signal summoned us on board; the wind was fair and fresh. We scudded along with great swiftness, passing many towns and fortresses. Each dome, each minaret, I thought was Constantinople. At last it came; we were in full sight. Masses of habitations, grouped on gentle acclivities, rose on all sides out of the water, part in Asia, part in Europe; a gay and confused vision of red buildings, and dark-green cypress groves, hooded domes, and millions of minarets. As we approached, the design became more obvious. The groups formed themselves into three considerable cities, intersected by arms of the sea. Down one of these, rounding the Seraglio point, our vessel held her course. We seemed to glide into the heart of the capital. The water was covered with innumerable boats, as swift as gondolas and far more gay, curiously carved and richly gilt. In all parts swarmed a showy population. The characteristic of the whole scene was brilliancy. The houses glittered, the waters sparkled, and flocks of white and sacred birds glanced in the golden air, and skimmed over the blue wave. On one side of the harbour was moored the Turkish fleet, dressed out in all their colours. Our course was ended, and we cast our anchor in the famous Golden Horn.

CHAPTER XXIII.

THE BOSPHORUS AND THE BAZAAR.

NO PICTURE can ever convey a just idea of Constantinople. I have seen several that are faithful, as far as they extend; but the most comprehensive can exhibit only a small portion of this extraordinary city. By land or by water, in every direction, passing up the Golden Horn to the valley of Fresh Waters, or preceding, on the other hand, down the famous Bosphorus to Buyukdere and Terapia, to the Euxine, what infinite novelty! New kiosks, new hills, new windings, new groves of cypress, and new forests of chestnut, open on all sides.

The two most remarkable things at Constantinople are the Bosphorus and the bazaar. Conceive the ocean a stream not broader than the Rhine, with shores presenting all the beauty and variety of that river, running between gentle slopes covered with rich woods, gardens, and summer-palaces, cemeteries and mosques, and villages, and bounded by sublime mountains. The view of the Euxine from the heights of Terapia, just seen through the end of the Straits, is like gazing upon eternity.

The bazaar is of a different order, but not less remarkable. I never could obtain from a Turk any estimate of the ground it covered. Several, in the habit of daily attendance, have mentioned to me that they often find themselves in divisions they have not before visited. Fancy a Parisian panorama passage, fancy perhaps a square mile covered with these arcades, intersecting each other in all directions, and full of every product of the empire, from diamonds to dates. This will give you some idea of the Great Bazaar at Constantinople. The dealers, in every possible costume, sit cross-legged in their stalls, and dealers in the same article usually congregate together. The armourers, the grocers, the pipe-makers, the jewellers, the shawl-sellers, the librarians, all have their distinct quarter. Now you walk along a range of stalls filled with fanciful slippers of cloth and leather, of all colours, embroidered with gold or powdered with pearls; now you are in a street of confectionery; and now you are cheapening a Damascus sabre in the bazaar of arms, or turning over a vividly illuminated copy of Hafiz in that last stronghold of Turkish bigotry, the quarter of the vendors of the Koran. The magnificence, novelty, and variety of the goods on sale, the whole nation of shopkeepers, all in different dress, the crowds of buyers from all parts of the world,—I only hint at these traits. Here every people has a characteristic costume. Turks, Greeks, Jews and Armenians are the staple population: the latter are numerous. The Armenians wear round and very unbecoming black caps and flowing robes; the Jews, a black hat wreathed with a white handkerchief; the Greeks, black turbans. The Turks are fond of dress, and indulge in all combinations of costume. Of late, among the young men in the capital, it has been the fashion to discard the huge turban and the ample robes, and they have formed an exceedingly ungraceful dress upon the Frank; but vast numbers cling to the national costume, especially the Asiatics, renowned for the prodigious height and multifarious folds of their headgear.

CHAPTER XXIV.

AN INTERVIEW WITH THE SULTAN.

ALIL PACHA paid me a visit one day at my residence on the Bosphorus, and told me that he had mentioned my name to the Sultan, who had expressed a desire to see me. As it is not etiquette for the Padishah to receive Franks, I was, of course, as sensible to the high honour as I was anxious to become acquainted with the extraordinary man who was about to confer it.

The Sultan was at this moment at a place on the Bosphorus, not far from Tophana. Hither on the appointed day I repaired with Halil and the drogueman of the Porte. We were ushered into a chamber, where a principal officer of the household received us, and where I smoked out of a pipe tipped with diamonds, and sipped coffee perfumed with roses out of cups studded with precious stones.

When we had remained here for about half an hour, Mustapha, the private secretary and favourite of the Sultan entered, and, after saluting us, desired us to follow him. We proceeded along a corridor, at the end of which stood two or three eunuchs, richly dressed, and then the door opened, and I found myself in an apartment of moderate size, painted with indifferent arabesques in fresco, and surrounded with a divan of crimson velvet and gold. Seated upon this, with his feet on the floor, his arms folded, and in a hussar dress, was the Grand Signor.

As we entered he slightly touched his heart, according to the fashions of the Orientals; and Mustapha, setting us an example, desired us to seat ourselves. I fancied, and I was afterwards assured of the correctness of my observation, that the Sultan was very much constrained, and very little at his ease. The truth is, he is totally unused to interviews with strangers, and this was for him a more novel situation than for me. His constraint wore off as conversation proceeded. He asked a great many questions, and often laughed, turning to Mustapha with a familiar nod when my replies pleased him. He inquired much about the Albanian war. Without flattering my late commander, it was in my power to do him service. He asked me what service I had before seen, and was evidently surprised when I informed him I was only an amateur. He then made many inquiries as to the European forces, and in answering them I introduced some opinions on politics, which interested him. He asked me who I was. I told him I was the son of the Prime Minister of——, a power always friendly to the Ottoman. His eyes sparkled, and he repeated several times, 'It is well, it is well;' meaning, I suppose, that he did not repent of the interview. He told me that in two years' time he should have two hundred thousand regular infantry; that, if the Russian war could have been postponed another year, he should have beat the Muscovites; that the object of the war was to crush his schemes of re-generation; that he was betrayed at Adrianople, as well as at Varna. He added that he had only done what Peter the Great had done before him, and that Peter was thwarted by unsuccessful wars, yet at last succeeded.

I, of course, expressed my conviction that his highness would be as fortunate.

The Padishah then abruptly said that all his subjects should have equal rights; that there should be no difference between Moslem and infidel; that all who contributed to the government had a right to the same protection.

Here Mustapha nodded to Halil, and we rose, and bowing, quitted the presence of a really great man.

I found at the portal a fine Arabian steed, two Cachemire shawls, a scarlet cloak of honour, with the collar embroidered with gold and fastened with diamond clasps, a sabre, and two superb pipes. This was my reward for charging with the Turkish cavalry at Bitoglia.

CHAPTER XXV.

STAMBOUL.

ONE of the most curious things at Constantinople is the power you have in the Capital of the East, of placing yourself in ten minutes in a lively Frank town. Such is Pera. I passed there the winter months of December and January in agreeable and intelligent society. My health improved, but my desire of wandering increased. I began to think that I should now never be able to settle in life. The desire of fame did not revive. I felt no intellectual energy; I required nothing more than to be amused. And having now passed four or five months at Stamboul, and seen all its wonders, from the interior of its mosques to the dancing dervishes, I resolved to proceed. So, one cold morning in February, I crossed over to Scutari, and pressed my wandering foot upon Asia.

PART THE SIXTH.

CHAPTER I.

THE INFLUENCE OF THE PAST.

I WAS now in the great Peninsula of Asia Minor, a country admirably fortified by Nature, abounding in vast, luxuriant, and enchanting plains, from which a scanty population derive a difficult subsistence, and watered by broad rivers rolling through solitude.

As I journeyed along I could not refrain from contrasting the desolation of the present with the refinement of the past, and calling up a vision of the ancient splendour of this famous country. I beheld those glorious Greek federations that covered the provinces of the coast with their rich cultivation and brilliant cities. Who has not heard of the green and bland Ionia, and its still more fruitful, although less picturesque, sister, the rich Æolis? Who has not heard of the fane of Ephesus, and the Anacreontic Teios; Chios, with its rosy wine; and Cnidos, with its rosy goddess; Colophon, Priene, Phocæa, Samos, Miletos, the splendid Halicarnassus, and the sumptuous Cos, magnificent cities, abounding in genius and luxury, and all the polished refinement that ennobles life! Everywhere around, these free and famous citizens disseminated their liberty and their genius; in the savage Tauris; and on the wild shores of Pontus; on the banks of the Borysthenes, and by the waters of the rapid Tyras. The islands in their vicinity shared their splendour and their felicity; the lyric Lesbos, and Tenedos with its woods and vines, and those glorious gardens, the fortunate Cyprus, and the prolific Rhodes.

Under the empire of Rome the Peninsula of Asia enjoyed a not less eminent prosperity. The interior provinces vied in wealth and civilisation with the ancient colonies of the coast. Then the cavalry of Cappadocia and Paphlagonia were famous as the Lycian mariners, the soldiers of Pontus, and the bowmen of Armenia; then Galatia sent forth her willing and welcome tribute of corn, and the fruitful Bithynia rivalled the Pamphylian pastures, the vines of Phrygia, and the Pisidian olives. Tarsus, Ancyra, Sardis, Cæsarea, Sinope, Amisus, were the great and opulent capitals of these flourishing provinces. Alexandria rose upon the ruins of Troy, and Nicæa and Nicomedia ranked with the most celebrated cities.

And now the tinkling bell of the armed and wandering caravan was the only indication of human existence!

It is in such scenes as these, amid the ruins of ancient splendour and the recollections of vanished empire, that philosophers have pondered on the nature of government, and have discovered, as they fancied, in the consequences of its various forms, the causes of duration or of decay, of glory or of humiliation.

Freedom, says the sage, will lead to prosperity, and despotism to destruction.

Yet has this land been regulated by every form of government that the ingenuity of man has devised. The federal republic, the military empire, the oriental despotism, have in turn controlled its fortunes. The deputies of free states have here assembled in some universal temple which was the bond of union between their cities. Here has the proconsul presided at his high tribunal: and here the pacha reposes in his divan. The Pagan fane, and the Christian church, and the Turkish mosque, have here alike been erected to form the opinions of the people. The legends of Chios and Olympus are forgotten, the sites of the seven churches cannot even be traced, and nothing is left but the revelations of the son of Abdallah, a volume, the whole object of which is to convert man into a fanatic slave.

Is there then no hope? Is it an irrevocable doom, that society shall be created only to be destroyed? When I can accept such a dogma, let me also believe that the beneficent Creator is a malignant demon. Let us meditate more deeply; let us at length discover that no society can long subsist that is based upon metaphysical absurdities.

The law that regulates man must be founded on a knowledge of his nature, or that law leads him to ruin. What is the nature of man? In every clime and in every creed we shall find a new definition.

Before me is a famous treatise on human nature, by a Professor of Königsberg. No one has more profoundly meditated on the attributes of his subject. It is evident that, in the deep study of his own intelligence, he has discovered a noble method of expounding that of others. Yet when I close his volumes, can I conceal from myself that all this time I have been studying a treatise upon the nature, not of man, but, of a German?

What then! Is the German a different animal from the Italian? Let me inquire in turn, whether you conceive the negro of the Gold Coast to be the same being as the Esquimau, who tracks his way over the polar snows?

The most successful legislators are those who have consulted the genius of the people. But is it possible to render that which is the occasional consequence of fine observation the certain result of scientific study?

One thing is quite certain, that the system we have pursued to attain a knowledge of man has entirely failed. Let us disembarrass ourselves of that 'moral philosophy' which has filled so many volumes with words. History will always remain a pleasant pastime; it never could have been a profitable study. To study man from the past is to suppose that man is ever the same animal, which I do not. Those who speculated on the career of Napoleon had ever a dog's-eared annalist to refer to. The past equally proved that he was both a Cromwell and a Washington. Prophetic Past! He turned out to be the first. But suppose he had been neither; suppose he had proved a Sylla?

Man is an animal, and his nature must be studied as that of all other animals. The almighty Creator has breathed His spirit into us; and we testify our gratitude for this choice boon by never deigning to consider what may be the nature of our intelligence. The philosopher, however, amid this darkness, will not despair. He will look forward to an age of rational laws and beneficent education. He will remember that all the truth he has attained has been by one process. He will also endeavour to become acquainted with himself by demonstration, and not by dogma.

CHAPTER II.

ONE fair spring morning, with a clear blue sky, and an ardent but not intense sun, I came in sight of the whole coast of Syria; very high and mountainous, with the loftiest ranges covered with snow.

I had sailed from Smyrna, through its lovely gulf, vaster and more beautiful than the Ambracian, found myself in a new archipelago, the Sporades; and, having visited Rhodes and Cyprus, engaged at the last island a pilot to take us to the most convenient Syrian port.

Syria is, in fact, an immense chain of mountains, extending from Asia Minor to Arabia. In the course of this great chain an infinity of branches constantly detach themselves from the parent trunk, forming on each side, either towards the desert or the sea, beautiful and fertile plains. Washed by the Levantine wave, on one side we behold the once luxurious Antioch, now a small and dingy Turkish town. The traveller can no longer wander in the voluptuous woods of Daphne. The palace and the garden pass away with the refined genius and the delicate taste that

(64)

create them; but Nature is eternal, and even yet the valley of the Orontes offers, under the glowing light of an eastern day, scenes of picturesque beauty that Switzerland cannot surpass. The hills of Laodicea, once famous for their wine, are now celebrated for producing the choicest tobacco of the East. Tripoli is a flourishing town, embosomed in wild groves of Indian figs, and famous for its fruits and silks. Advancing along the coast we reach the ancient Berytus, whose tobacco vies with Laodicea, and whose silk surpasses that of Tripoli. We arrive at all that remains of the superb Tyre; a small peninsula and a mud village. The famous Acre is still the most important place upon the coast; and Jaffa, in spite of so many wars, is yet fragrant amid its gardens and groves of lemon trees.

The towns on the coast have principally been built on the sites and ruins of the ancient cities whose names they bear. None of them have sufficient claims to the character of a capital; but on the other side of the mountains we find two of the most important of oriental cities, the populous Aleppo, and the delicious Damascus; nor must we forget Jerusalem, that city sacred in so many creeds!

In ancient remains, Syria is inferior only to Egypt. All have heard of the courts of Baalbec and the columns of Palmyra. Less known, because only recently visited, and visited with extreme danger, are the vast ruins of magnificent cities in the Arabian vicinity of the lake Asphaltites.

The climate of this country is various as its formation. In the plains is often experienced that intense heat so fatal to the European invader; yet the snow, that seldom falls upon the level ground, or falls

only to vanish, rests upon the heights of Lebanon,
and, in the higher lands, it is not difficult at all times
to discover exactly the temperature you desire. I
travelled in Syria at the commencement of the year,
when the short but violent rainy season had just
ceased. It is not easy to conceive a more beautiful
and fruitful land. The plains were covered with that
fresh green tint so rare under an Eastern sky; the
orange and lemon trees were clothed both with fruit
and blossom; and then, too, I first beheld the huge
leaf of the banana, and tasted for the first time the
delicate flavour of its unrivalled fruit. From the great
extent of the country, and the consequent variation
of clime, the Syrian can always command a succession, as well as a variety, of luxuries. The season of
the pomegranate will commence in Antioch when it
ends in Jaffa; and when you have exhausted the figs
of Beyroot, you can fly to the gardens of Damascus.
Under the worst government that perhaps ever oppressed its subjects, Syria still brings forth the choice
productions of almost every clime; corn and cotton,
maize and rice, the sugar-cane of the Antilles, and the
indigo and cochineal of Mexico. The plains of Antioch and of Palestine are covered with woods of the
finest olives, the tobaccoes of the coast are unrivalled
in any country; and the mountains of Lebanon are
clothed with white mulberry-trees that afford the
richest silks, or with vineyards that yield a wine
which justly bears the name of Golden.

The inhabitants of this country are various as its
productions and its mutable fortunes. The Ottoman
conqueror is now the lord, and rules the posterity of
the old Syrian Greeks and of the Arabs, who were
themselves once predominant. In the mountains the

independent and mysterious Druses live in freedom under their own Emir; and in the ranges near Antioch we find the Ansaree tribes, who, it is whispered, yet celebrate the most singular rites of Paganism. In the deserts around Aleppo wander the pastoral Kourd and the warlike Turkoman; and from Tadmor to Gaza the whole Syrian desert is traversed by the famous Bedouin.

There is a charm in oriental life, and it is Repose. Upon me, who had been bred in the artificial circles of corrupt civilisation, and who had so freely indulged the course of his impetuous passions, this character made a forcible impression. Wandering over those plains and deserts, and sojourning in those silent and beautiful cities, I experienced all the serenity of mind which I can conceive to be the enviable portion of the old age of a virtuous life. The memory of the wearing cares, and corroding anxieties, and vaunted excitement of European life, filled me with pain. Keenly I felt the vanity and littleness of all human plans and aspirations. Truly may I say that on the plains of Syria I parted forever with my ambition. The calm enjoyment of existence appeared to me, as it now does, the highest attainable felicity; nor can I conceive that anything could tempt me from my solitude, and induce me once more to mingle with mankind, with whom I have little in common, but the strong conviction that the fortunes of my race depended on my effort, or that I could materially advance that great amelioration of their condition, in the practicability of which I devoutly believe.

CHAPTER III.

THE BANKS OF THE EUPHRATES.

GALLOPED over an illimitable plain, covered with a vivid though scanty pasture, and fragrant with aromatic herbs. A soft, fresh breeze danced on my cheek, and brought vigour to my frame. Day after day I journeyed and met with no sign of human existence; no village, no culture, no resting-place, not even a tree. Day after day I journeyed, and the land indicated no termination. At an immense distance the sky and the earth blended in a uniform horizon. Sometimes, indeed, a rocky vein shot out of the soil; sometimes, indeed, the land would swell into long undulations; sometimes, indeed, from a dingle of wild bushes a gazelle would rush forward, stare, and bound away.

Such was my first wandering in the Syrian desert! But remember it was the burst of spring. I could conceive nothing more delightful, nothing more unlike what I had anticipated. The heat was never intense, the breeze was ever fresh and sweet, the nocturnal heavens luminous and clear to a degree which it is impossible to describe. Instead of that uniform appearance and monotonous splendour I had hitherto so often gazed on, the stars were of different tints and forms. Some were green, some white, some red; and, instead of appearing as if they only studded a vast and azure vault, I clearly distinguished them, at different distances, floating in ether.

I no longer wondered at the love of the Bedouins for their free and unsophisticated earth. It appeared to me that I could have lived in the desert for ever. At night we rested. Our camels bore us water in goat-skins, cakes of fuel, which they themselves produced, and scanty, although sufficient, provisions. We lit our fire, pounded our coffee, and smoked our pipes, while others prepared our simple meal, bread made at the instant, and on the cinders, a slice of dried meat, and a few dates.

I have described the least sterile of the deserts, and I have described it at the most favourable period. In general the soil of the Syrian wilderness is not absolutely barren. The rains cover it with verdure, but these occur only for a few weeks, when the rigour of a winter day arrests the clouds, and they dissolve into showers. At all other seasons they glide over the scorched and heated plain, which has neither hills nor trees to attract them. It is the want of water which is the occasion of this sterility. In the desert there is not even a brook; springs are rare and generally brackish; and it is on the artificial wells, stored by the rains, that the wanderer chiefly depends.

From the banks of the Euphrates to the shores of the Red Sea; from the banks of the Nile to the Persian Gulf, over a spread of country three times the extent of Germany, Nature, without an interval, ceases to produce. Beneficent Nature! Let us not wrong her; for, even in a land apparently so unfavoured, exists a numerous and happy race. As you wander along, the appearance of the desert changes. The wilderness, which is comparatively fertile in Syria, becomes rocky when you enter Arabia, and sandy as you proceed. Here in some degree we meet with the terrible idea of the desert prevalent in Europe; but it is in Africa, in the vast and unexplored regions of Libya and Zahara, that we must seek for the illimitable and stormy ocean of overwhelming sand which we associate with the popular idea of the desert.

The sun was nearly setting, when an Arab horseman, armed with his long lance, was suddenly observed on an eminence in the distance. He galloped towards us, wheeled round and round, scudded away, again approached, and our guide, shouting, rode forward to meet him. They entered into earnest conversation, and then joined us. Abdallah, the guide, informed me that this was an Arab of the tribe I intended to visit, and that we were very near their encampment.

The desert was here broken into bushy knolls, which limited the view. Advancing and mounting the low ridge on which we had first observed the Bedouin, Abdallah pointed out to me at no great distance a large circle of low black tents, which otherwise I might not have observed, or have mistaken them in the deceptive twilight for some natural formation. On the left of the encampment was a small grove of palm trees; and when we had nearly gained the settlement, a procession of women in long blue robes, covering with one hand their faces with their veils, and with the other supporting on their heads a tall and classically formed vase, advanced with a beautiful melody to the fountain, which was screened by the palm trees.

The dogs barked· some dark faces and long matchlocks suddenly popped up behind the tents.

The Bedouin, with a shout, galloped into the encampment, and soon reappeared with several of his tribe. We dismounted, and entered the interior court of the camp, which was filled with camels and goats. There were few persons visible, although, as I was conducted along to the tent of the chief, I detected many faces staring at me from behind the curtains of their tents. The pavilion of the sheikh was of considerable size. He himself was a man advanced in years, but hale and lively; his long white beard curiously contrasting with his dark visage. He received me, sitting on a mat, his son standing on his right hand without his slippers, and a young grandchild squatting by his side.

He welcomed me with the usual oriental salutation; touching his forehead, his mouth, and his heart, while he exclaimed 'Salaam;' thus indicating that all his faculties and feelings were devoted to me. He motioned that we should seat ourselves on the unoccupied mats, and taking from his mouth a small pipe of date wood, gave it to his son to bear to me. A servant instantly began pounding coffee. I then informed him, through Abdallah, that, having heard of his hospitality and happy life, I had journeyed even from Damascus to visit him; that I greatly admired the Bedouin character, and eulogised their valour, their independence, their justice, and their simplicity.

He answered that he liked to be visited by Franks, because they were wise men, and requested that I would feel his pulse.

I performed this ceremony with becoming gravity, and inquired whether he were indisposed. He said that he was well, but that he might be better. I told him that his pulse was healthy and strong for one of his age, and I begged to examine his tongue, which greatly pleased him; and he observed that he was eighty years of age, and could ride as well and as long as his son.

Coffee was now brought. I ventured to praise it. He said it was well for those who had not wine. I observed that wine was not suited to these climes, and that, although a Frank, I had myself renounced it. He answered that the Franks were fond of wine, but that, for his part, he had never tasted it, although he should like once to do so.

I regretted that I could not avail myself of this delicate hint, but Lausanne produced a bottle of eau-de-Cologne, and I offered him a glass. He drank it with great gravity, and asked for some for his son, observing it was good raki, but not wine. I suspected from this that he was not totally unacquainted with the flavour of the forbidden liquor, and I dared to remark with a smile, that raki had one advantage over wine, that it was not forbidden by the prophet. Unlike the Turks, who never understand a jest, he smiled, and then said that the Book (meaning the Koran) was good for men who lived in cities, but that God was everywhere.

Several men now entered the tent, leaving their slippers on the outside, and some saluting the sheikh as they passed, seated themselves.

I now inquired after horses, and asked him whether he could assist me in purchasing some of the true breed. The old sheikh's eyes sparkled as he informed

me that he possessed four mares of pure blood, and
that he would not part with one, not even for fifty thousand piastres. After this hint, I was inclined to drop
the subject, but the sheikh seemed interested by it,
and inquired if the Franks had any horses.

I answered, that some Frank nations were famous
for their horses, and mentioned the English, who had
a superb race from the Arabs. He said he had heard
of the English; and asked me which was the greatest
nation of the Franks. I told him there were several
equally powerful, but perhaps that the English nation
might be fairly described as the most important. He
answered, 'Ay! on the sea, but not on land.'

I was surprised by the general knowledge indicated by this remark, and more so when he further
observed that there was another nation stronger by
land. I mentioned the Russians. He had not heard
of them, notwithstanding the recent war with
the Porte. The French? I inquired. He knew the
French, and then told me that he had been at the
siege of Acre, which explained all this intelligence.
He then inquired if I were an Englishman. I told
him my country, but was not astonished that he had
never heard of it. I observed that, when the old man
spoke, he was watched by his followers with the
greatest attention, and they grinned with pride and
exultation at his knowledge of the Franks, showing
their white teeth, elevating their eyes, and exchanging looks of wonder.

Two women now entered the tent, at which I
was surprised. They had returned from the fountain,
and wore small black masks, which covered the upper
part of the face. They knelt down at the fire, and
made a cake of bread, which one of them handed to

me. I now offered to the sheikh my own pipe, which
Lausanne had prepared. Coffee was again handed, and
a preparation of sour milk and rice, not unpalatable.

I offered the sheikh renewed compliments on his
mode of life, in order to maintain conversation; for
the chief, although, like the Arabs in general, of a
lively temperament, had little of the curiosity of what
are considered the more civilised Orientals, and asked
very few questions.

'We are content,' said the sheikh.

'Then, believe me, you are in the condition of no
other people,' I replied.

'My children,' said the sheikh, 'hear the words of
this wise man! If we lived with the Turks,' continued the chieftain, 'we should have more gold and
silver, and more clothes, and carpets, and baths; but
we should not have justice and liberty. Our luxuries
are few, but our wants are fewer.'

'Yet you have neither priests nor lawyers?'

'When men are pure, laws are useless; when men
are corrupt, laws are broken.'

'And for priests?'

'God is everywhere.'

The women now entered with a more substantial
meal, the hump of a young camel. I have seldom eaten
anything more delicate and tender. This dish was a
great compliment, and could only have been offered
by a wealthy sheikh. Pipes and coffee followed.

The moon was shining brightly, when, making my
excuses, I quitted the pavilion of the chieftain, and
went forth to view the humours of the camp. The
tall camels, crouching on their knees in groups, with
their outstretched necks and still and melancholy visages, might have been mistaken for works of art had

it not been for the process of rumination. A crowd was assembled round a fire, before which a poet recited impassioned verses. I observed the slight forms of the men, short and meagre, agile, dry, and dark, with teeth dazzling white, and quick, black, glancing eyes. They were dressed in cloaks of coarse black cloth, apparently the same stuff as their tents, and few of them, I should imagine, exceeded five feet six inches in height. The women mingled with the men, although a few affected, to conceal their faces on my approach. They were evidently deeply interested in the poetic recital. One passage excited their loud applause. I inquired its purport of Abdallah, who thus translated it to me. A lover beholds his mistress, her face covered with a red veil. Thus he addresses her!

'OH! WITHDRAW THAT VEIL, WITHDRAW THAT RED VEIL! LET ME BEHOLD THE BEAUTY THAT IT SHROUDS! YES! LET THAT ROSY TWILIGHT FADE AWAY, AND LET THE FULL MOON RISE TO MY VISION.'

Beautiful! Yet more beautiful in the language of the Arabs; for in that rich tongue, there are words to describe each species of twilight, and where we are obliged to have recourse to an epithet, the Arabs reject the feeble and unnecessary aid.

It was late ere I retired, and I stretched myself on my mat, musing over this singular people, who combined primitive simplicity of habits with the refined feelings of civilisation, and who, in a great degree, appeared to me to offer an evidence of that community of property and that equality of condition, which have hitherto proved the despair of European sages, and fed only the visions of their fanciful Utopias.

CHAPTER IV.

A Syrian Village.

SYRIAN village is beautiful in the centre of a fertile plain. The houses are isolated, and each surrounded by palm trees; the meadows divided by rich plantations of Indian fig, and bounded by groves of olive. In the distance rose a chain of severe and savage mountains. I was soon wandering, and for hours, in the wild, stony ravines of these shaggy rocks. At length, after several passes, I gained the ascent of a high mountain. Upon an opposite height, descending as a steep ravine, and forming, with the elevation on which I rested, a dark and narrow gorge, I beheld a city entirely surrounded by what I should have considered in Europe an old feodal wall, with towers and gates. The city was built upon an ascent, and, from the height on which I stood, I could discern the terrace and the cupola of almost every house, and the wall upon the other side rising from the plain; the ravine extending only on the side to which I was opposite. The city was in a bowl of mountains. In the front was a magnificent mosque, with beautiful gardens, and many light and lofty

gates of triumph; a variety of domes and towers rose
in all directions from the buildings of bright stone.

Nothing could be conceived more wild, and terrible, and desolate than the surrounding scenery, more
dark, and stormy, and severe; but the ground was
thrown about in such picturesque undulations, that
the mind, full of the sublime, required not the beautiful; and rich and waving woods and sparkling
cultivation would have been misplaced. Except
Athens, I had never witnessed any scene more essentially impressive. I will not place this spectacle be-
low the city of Minerva. Athens and the Holy City
in their glory must have been the finest representations of the beautiful and the sublime; the Holy City,
for the elevation on which I stood was the Mount of
Olives, and the city on which I gazed was JERUSALEM.

CHAPTER V.

THE CITY OF PEACE.

HE dark gorge beneath me was the vale of Jehoshaphat; farther on was the fountain of Siloah. I entered by the gate of Bethlehem, and sought hospitality at the Latin Convent of the Terra Santa.

Easter was approaching, and the city was crowded with pilgrims. I had met many caravans in my progress. The convents of Jerusalem are remarkable. That of the Armenian Christians at this time afforded accommodation for four thousand pilgrims. It is a town of itself, and possesses within its walls streets and shops. The Greek Convent held perhaps half as many. And the famous Latin Convent of the Terra Santa, endowed by all the monarchs of Catholic Christendom, could boast of only one pilgrim, myself! The Europeans have ceased to visit the Holy Sepulchre.

As for the interior of Jerusalem, it is hilly and clean. The houses are of stone and well built, but like all Asiatic mansions, they offer nothing to the eye but blank walls and dull portals. The mosque I had admired was the famous Mosque of Omar, built upon the supposed site of the Temple. It is perhaps the most beautiful of Mahomedan temples, but the Frank, even in the Eastern dress, will enter it at the risk of his life. The Turks of Syria have not been contaminated by the heresies of their enlightened Sultan. In Damascus it is impossible to appear in the Frank dress without being pelted; and although they would condescend, perhaps, at Jerusalem to permit an infidel dog to walk about in his national dress, he would not escape many a curse and many a scornful exclamation of 'Giaour!' There is only one way to travel in the East with ease, and that is with an appearance of pomp. The Turks are much influenced by the exterior, and although they are not mercenary, a well-dressed and well-attended infidel will command respect.*

---

* The reader will be kind enough to remember that these observations were made in Syria in the year 1830. Since that period the Levant has undergone great vicissitudes.

CHAPTER VI.

CHURCH OF THE HOLY SEPULCHRE.

HE Church of the Holy Sepulchre is nearly in the middle of the city, and professedly built upon Mount Calvary, which, it is alleged, was levelled for the structure. Within its walls they have contrived to assemble the scenes of a vast number of incidents in the life of the Saviour, with a highly romantic violation of the unity of place. Here the sacred feet were anointed, there the sacred garments parcelled; from the pillar of the scourging to the rent of the rock, all is exhibited in a succession of magical scenes. The truth is, the whole is an ingenious imposture of a comparatively recent date, and we are indebted to that favoured individual, the Empress Helen, for this exceedingly clever creation, as well as for the discovery of the true cross. The learned believe, and with reason, that Calvary is at present, as formerly, without the walls, and that we must seek this celebrated elevation in the lofty hill now called Sion.

The church is a spacious building, surmounted by a dome. Attached to it are the particular churches of the various Christian sects, and many chapels and sanctuaries. Mass in some part or other is constantly celebrating, and companies of pilgrims may be observed in all directions, visiting the holy places and offering their devotions. Latin and Armenian and Greek friars are everywhere moving about. The court is crowded with the vendors of relics and rosaries. The Church of the Sepulchre itself is a point of common union, and in its bustle and lounging character rather reminded me of an exchange than a temple.

One day as I was pacing up and down this celebrated building, in conversation with an ingenious Neapolitan friar, experienced in the East, my attention was attracted by one who, from his sumptuous dress, imposing demeanour, self-satisfied air, and the coolness with which, in a Christian temple, he waved in his hand a rosary of Mecca, I for a moment considered a Moslem. 'Is it customary for the Turks to visit this place?' I inquired, drawing the attention of my companion to the stranger.

'The stranger is not a Turk,' answered the friar, 'though I fear I cannot call him a Christian. It is Marigny, a French traveller. Do you not know him? I will introduce you. He is a man of distinguished science, and has resided some months in this city, studying Arabic.'

We approached him, and the friar made us acquainted.

'Salaam Aleikoum! Count. Here at last is no inquisition. Let us enjoy ourselves. How mortifying, my good Brother Antony, that you cannot burn me!'

The friar smiled, and was evidently used to this raillery.

'I hope yet to behold the Kaaba,' said Marigny; 'it is at least more genuine than anything we here see.'

'Truth is not truth to the false,' said Brother Antony.

'What, you reason!' exclaimed Marigny. 'Stick to faith and infallibility, my good friend Antonio. I have just been viewing the rent in the rock. It is a pity, holy father, that I have discovered that it is against the grain.'

'The greater the miracle,' said the friar.

'Bravo! you deserve to be a bishop.'

'The church has no fear of just reasoners,' observed Brother Antony.

'And is confuted, I suppose, only by the unjust,' rejoined Marigny.

'Man without religion is a wild beast,' remarked the friar.

'Which religion?' inquired Marigny.

'There is only one true religion,' said Brother Antony.

'Exactly; and in this country, Master Antony, remember you are an infidel.'

'And you, they say, are a Moslem.'

'They say wrong. I believe in no human revelation, because it obtrudes the mind of another man into my body, and must destroy morality, which can only be discovered by my own intelligence.'

'All is divine revelation,' said a stranger who joined us.

'Ah, Werner!' said Marigny, 'you see we are at our old contests.'

'All is divine revelation,' repeated Werner, 'for all comes from God.'

'But what do you mean by God?'

'I mean the great luminous principle of existence, the first almighty cause from whom we are emanations, and in whose essence we shall again mingle.'

'I asked for bread, and you gave me a stone. I asked for a fact, and you give me a word. I cannot annex an idea to what you say. Until my Creator gift me with an intelligence that can comprehend the idea of his existence, I must conclude that he does not desire that I should busy myself about it.'

'That idea is implanted in our breasts,' said Werner.

'Innate!' exclaimed Marigny, with a sneer.

'And why not innate?' replied Werner solemnly. 'Is it impossible for the Great Being who created us to create us with a sense of his existence?'

'Listen to these philosophers,' said Brother Antony; 'I never heard two of them agree. I must go to mass.'

'Mr. Werner and myself, Count,' said Marigny, 'are about to smoke a pipe with Besso, a rich Hebrew merchant here. He is one of the finest-hearted fellows in the world, and generous as he is rich. Will you accompany us? You will greatly honour him and find in his divan some intelligent society.'

CHAPTER VII.

TRAVEL TEACHES TOLERATION.

ARIGNY was a sceptic and an absolute materialist, yet he was influenced by noble views, for he had devoted his life to science, and was now, at his own charge, about to penetrate into the interior of Africa by Sennaar. Werner was a German divine and a rationalist, tauntingly described by his companion as a devout Christian, who did not believe in Christianity. Yet he had resided in Palestine and Egypt nearly four years, studying their languages and customs, and accumulating materials for a history of the miraculous creed whose miracles he explained. Both were men of remarkable intellectual powers, and the ablest champions of their respective systems.

I accompanied these new acquaintances to the house of Besso, and was most hospitably received, and sumptuously entertained. I have seldom met with a man of more easy manners and a more gracious carriage than Besso, who, although sincere in his creed, was the least bigoted of his tribe. He introduced us to his visitor, his friend and correspondent, Sheriff Effendi, an Egyptian merchant, who fortunately spoke the lingua Franca with facility. The other guest was an Englishman, by name Benson, a missionary, and a learned, pious, and acute man.

Such was the party in whose society I generally spent a portion of my day during my residence at Jerusalem: and I have often thought that, if the conversations to which I have there listened were recorded, a volume might be sent forth of more wit and wisdom than is now usually met with. The tone of discussion was, in general, metaphysical and scientific, varied with speculations principally on African travel, a subject with which Sheriff Effendi was well acquainted. In metaphysics, sharp were the contests between Benson, Marigny, and Werner, and on all sides ably maintained. I listened to them with great interest. Besso smiled, and Sheriff Effendi shrugged his shoulders.

Understanding that this mild and intelligent Moslem was in a few days about to join the caravan over the desert through Gaza, to Egypt, I resolved to accompany him. I remember well that, on the eve of our departure, one of those metaphysical discussions arose in which Marigny delighted. When it terminated, he proposed that, as our agreeable assembly was soon about to disperse, each of us should inscribe on a panel of the wall some sentence as a memorial of his sojourn.

Benson wrote first, *'For as in Adam all die, so in Christ all men shall be made alive.'*

Werner wrote, *'Glory to Christ! The supernatural has destroyed the natural.'*

Marigny wrote, *'Knowledge is human.'*

Besso wrote, '*I will not believe in those who must believe in me.*'

Sheriff Effendi wrote, '*God is great; man should be charitable.*'

Contarini Fleming wrote, '*Time.*'

These are the words that were written in the house of Besso, the Hebrew, residing at Jerusalem, near the Gate of Sion. Amen! Travel teaches toleration.

CHAPTER VIII.

ERCHANCE, while I am writing these pages, some sage may be reading, in the once mysterious inscriptions of the most ancient of people, some secret which may change the foundations of human knowledge. Already the chronology of the world assumes a new aspect; already, in the now intelligible theology of Egypt, we have discovered the origin of Grecian polytheism; already we have penetrated beyond the delusive veil of Ptolemaic transmutation: Isis has yielded to Athor, and Osiris to Knepth. The scholar discards the Grecian nomenclature of Sesostris and Memnon. In the temples of Carnac he discovers the conquests of Rameses, and in the palaces of Medinet Abou, the refined civilisation of Amenoph.

Singular fate of modern ages, that beneficent Omnipotence has willed that for all our knowledge we should be indebted to the most insignificant of ancient states. Our divine instruction is handed down to us by an Arabian tribe, and our profane learning flows only from the clans of the Ægean!

(87)

Where are the records of the Great Assyrian
monarchy? Where are the books of the Medes and
Persians? Where the learned annals of the Pha-
raohs?

Fortunate Jordan! Fortunate Ilissus! I have waded
through the sacred waters; with difficulty I traced the
scanty windings of the classic stream. Alas! for the
exuberant Tigris; alas! for the mighty Euphrates; alas!
for the mysterious Nile!

A river is suddenly found flowing through the
wilderness; its source is unknown. On one side are
interminable wastes of sand; on the other, a rocky
desert and a narrow sea. Thus it rolls on for five
hundred miles, throwing up on each side, to the extent of about three leagues, a soil fertile as a garden.
Within a hundred and fifty miles of the sea it divides
into two branches, which wind through an immense
plain, once the granary of the world. Such is Egypt!

From the cataracts of Nubia to the gardens of the
Delta, in a course of twelve hundred miles, the banks
of the Nile are covered at slight intervals with temples and catacombs, pyramids and painted chambers.
The rock temples of Ipsambol, guarded by colossal
forms, are within the roar of the second cataract:
avenues of sphinxes lead to Derr, the chief town of
Nubia: from Derr to the first cataract, the Egyptian
boundary, a series of rock temples conduct to the
beautiful and sacred buildings of Philöe: Edfou and
Esneh are a fine preparation for the colossal splendour
and the massy grace of ancient Thebes.

Even after the inexhaustible curiosity and varied
magnificence of this unrivalled record of ancient art,
the beautiful Dendera, consummate blending of Egyptian imagination and Grecian taste, will command

your enthusiastic gaze; and, if the catacombs of Siout and the chambers of Benihassan prove less fruitful of interest after the tombs of the kings and the cemeteries of Gornou, before you are the obelisks of Memphis, and the pyramids of Gizeh, Saccarah, and Dashour!

CHAPTER IX.

ARABIAN WOMEN.

THE traveller who crosses the desert and views the Nile with its lively villages, clustered in groves of palm, and its banks entirely lined with that graceful tree, will bless with sincerity 'the Father of Waters.' 'Tis a rich land, and indeed flowing with milk and honey. The Delta in its general appearance somewhat reminded me of Belgium. The soil everywhere is a rich black mud and without a single stone. The land is so uniformly flat that those who arrive by sea do not descry it until within half a dozen miles, when a palm tree creeps upon the horizon, and then you observe the line of land that supports it. The Delta is intersected by canals, which are filled by the rising Nile. It is by their medium, and not by the absolute overflowing of the river, that the country is periodically deluged.

The Arabs are gay, witty, vivacious, and susceptible and acute. It is difficult to render them miserable, and a beneficent government may find in them the most valuable subjects. A delightful climate is some compensation for a grinding tyranny. Every

night, as they row along the moonlit river, the boatmen join in a melodious chorus; shouts of merriment
burst from each illumined village; everywhere are
heard the sounds of laughter and of music, and,
wherever you stop, you are saluted by the dancing
girls. These are always graceful in their craft; sometimes agreeable in their persons. They are gaily, even
richly dressed in bright colours, with their hair braided
with pearls, and their necks and foreheads adorned
with strings of gold coin. In their voluptuous dance,
we at once detect the origin of the bolero and fan-
dango and castanets of Spain.

I admire much the Arab women. They are deli-
cately moulded. Never have I seen such twinkling
feet and such small hands. Their complexion is clear,
and not dark; their features beautifully formed and
sharply defined; their eyes liquid with passion, and
bright with intelligence. The traveller is delighted to
find himself in an oriental country where the women
are not imprisoned and scarcely veiled. For a long
time, I could not detect the reason why I was so
charmed with Egyptian life. At last I recollected that
I had recurred, after a long estrangement, to the cheerful influence of women.

CHAPTER X.

CAIRO.

FOLLOWED the course of the Nile far into Nubia, and did not stop until I was under the tropic of Cancer. Shortly after quitting Egypt, the landscape changes. It is perfectly African; mountains of burning sand, vegetation unnaturally vivid, groves of cocoa trees, groups of crocodiles, and an ebony population in a state of nudity, armed with spears of reeds and shields of the hide of the hippopotamus and the giraffe.

The voyage back was tedious, and I was glad after so much wandering to settle down in Cairo.

CHAPTER XI.

THE CITY OF THE DEAD.

CAIRO is situate on the base of considerable hills, whose origin cannot be accounted for, but which are undoubtedly artificial. They are formed by the ruins and the rubbish of long centuries. When I witness these extraordinary formations, which are not uncommon in the neighbourhood of Eastern cities, I am impressed with the idea of the immense antiquity of oriental society.

There is a charm about Cairo, and it is this, that it is a capital in a desert. In one moment you are in the stream of existence, and in another in boundless solitude, or, which is still more awful, the silence of tombs. I speak of the sepulchres of the Mamlouk sultans without the city. They form what may indeed be styled a City of the Dead, an immense Necropolis, full of exquisite buildings, domes covered with fretwork, and minarets carved and moulded with rich and elegant fancy. To me they proved much more interesting than the far-famed pyramids, although their cones in a distance are indeed sublime, their grey cones soaring in the light blue sky.

(93)

The genius that has raised the tombs of the sultans may also be traced in many of the mosques of the city, splendid specimens of Saracenic architecture. In gazing upon these brilliant creations, and also upon those of ancient Egypt, I have often been struck by the felicitous system which they display, of ever forming the external ornaments by inscriptions. How far excelling the Grecian and Gothic method! Instead of a cornice of flowers, or an entablature of unmeaning fancy, how superior to be reminded of the power of the Creator, or the necessity of government, the deeds of conquerors, or the discoveries of arts!

CHAPTER XII.

A SUMMONS FROM HOME.

T WAS in these solitary rides in the desert of Cairo, and in these lone wanderings amid the tombs of the sultans, that I first again felt the desire of composition. My mind appeared suddenly to have returned. I became restless, disquieted. I found myself perpetually indulging in audible soliloquy, and pouring forth impassioned monologues. I was pleased with the system of oriental life, and the liberty in which, in Egypt, Franks can indulge. I felt no inclination to return to Europe, and I determined to cast my lot in this pleasant and fruitful land. I had already spent in Cairo several months, and I now resolved to make it my permanent residence, when I received strange letters from my father. I style them strange, for there breathed throughout a tone of melancholy which with him was unusual, and which perplexed me. He complained of ill health, and expressed a hope that my wanderings were drawing to a close, and that we might again meet. I had been nearly six years absent. Was it possible? Was it indeed six years since I stood upon Mount Jura? And yet in that time how much had happened! How much had I seen, and felt, and learnt! What violent passions, what strange countries, what lively action, and what long meditation!

Strange as may have appeared my conduct to my father, I loved him devotedly. An indication of sentiment on his part ever called forth all my latent affection. It was the conviction, of which I could never divest myself, that he was one who could spare no portion of his sense for the softer feelings, and that his conduct to me was rather in accordance with a system of society than instigated by what I should consider the feelings of a father: it was this conviction that had alone permitted me so long to estrange myself from his hearth. But now he called me back, and almost in sorrow. I read his letter over and over again, dwelt on all its affection and all its suppressed grief. I felt an irresistible desire to hasten to him without a moment's delay. I longed to receive his blessing and his embrace.

I quitted Cairo. The Mahmadie canal was not yet open. I was obliged, therefore, to sail to Rosetta. Thence I crossed the desert in a constant mirage, and arrived at the famous Alexandria. In this busy port I was not long in finding a ship. One was about to sail for Ancona. I engaged a passage, and soon the palms and sands of Egypt vanished from my sight.

CHAPTER XIII.

THE ORANGE GROVE.

OUR passage was tedious. The captain was afraid of pirates, and, alarmed in the night, suddenly changed his course, and made for the Barbary coast, by which we lost our wind. We were becalmed off Candia. I once more beheld Mount Ida.

Having induced the captain to run into port, I landed once more on that fatal coast. The old consul and his family were still there, and received me with a kindness which reminded me of our first happy meeting. I slept in the same chamber. When I awoke in the morning the sun was still shining, the bright plants still quivering in its beams. But the gazelle had gone, the white gazelle had died. And my gazelle, where was she?

I beheld our home, our once happy home. Spiro only was with me, and his family came forth with joy to greet him. I left them, and hastened with tremulous steps to the happy valley. I passed by the grove of orange trees. My strength deserted me. I leant nearly fainting against a tree. At last I dared to advance a step, and look forward.

I beheld it: yes! I beheld it, green and verdant, and covered with white roses; but I dared not approach. I wafted it an embrace and a blessing, and rushed to the shore.

At Ancona I entered the lazaretto to perform a long quarantine. I instantly wrote to my father, and despatched a courier to my banker at Florence. I received from him in a few days a packet. I opened it with a sad foreboding. A letter in my father's handwriting reassured me. I tore it open; I read.

CHAPTER XIV.

A Tender Letter.

Y BELOVED Contarini, the hand of death is upon me. Each day my energies decrease. I can conceal from others, but not from myself, my gradual but certain decay. We shall not meet again, my child; I have a deep conviction we shall not meet again. Yet I would not die without expressing to you my love, without yielding to feelings which I have too long suppressed.

'Child of my affections! receive my blessing. Offspring of my young passion! let me press you, in imagination, to my lone bosom!

'Ah! why are you not with me? why is not my hand in yours? There is much to say, more than I can ever express; yet I must write, for I would not die without my son doing justice to his father.

'As a child, you doubted my love; as a man, in spite of all your struggles, I am conscious you never divested yourself of the agonising idea. What is this life, this life of error and misconception and woe!

'My feeble pen trembles in my hand. There is much to write, much, alas! that never can be written. Why are we parted?

'You think me cold; you think me callous; you think me a hollow-hearted worldling. Contarini! recall the doubt and misery of your early years, and all your wild thoughts, and dark misgivings, and vain efforts; recall all these, and behold the boyhood of your father!

'I, too, believed myself a poet; I, too, aspired to emancipate my kind; I, too, looked forward to a glorious future, and the dazzling vista of eternal fame. The passions of my heart were not less violent than yours, and not less ardent was my impetuous love.

'Woe! woe! the father and the son have been alike stricken. I know all; I know all, my child. I would have saved you from the bitter lot; I alone would have borne the deep despair.

'Was she fair? Was she beautiful? Alas! there was once one as bright and as glorious; you knew not your mother.

'I can remember the day but as yesterday when I first gazed upon the liquid darkness of her eye. It was in that fatal city I will not name; horrible Venice!

'I found her surrounded by a thousand slaves; I won her from amid this band; against the efforts and opposition of all her family I won her. Yes! she was my bride; the beautiful daughter of this romantic land; a land to which I was devoted, and for which I would have perilled my life. Alas! I perilled my love! My imagination was fired by that wondrous and witching city. My love of freedom, my hatred of oppression, burned each day with a brighter and more vehement flame. I sighed over its past glory and present degradation; and when I mingled my blood with the veins of the Contarini, I vowed I would revive the glory they had themselves created.

'Venice was at that time under the yoke of the French. The recollection of the republic was still fresh in men's minds; the son of the last doge was my relative and my friend. Unhappy Manini! thy memory demands a tear.

'We conspired. Even now my blood seems to flow with renewed force, when I recall the excitement of our secret meetings in the old Palazzo Contarini, on the Grand Lagune. How often has daylight on the waters reminded us of our long councils!

'We were betrayed. Timely information permitted me to escape. I bore away my wife. We reached Mantua in safety. Perhaps it was the agitation of the event and the flight; since the tragedy of Candia I have sometimes thought it might have been a constitutional doom. But that fatal night: why, why recall it? We have both alike suffered. No, not alike, for I had my child.

'My child, my darling child, even now your recollection maintains me; even now my cheek warms, as I repose upon the anticipation of your glory.

'I will not dwell upon what I then endured. Alas! I cannot leave it to your imagination. Your reality has taught you all. I roved a madman amid the mountains of the Tyrol. But you were with me, my child, and I looked upon your mild and pensive eyes, and the wildness of my thoughts died away.

'I recurred to those hopes of poetic fame which had soothed the dull wretchedness of my boyhood. Alas! no flame from heaven descended on my lyre. I experienced only mortification; and so complete was my wretchedness, so desolate my life, so void of hope and cheerfulness, and even the prospect of that common ease which the merest animals require, that, had it not been for you, I would have freed myself from the indescribable burden of my existence. My hereditary estates were confiscated; my friends, like myself, were in exile. We were, in fact, destitute, and I had lost all confidence in my energies.

'Thus woe-begone, I entered Vienna, where I found a friend. Mingling in the artificial society of that refined city, those excited feelings, fed by my strange adventures and solitary life, subsided. I began to lose what was peculiar in me, and to share much that was general. Worldly feelings sprang up. Some success brought back my confidence. I believed that I was not destitute of power, but had only mistaken its nature. It was a political age. A great theatre seemed before me. I had ever been ambitious. I directed my desires into a new channel, and I determined to be a statesman.

'I had attracted the attention of the Austrian minister. I became his secretary. You know the rest.

'I resolved that my child should be happy. I desired to save him from the misery that clouded my own youth. I would have preserved him from the tyranny of impetuous passions, and the harrowing woe that awaits an ill-regulated mind. I observed in him a dangerous susceptibility that alarmed me. I studied to prevent the indulgence of his feelings. I was kind, but I was calm. His imaginative temperament did not escape me. I perceived only hereditary weakness, and would have prevented hereditary woe. It was my aim to make him a practical man. Contarini, it was the anxiety of affection that prevented me from doing justice to your genius.

'My son, could I but once press you in my arms, I should die happy. And even now the future supports me, and I feel the glory of your coming fame irradiating my tomb.

'Why cannot we meet? I could say so much, although I would say only I loved you. The pen falls from my hand, the feeble pen, that has signified nothing. Imagine what I would express. Cherish my memory, while you receive my blessing.'

'Let me fly, let me fly to him instantly!' I felt the horrors of imprisonment; I wrung my hands, and stamped from helplessness. There was a packet. I opened it; a lock of rich dark hair, whose colour was not strange to me, and a beautiful miniature, that seemed a portrait of my beloved, yet I gazed upon the countenance of my mother.

CHAPTER XV.

 HERE was yet a letter from my banker which I long neglected to open. I opened it at last, and learned the death of my remaining parent.

The age of tears was past; that relief was denied me. I looked up to Heaven in despair. I flew to a darkened chamber. I buried my face in my hands; and, lone and speechless, I delivered myself up for days to the silent agony of the past.

PART THE SEVENTH.

CHAPTER I.

In Rome.

LEANT against a column of the Temple of Castor. On one side was the Palace of the Cæsars; on the other, the colossal amphitheatre of Vespasian. Arches of triumph, the pillars of Pagan temples, and the domes of Christian churches rose around me. In the distance was the wide Campagna, the Claudian Aqueduct, and the Alban Mount.

Solitude and silence reigned on that sacred road once echoing with the shouts and chariots of three hundred triumphs; solitude and silence, meet companions of imperial desolation! Where are the spoils of Egypt and of Carthage? Where the golden tribute of Iberia? Where the long Gallic trophies? Where are the rich armour and massy cups of Macedon? Where are the pictures and statues of Corinth? Where the libraries of Athens? Where is the broken bow of Parthia? Where are the elephants of Pontus, and the gorgeous diadems of the Asian Kings?

And where is Rome? All nations rose and flourished only to swell her splendour, and now I stand amid her ruins.

In such a scene what are our private griefs and petty sorrows? And what is man? I felt my nothingness. Life seemed flat, and dull, and trifling. I could not conceive that I could again become interested in its base pursuits. I believed that I could no longer be influenced by joy or by sorrow. Indifference alone remained.

A man clambered down the steep of the Palatine. It was Winter, flushed and eager from a recent excavation.

'What, Count,' he exclaimed, 'moralising in the Forum!'

'Alas, Winter, what is life?'

'An excellent thing, so long as one can discover as pretty a Torso as I have stumbled upon this morning.'

'A Torso! a maimed memorial of the past. The very name is melancholy.'

'What is the past to me? I am not dead. You may be. I exist in the present.'

'The vanity of the present overpowers me.

'Pooh! I tell you what, my friend, the period has arrived in your life, when you must renounce meditation. Action is now your part. Meditation is culture. It is well to think until a man has discovered his genius, and developed his faculties, but then let him put his intelligence in motion. Act, act, act; act without ceasing, and you will no longer talk of the vanity of life.'

'But how am I to act?'

'Create. Man is made to create, from the poet to the potter.'

CHAPTER II.

CREATION OF THE BEAUTIFUL.

MY FATHER bequeathed me his entire property, which was more considerable than I imagined; the Countess and her children being amply provided for by her own estate. In addition to this, I found that he had claimed in my favour the Contarini estates, to which, independently of the validity of my marriage, I was entitled through my mother. After much litigation, the question had been decided in my behalf a few months before my return to Italy. I found myself, therefore, unexpectedly a rich man. I wrote to the Countess, and received from her an affectionate reply; nor should I omit that I was honoured by an autograph letter of condolence from the King and an invitation to re-enter his service.

As I was now wearied with wandering, and desirous of settling down in life; and as I had been deprived of those affections which render home delightful, I determined to find in the creations of art some consolation, and some substitute for that domestic bliss which I value above all other blessings. I resolved to create a paradise. I purchased a large

estate in the vicinity of Naples, with a palace and
beautiful gardens. I called in the assistance of the
first artists in the country; and I availed myself, above
all, of the fine taste of my friend Winter. The palace
was a Palladian pile, built upon a stately terrace covered with orange and citron trees, and to which you
ascended by broad flights of marble steps. The formation of the surrounding country was highly picturesque, hills beautifully peaked or undulating, and
richly wooded, covered with the cypress and the
ilex, and crowned with the stone pine. Occasionally
you caught a glimpse of the blue sea and the brilliant
coast.

Upon the terrace upon each side of the portal, I
have placed a colossal sphinx, which were excavated
when I was at Thebes, and which I was fortunate
enough to purchase. They are of rose-coloured granite,
and as fresh and sharp as if they were finished yesterday. There is a soft majesty and a serene beauty
in the countenances, which are remarkable.

It is my intention to build in these beautiful do-
mains a Saracenic palace, which my oriental collec-
tions will befit, but which I hope also to fill with the
masterpieces of Christian art. At present I have
placed in a gallery some fine specimens of the Venetian, Roman, and Eclectic schools, and have ranged
between them copies in marble, by Bertolini, of the
most celebrated ancient statues. In one cabinet, by
itself, is the gem of my collection, a Magdalen by
Murillo; and, in another, a sleeping Cupid, by Canova,
over which I have contrived, by a secret light, to
throw a rosy flush, that invests the ideal beauty of
the sculptor with a still more ideal life. At the end
of the gallery I have placed the portraits of my father

and of my mother; the latter copied by an excellent artist from a miniature. Between them is a frame of richly carved ivory, enclosing a black velvet veil, studded with white roses worked in pearls.

Around me, I hope in time to create a scene which may rival in beauty and variety, although not in extent, the villa of Hadrian, whom I have always considered the most sumptuous and accomplished character of antiquity. I have already commenced the foundation of a tower which shall rise at least one hundred and fifty feet, and which, I trust, will equal in the beauty of the design and in the solidity of the masonry the most celebrated works of antiquity. This tower I shall dedicate to the Future, and I intend that it shall be my tomb.

Lausanne has married, and will never quit me. He has promised also to form a band of wind instruments, a solace necessary to solitude. Winter is my only friend and my only visitor. He is a great deal with me, and has a studio in the palace. He is so independent, that he often arrives and quits it without my knowledge; yet I never converse with him without pleasure.

Here let me pass my life in the study and the creation of the beautiful. Such is my desire; but whether it will be my career is, I feel, doubtful. My interest in the happiness of my race is too keen to permit me for a moment to be blind to the storms that lour on the horizon of society. Perchance also the political regeneration of the country to which I am devoted may not be distant, and in that great work I am resolved to participate. Bitter jest, that the most civilised portion of the globe should be considered incapable of self-government!

When I examine the state of European society with the unimpassioned spirit which the philosopher can alone command, I perceive that it is in a state of transition, a state of transition from feodal to federal principles. This I conceive to be the sole and secret cause of all the convulsions that have occurred and are · to occur.

Circumstances are beyond the control of man; but his conduct is in his own power. The great event is as sure as that I am now penning this prophecy of its occurrence. With us it rests whether it shall be welcomed by wisdom or by ignorance, whether its beneficent results shall be accelerated by enlightened minds, or retarded by our dark passions.

What is the arch of the conqueror, what the laurel of the poet! I think of the infinity of space, I feel my nothingness. Yet if I am to be remembered, let me be remembered as one who, in a sad night of gloomy ignorance and savage bigotry was prescient of the flaming morning-break of bright philosophy, as one who deeply sympathised with his fellow-men, and felt a proud and profound conviction of their perfectibility; as one who devoted himself to the amelioration of his kind, by the destruction of error and the propagation of truth.

COUNT ALARCOS:

A TRAGEDY.

ADVERTISEMENT

———

As THERE is no historical authority for the events of the celebrated Ballad on which this Tragedy is founded, I have fixed upon the thirteenth century for the period of their occurrence. At that time the kingdom of Castille had recently obtained that supremacy in Spain which led, in a subsequent age, to the political integrity of the country. Burgos, its capital, was a magnificent city; and then also arose that masterpiece of Christian architecture, its famous Cathedral.

This state of comparative refinement and civilisation permitted the introduction of more complicated motives than the rude manners of the Ballad would have authorised; while the picturesque features of the Castillian middle ages still flourished in full force; the factions of a powerful nobility, renowned for their turbulence, strong passions, enormous crimes, profound superstition.

Δ.

LONDON: *May*, 1839.

DRAMATIS PERSONÆ.

THE KING OF CASTILLE.
COUNT ALARCOS, a Prince of the Blood.
COUNT OF SIDONIA.
COUNT OF LEON.
PRIOR OF BURGOS.
ORAN, a Moor.
FERDINAND, a Page.
GUZMAN JACA, a Bravo.
GRAUS, the Keeper of a Posada.

SOLISA, Infanta of Castille, only child of the King.
FLORIMONDE, Countess Alarcos.
FLIX, a Hostess.

Courtiers, Pages, Chamberlains, Bravos, and Priests.

Time : The 13th Century.
Scene : Burgos, the Capital of Castille, and its vicinity.

COUNT ALARCOS:

A TRAGEDY.

ACT I.

SCENE I.

A Street in Burgos; the Cathedral in the distance
Enter TWO COURTIERS.

1ST COUR.

HE Prince of Hungary dismissed?

2ND COUR.
Indeed

So runs the rumour.

1ST COUR.
Why, the spousal note

Still floats upon the air!

2ND COUR.

Myself this morn
Beheld the Infanta's entrance, as she threw,
Proud as some bitless barb, her haughty glance
On our assembled chiefs.

1ST COUR.
The Prince was there?

2ND COUR.

Most royally; nor seemed a man more fit
To claim a kingdom for a dower. He looked
Our Gadian Hercules, as the advancing peers
Their homage paid. I followed in the train
Of Count Alarcos, with whose ancient house
My fortunes long have mingled.

1ST COUR.

'Tis the same,
But just returned?

2ND COUR.

Long banished from the Court
And only favoured since the Queen's decease,
His ancient foe.

1ST COUR.

A very potent Lord?

2ND COUR.

Near to the throne; too near perchance for peace
You're young at Burgos, or indeed 'twere vain
To sing Alarcos' praise, the brightest knight
That ever waved a lance in Old Castille.

1ST COUR.

You followed in his train?

2ND COUR.

And as we passed,
Alarcos bowing to the lowest earth,
The Infanta swooned; and pale as yon niched
saint,
From off the thronèd step, her seat of place,
Fell in a wild and senseless agony.

1ST COUR.

Sancta Maria! and the King—

2ND COUR.

Uprose

And bore her from her maidens, then broke up
The hurried Court; indeed I know no more:
For like a turning tide the crowd pressed on,
And scarcely could I gain the grateful air.
Yet on the Prado's walk came smiling by
The Bishop of Ossuna; as he passed
He clutched my cloak, and whispered in my ear,
'The match is off.'

Enter PAGE.

1ST COUR.

Hush! hush! a passenger.

PAGE.

Most noble Cavaliers, I pray, inform me
Where the great Count Alarcos holds his quarter.

2ND COUR.

In the chief square. His banner tells the roof;
Your pleasure with the Count, my gentle youth?

PAGE.

I were a sorry messenger to tell
My mission to the first who asks its aim.

2ND COUR.

The Count Alarcos is my friend and chief.

PAGE.

Then better reason I should trusty be.
For you can be a witness to my trust.

1ST COUR.

A forward youth!

2ND COUR.

A page is ever pert.

PAGE.

Ay! ever pert is youth that baffles age.

[*Exit* PAGE.

1ST COUR.

The Count is married?

2ND COUR.

To a beauteous lady;
And blessed with a fair race.   A happy man
Indeed is Count Alarcos.

[*A trumpet sounds.*

1ST COUR.

Prithee, see;
Passes he now?

2ND COUR.

Long since.   Yon banner tells
The Count Sidonia.   Let us on, and view
The passage of his pomp.   His Moorish steeds,
They say, are very choice.

[*Exeunt* TWO COURTIERS.

————

SCENE 2.

A Chamber in the Palace of Alarcos.   The COUNTESS
seated and working at her tapestry; the
COUNT *pacing the Chamber.*

COUN.

You are disturbed, Alarcos?

ALAR.

'Tis the stir
And tumult of this morn. I am not used
To Courts.

COUN.

I know not why, it is a name
That makes me tremble.

ALAR.

Tremble, Florimonde,
Why should you tremble?

COUN.

Sooth I cannot say.
Methinks the Court but little suits my kind;
I love our quiet home.

ALAR.

This is our home.

COUN.

When you are here.

ALAR.

I will be always here.

COUN.

Thou canst not, sweet Alarcos. Happy hours,
When we were parted but to hear thy horn
Sound in our native woods!

ALAR.

Why, this is humour!
We're courtiers now; and we must smile and
    smirk.

COUN.

Methinks your tongue is gayer than your glance.
The King, I hope, was gracious?

ALAR.

Were he not,
My frown's as prompt as his. He was most
gracious.

COUN.

Something has chafed thee?

ALAR.

What should chafe me, child,
And when should hearts be light, if mine be dull?
Is not mine exile over? Is it naught
To breathe in the same house where we were
born,
And sleep where slept our fathers? Should that
chafe?

COUN.

Yet didst thou leave my side this very morn,
And with a vow this day should ever count
Amid thy life most happy; when we meet
Thy brow is clouded.

ALAR.

Joy is sometimes grave,
And deepest when 'tis calm. And I am joyful,
If it be joy, this long forbidden hall
Once more to pace, and feel each fearless step
Tread on a baffled foe.

COUN.

Hast thou still foes?

ALAR.

I trust so; I should not be what I am,
Still less what I will be, if hate did not
Pursue me as my shadow. Ah! fair wife,

Thou knowest not Burgos. Thou hast yet to
    fathom
The depths of thy new world.

Coun.

I do recoil
As from some unknown woe, from this same world.
I thought we came for peace.

Alar.

Peace dwells within
No lordly roof in Burgos. We have come
For triumph.

Coun.

So I share thy lot, Alarcos,
All feelings are the same.

Alar.

My Florimonde,
I took thee from a fair and pleasant home
In a soft land, where, like the air they live in,
Men's hearts are mild. This proud and fierce
    Castille
Resembles not thy gentle Aquitaine,
More than the eagle may a dove, and yet
It is my country. Danger in its bounds
Weighs more than foreign safety. But why speak
Of what exists not?

Coun.

And I hope may never!

Alar.

And if it come, what then? This chance shall
    find me
Not unprepared.

COUN.

But why should there be danger?
And why should'st thou, the foremost prince of
    Spain,
Fear or make foes? Thou standest in no light
Would fall on other shoulders; thou hast no height
To climb, and naught to gain.   Thou art complete;
The King alone above thee, and thy friend.

ALAR.

So I would deem. I did not speak of fear.

COUN.

Of danger?

ALAR.

That's delight, when it may lead
To mighty ends. Ah, Florimonde! thou art too
    pure;
Unsoiled in the rough and miry paths
Of this same trampling world; unskilled in heats
Of fierce and emulous spirits. There's a rapture
In the strife of factions, that a woman's soul
Can never reach. Men smiled on me to-day
Would gladly dig my grave; and yet I smiled,
And gave them coin as ready as their own,
And not less base.

COUN.

And can there be such men,
And canst thou live with them?

ALAR.

Ay! and they saw
Me ride this morning in my state again;
The people cried 'Alarcos and Castille!'
The shout will dull their feasts.

COUN.

There was a time
Thou didst look back as on a turbulent dream
On this same life.

ALAR.

I was an exile then.
This stirring Burgos has revived my vein.
Yea, as I glanced from off the Citadel
This very morn, and at my feet outspread
Its amphitheatre of solemn towers
And groves of golden pinnacles, and marked
Turrets of friends and foes; or traced the range,
Spread since my exile, of our city's walls
Washed by the swift Arlanzon: all around
The flash of lances, blaze of banners, rush
Of hurrying horsemen, and the haughty blast
Of the soul-stirring trumpet, I renounced
My old philosophy, and gazed as gazes
The falcon on his quarry!

COUN.

Jesu grant
The lure will bear no harm! [*A trumpet sounds.*

ALAR.

Whose note is that?
I hear the tramp of horsemen in the court;
We have some guests.

COUN.

Indeed!

Enter the COUNT OF SIDONIA, *and the* COUNT OF LEON.

ALAR.

My noble friends,
My Countess greets ye!

SIDO.

                   And indeed we pay
To her our homage.

          LEON.

                   Proud our city boasts
So fair a presence.

          COUN.

                   Count Alarcos' friends
Are ever welcome here.

          ALAR.

          No common wife,
Who welcomes with a smile her husband's friends.

          SIDO.

Indeed a treasure! When I marry, Count,
I'll claim your counsel.

          COUN.

          'Tis not then your lot?

          SIDO.

Not yet, sweet dame; tho' sooth to say, full often
I dream such things may be.

          COUN.

          Your friend is free?

          LEON.

And values freedom: with a rosy chain
I still should feel a captive.

          SIDO.

          Noble Leon
Is proof against the gentle passion, lady,
And will ere long, my rapier for a gage,
Marry a scold.

LEON.

In Burgos now, methinks,
Marriage is scarce the mode. Our princess frowns,
It seems, upon her suitors.

SIDO.

Is it true

The match is off?

LEON.

'Tis said.

COUN.

The match is off!
You did not tell me this strange news, Alarcos.

SIDO.

Did he not tell you how —

ALAR.

In truth, good sirs,
My wife and I are somewhat strangers here,
And things that are of moment to the minds
That long have dwelt on them, to us are naught.
    (*To the* COUNTESS.)
There was a sort of scene to-day at Court;
The Princess fainted: we were all dismissed,
Somewhat abruptly; but, in truth, I deem
These rumours have no source but in the tongues
Of curious idlers.

SIDO.

Faith, I hold them true.
Indeed they're very rife.

LEON.

Poor man, methinks
His is a lot forlorn, at once to lose
A mistress and a crown!

Coun.

       Yet both may bring
Sorrow and cares. But little joy, I ween,
Dwells with a royal bride, too apt to claim
The homage she should yield.

Sido.

       I would all wives
Held with your Countess in this pleasing creed.

Alar.

She has her way: it is a cunning wench
That knows to wheedle. Burgos still maintains
Its fame for noble fabrics. Since my time
The city's spread.

Sido.

       Ah! you're a traveller, Count.
And yet we have not lagged.

Coun.

       The Infanta, sirs,
Was it a kind of swoon?

Alar.

       Old Lara lives
Still in his ancient quarter?

Leon.

       With the rats
That share his palace. You spoke, Madam?

Coun.

                        She
Has dainty health, perhaps?

Leon.

       All ladies have.
And yet as little of the fainting mood
As one could fix on —

ALAR.

Mendola left treasure?

SIDO.

Wedges of gold, a chamber of sequins
Sealed up for ages, flocks of Barbary sheep
Might ransom princes, tapestry so rare
The King straight purchased, covering for the price
Each piece with pistoles.

COUN.

Is she very fair?

LEON.

As future queens must ever be, and yet
Her face might charm uncrowned.

COUN.

It grieves me much
To hear the Prince departs.   'Tis not the first
Among her suitors?

ALAR.

Your good uncle lives—
Nunez de Leon?

LEON.

To my cost, Alarcos;
He owes me much.

SIDO.

Some promises his heir
Would wish fulfilled.

COUN.

In Gascony, they said,
Navarre had sought her hand.

LEON.

He loitered here
But could not pluck the fruit: it was too high.

Sidonia threw him in a tilt one day.
The Infanta has her fancies; unhorsed knights
Count not among them.

Enter a CHAMBERLAIN *who whispers* COUNT ALARCOS.

ALAR.
Urgent, and me alone
Will commune with! A Page! Kind guests, your
    pardon,
I'll find you here anon. My Florimonde,
Our friends will not desert you, like your spouse.
[*Exit* ALARCOS.

COUN.
My Lords, will see our gardens?

SIDO.
We are favoured.
We wait upon your steps.

LEON.
And feel that roses
Will spring beneath them.

COUN.
You are an adept, sir,
In our gay science.

LEON.
Faith, I stole it, lady,
From a loose Troubadour Sidonia keeps
To write his sonnets.   [*Exeunt omnes.*

SCENE 3.

A Chamber.

Enter ALARCOS *and* PAGE.

PAGE.

Will you wait here, my Lord?

ALAR.

I will, sir Page.

[*Exit* Page.

The Bishop of Ossuna: what would he?
He scents the prosperous ever. Ay! they'll cluster
Round this new hive. But I'll not house them yet.
Marry, I know them all; but me they know,
As mountains might the leaping stream that meets
The ocean as a river. Time and exile
Change our life's course, but is its flow less deep
Because it is more calm? I've seen to-day
Might stir its pools. What if my phantom flung
A shade on their bright path? 'Tis closed to me
Although the goal's a crown. She loved me once;
Now swoons, and now the match is off. She's true.
But I have clipped the heart that once could soar
High as her own! Dreams, dreams! And yet en-
      tranced,
Unto the fair phantasma that is fled,
My struggling fancy clings; for there are hours
When memory with her signet stamps the brain
With an undying mint; and these were such,
When high Ambition and enraptured Love,
Twin Genii of my daring destiny,

Bore on my sweeping life with their full wing,
Like an angelic host:

> [*In the distance enter a lady veiled.*
> Is this their priest?

Burgos unchanged I see.

> [*Advancing towards her.*
> A needless veil

To one prophetic of thy charms, fair lady.
And yet they fall on an ungracious eye.

> [*Withdraws the veil.*

Solisa!

SOL.

> Yes! Solisa; once again
O say Solisa! let that long lost voice
Breathe with a name too faithful!

ALAR.

> Oh! what tones,
What amazing sight is this! The spellbound forms
Of my first youth rise up from the abyss
Of opening time. I listen to a voice
That bursts the sepulchre of buried hope
Like an immortal trumpet.

SOL.

> Thou hast granted,
MARY, my prayers!

ALAR.

> Solisa, my Solisa!

SOL.

Thine, thine, Alarcos. But thou: whose art thou?

ALAR.

Within this chamber is my memory bound;
I have no thought, no consciousness beyond
Its precious walls.

SOL.

Thus did he look, thus speak,
When to my heart he clung, and I to him
Breathed my first love —— and last.

ALAR.

Alas! alas!
Woe to thy Mother, maiden.

SOL.

She has found
That which I oft have prayed for.

ALAR.

But not found
A doom more dark than ours.

SOL.

I sent for thee,
To tell thee why I sent for thee; yet why,
Alas! I know not. Was it but to look
Alone upon the face that once was mine?
This morn it was so grave. O! was it woe,
Or but indifference, that inspired that brow
That seemed so cold and stately? Was it hate?
O! tell me anything, but that to thee
I am a thing of nothingness.

ALAR.

O spare!
Spare me such words of torture.

SOL.

Could I feel
Thou didst not hate me, that my image brought
At least a gentle, if not tender thought,
I'd be content. I cannot live to think,
After the past, that we should meet again

And change cold looks.   We are not strangers, say
At least we are not strangers?

ALAR.

Gentle Princess —

SOL.

Call me Solisa; tho' we meet no more
Call me Solisa now.

ALAR.

Thy happiness —

SOL.

O! no, no, no, not happiness, at least
Not from those lips.

ALAR.

Indeed it is a name
That ill becomes them.

SOL.

Yet they say, thou'rt happy,
And bright with all prosperity, and I
Felt solace in that thought.

ALAR.

Prosperity!
Men call them prosperous whom they deem enjoy
That which they envy; but there's no success
Save in one master-wish fulfilled, and mine
Is lost forever.

SOL.

Why was it?   O, why
Didst thou forget me?

ALAR.

Never, lady, never —
But ah! the past, the irrevocable past —
We can but meet to mourn.

SOL.

No, not to mourn,
I came to bless thee, came to tell to thee
I hoped that thou wert happy.

ALAR.

Come to mourn.
I'll find delight in my unbridled grief:
Yes! let me fling away at last this mask,
And gaze upon my woe.

SOL.

O, it was rash,
Indeed, 'twas rash, Alarcos; what, sweet sir,
What, after all our vows, to hold me false,
And place this bar between us! I'll not think
Thou ever loved'st me as thou did'st profess,
And that's the bitter drop.

ALAR.

Indeed, indeed —

SOL.

I could bear much, I could bear all, but this
My faith in thy past love, it was so deep,
So pure, so sacred, 'twas my only solace;
I fed upon it in my secret heart,
And now e'en that is gone.

ALAR.

Doubt not the past,
'Tis sanctified. It is the green fresh spot
In my life's desert.

SOL.

There is none to thee
As I have been? Speak, speak, Alarcos, tell me
Is't true? Or, in this shipwreck of my soul,

Do I cling wildly to some perishing hope
That sinks like me?

ALAR.

The May-burst of the heart
Can bloom but once; and mine has fled, not faded.
That thought gave fancied solace, ah, 'twas fancy,
For now I feel my doom.

SOL.

Thou hast no doom
But what is splendid as thyself.   Alas!
Weak woman, when she stakes her heart, must play
Ever a fatal chance.   It is her all,
And when 'tis lost, she's bankrupt; but proud man
Shuffles the cards again, and wins to-morrow
What pays his present forfeit.

ALAR.

But alas!

What have I won?

SOL.

A country and a wife.

ALAR.

A wife!

SOL.

A wife, and very fair, they say.
She should be fair, who could induce thee break
Such vows as thine.   O! I am very weak.
Why came I here?   Was it indeed to see
If thou could'st look on me?

ALAR.

My own Solisa.

SOL.

Call me not thine; why, what am I to thee
That thou should'st call me thine?

ALAR.

              Indeed, sweet lady,
Thou lookest on a man as bruised in spirit,
As broken-hearted, and subdued in soul,
As any breathing wretch that deems the day
Can bring no darker morrow. Pity me!
And if kind words may not subdue those lips
So scornful in their beauty, be they touched
At least by Mercy's accents! Was't a crime,
I could not dare believe that royal heart
Retained an exile's image? that forlorn,
Harassed, worn out, surrounded by strange aspects
And stranger manners, in those formal ties
Custom points out, I sought some refuge, found
At least companionship, and, grant t'was weak,
Shrunk from the sharp endurance of the doom
That awaits on exile, utter loneliness!

SOL.

His utter loneliness!

ALAR.

           And met thy name,
Most beauteous lady, prithee think of this,
Only to hear the princes of the world
Were thy hot suitors, and that one would soon
Be happier than Alarcos.

SOL.

           False, most false,
They told thee false.

ALAR.

           At least, then, pity me,
Solisa!

Sol.

       Ah! Solisa, that sweet voice,
Why should I pity thee? 'Tis not my office.
Go, go to her that cheered thy loneliness,
Thy utter loneliness. And had I none?
Had I no pangs of solitude? Exile!
O! there were moments I'd have gladly given
My crown for banishment. A wounded heart
Beats freer in a desert; 'tis the air
Of palaces that chokes it.

Alar.

          Fate has crossed,
Not falsehood, our sweet loves. Our lofty passion
Is tainted with no vileness. Memory bears
Convulsion, not contempt; no palling sting
That waits on base affections. It is something
To have loved thee; and in that thought I find
My sense exalted; wretched though I be.

Sol.

Is he so wretched? Yet he is less forlorn
Than when he sought, what I would never seek,
A partner in his woe! I'll ne'er believe it;
Thou art not wretched. Why, thou hast a friend,
A sweet companion in thy grief to soothe
Thy loneliness, and feed on thy bright smiles,
Thrill with thine accents, with impassioned rever-
      ence
Enclasp thine hand, and with enchained eyes
Gaze on thy glorious presence. O, Alarcos!
Art thou not worshipped now? What, can it be,
That there is one, who walks in Paradise,
Nor feels the air immortal?

ALAR.

Let my curse
Descend upon the hour I left thy walls,
My father's town!

SOL.

My blessing on thy curse!
Thou hast returned, thou hast returned, Alarcos?

ALAR.

To despair.

SOL.

Yet 'tis not the hour he quitted
Our city's wall, it is the tie that binds him
Within those walls, my lips would more denounce,
But ah, that tie is dear!

ALAR.

Accursèd be
The wiles that parted us; accursèd be
The ties that sever us!

SOL.

Thou'rt mine.

ALAR.

For ever.
Thou unpolluted passion of my youth,
My first, my only, my enduring love!
(*They embrace.*)

Enter FERDINAND, *the Page.*

FER.

Lady, a message from thy royal father;
He comes —

SOL.

(*Springing from the arms of* ALARCOS.)

My father! word of fear! Why now
To cloud my light? I had forgotten fate;
But he recalls it. O my bright Alarcos!
My love must fly. Nay, not one word of care;
Love only from those lips. Yet, ere we part,
Seal our sweet faith renewed.

ALAR.

And never broken.
[*Exit* ALARCOS.

SOL.

Why has he gone? Why did I bid him go?
And let this jewel I so daring plucked
Slip in the waves again? I'm sure there's time
To call him back, and say farewell once more.
I'll say farewell no more; it was a word
Ever harsh music when the morrow brought
Welcomes renewed of love. No more farewells.
O when will he be mine! I cannot wait,
I cannot tarry, now I know he loves me;
Each hour, each instant that I see him not,
Is usurpation of my right. O joy!
Am I the same Solisa, that this morn
Breathed forth her orison with humbler spirit
Than the surrounding acolytes? Thou'st smiled,
Sweet Virgin, on my prayers. Twice fifty tapers
Shall burn before thy shrine. Guard over me
O! mother of my soul, and let me prosper
In my great enterprise! O hope! O love!
O sharp remembrance of long baffled joy!
Inspire me now.

SCENE 4.

The KING; *the* INFANTA.

KING.

I see my daughter?

SOL.

Sir, your duteous child.

KING.

Art thou indeed my child? I had some doubt
I was a father.

SOL.

These are bitter words.

KING.

Even as thy conduct.

SOL.

Then it would appear
My conduct and my life are but the same.

KING.

I thought thou wert the Infanta of Castille,
Heir to our realm, the paragon of Spain;
The Princess for whose smiles crowned Christen-
    dom
Sends forth its sceptred rivals. Is that bitter?
Or bitter is it with such privilege,
And standing on life's vantage ground, to cross
A nation's hope, that on thy nice career
Has gaged its heart?

SOL.

Have I no heart to gage?
A sacrificial virgin, must I bind

My life to the altar, to redeem a state,
Or heal some doomèd people?

KING.

                    Is it so?
Is this an office alien to thy sex?
Or what thy youth repudiates? We but ask
What nature sanctions.

SOL.

                    Nature sanctions Love;
Your charter is more liberal. Let that pass.
I am no stranger to my duty, sir,
And read it thus. The blood that shares my sceptre
Should be august as mine. A woman loses
In love what she may gain in rank, who tops
Her husband's place; though throned, I would
      exchange
An equal glance. His name should be a spell
To rally soldiers. Politic he should be;
And skilled in climes and tongues; that stranger
      knights
Should bruit our high Castillian courtesies.
Such chief might please a state?

KING.

                    Fortunate realm!

SOL.

And shall I own less niceness than my realm?
No! I would have him handsome as a god;
Hyperion in his splendour, or the mien
Of conquering Bacchus, one whose very step
Should guide a limner, and whose common words
Are caught by Troubadours to frame their songs!
And O, my father, what if this bright prince

Should have a heart as tender as his soul
Was high and peerless? If with this same heart
He loved thy daughter?

KING.

Close the airy page
Of thy romance; such princes are not found
Except in lays and legends! yet a man
Who would become a throne, I found thee, girl;
The princely Hungary.

SOL.

A more princely fate,
Than an unwilling wife, he did deserve.

KING.

Yet wherefore didst thou pledge thy troth to him?

SOL.

And wherefore do I smile when I should sigh?
And wherefore do I feed when I would fast?
And wherefore do I dance when I should pray?
And wherefore do I live when I should die?
Canst answer that, good Sir? O there are women
The world deems mad, or worse, whose life but
    seems
One vile caprice, a freakish thing of whims
And restless nothingness; yet if we pierce
The soul, may be we'll touch some cause profound
For what seems causeless. Early love despised,
Or baffled, which is worse; a faith betrayed,
For vanity or lucre; chill regards,
Where to gain constant glances we have paid
Some fearful forfeit: here are many springs,
Unmarked by shallow eyes, and some, or all

Of these, or none, may prompt my conduct now —
But I'll not have thy prince.

KING.

My gentle child —

SOL.

I am not gentle. I might have been once;
But gentle thoughts and I have parted long;
The cause of such partition thou shouldst know
If memories were just.

KING.

Harp not, I pray,

On an old sorrow.

SOL.

Old! he calls it old!
The wound is green, and staunch it, or I die.

KING.

Have I the skill?

SOL.

Why! art thou not a King?
Wherein consists the magic of a crown
But in the bold achievement of a deed
Would scare a clown to dream?

KING.

I'd read thy thought.

SOL.

Then have it; I would marry.

KING.

It is well:

It is my wish.

SOL.

And unto such a prince
As I've described withal. For though a prince

Of Fancy's realm alone, as thou dost deem,
Yet doth he live indeed.

KING.

To me unknown.

SOL.

O! father mine, before thy reverend knees
Ere this we twain have knelt.

KING.

Forbear, my child;
Or can it be my daughter doth not know
He is no longer free?

SOL.

The power that bound him,
That bondage might dissolve? To holy Church
Thou hast given great alms?

KING.

There's more to gain thy wish,
If more would gain it; but it cannot be,
Even were he content.

SOL.

He is content.

KING.

Hah!

SOL.

For he loves me still.

KING.

I would do much
To please thee. I'm prepared to bear the brunt
Of Hungary's ire; but do not urge, Solisa,
Beyond capacity of sufferance
My temper's proof.

SOL.

Alarcos is my husband,
Or shall the sceptre from our line depart.
Listen, ye saints of Spain, I'll have his hand,
Or by our faith, my fated womb shall be
As barren as thy love, proud king.

KING.

Thou'rt mad!

Thou'rt mad!

SOL.

Is he not mine? Thy very hand,
Did it not consecrate our vows? What claim
So sacred as my own?

KING.

He did conspire —

SOL.

'Tis false, thou know'st 'tis false: against them-
selves
Men do not plot: I would as soon believe
My hand could hatch a treason 'gainst my sight,
As that Alarcos would conspire to seize
A diadem I would myself have placed
Upon his brow.

KING (*taking her hand*).

Nay, calmness. Say 'tis true
He was not guilty, say perchance he was not —

SOL.

Perchance, O! vile perchance. Thou know'st full
well,
Because he did reject her loose desires
And wanton overtures —

KING.

Hush, hush, O hush!

SOL.

The woman called my mother —

KING.

Spare me, spare —

SOL.

Who spared me?
Did not I kneel, and vouch his faith, and bathe
Thy hand with my quick tears, and clutch thy
robe
With frantic grasp? Spare, spare indeed? In
faith
Thou hast taught me to be merciful, thou hast, —
Thou and my mother!

KING.

Ah! no more, no more!
A crownèd King cannot recall the past,
And yet may glad the future. She thou namest,
She was at least thy mother; but to me,
Whate'er her deeds, for truly, there were times
Some spirit did possess her, such as gleams
Now in her daughter's eye, she was a passion,
A witching form that did inflame my life
By a breath or glance. Thou art our child; the link
That binds me to my race; thou hast her place
Within my shrinèd heart, where thou'rt the priest
And others are unhallowed; for, indeed,
Passion and time have so dried up my soul,
And drained its generous juices, that I own
No sympathy with man, and all his hopes
To me are mockeries.

SOL.

        Ah! I see, my father,
That thou wilt aid me!

KING.

        Thou canst aid thyself.
Is there a law to let him from thy presence?
His voice may reach thine ear; thy gracious
    glance
May meet his graceful offices. Go to.
Shall Hungary frown, if his right royal spouse
Smile on the equal of her blood and state,
Her gentle cousin?

SOL.

        And is this thine aid!

KING.

What word has roughed the brow, but now con-
    fiding
In a fond father's love?

SOL.

        Alas! what word?
What have I said? what done? that thou should'st
    deem
I could do this, this, this, that is so foul,
My baffled tongue deserts me. Thou should'st
    know me,
Thou hast set spies on me. What! have they
    told thee
I am a wanton? I do love this man
As fits a virgin's heart. Heaven sent such thoughts
To be our solace. But to act a toy
For his loose hours, or worse, to find him one
Procured for mine, grateful for opportunities

Contrived with decency, spared skilfully
From claims more urgent; not to dare to show
Before the world my homage; when he's ill
To be away, and only share his gay
And lusty pillow; to be shut out from all
That multitude of cares and charms that waits
But on companionship; and then to feel
These joys another shares, another hand
These delicate rites performs, and thou'rt remem-
    bered,
In the serener heaven of his bliss,
But as the transient flash: this is not love;
This is pollution.

                KING.

               Daughter, I were pleased
My cousin could a nearer claim prefer
To my regard. Ay, girl, 'twould please me well
He were my son, thy husband; but what then?
My pleasure and his conduct jar; his fate
Baulks our desire. He's married and has heirs.

                SOL.

Heirs, didst thou say heirs?

                KING.

             What ails thee?

                SOL.

                    Heirs, heirs?

                KING.

Thou art very pale!

                SOL.

              The faintness of the morn
Clings to me still; I pray thee, father, grant
Thy child one easy boon.

KING.

>   She has to speak
> But what she wills.

SOL.

>   Why, then, she would renounce
> Her heritage; yes, place our ancient crown
> On brows it may become.   A veil more suits
> This feminine brain; in Huelgas' cloistered shades
> I'll find oblivion.

KING.

>   Woe is me!   The doom
> Falls on our house.   I had this daughter left
> To lavish all my wealth on and my might.
> I've treasured for her; for her I have slain
> My thousands, conquered provinces, betrayed,
> Renewed, and broken faith.   She was my joy;
> She has her mother's eyes, and when she speaks
> Her voice is like Brunhalda's.   Cursèd hour,
> That a wild fancy touched her brain to cross
> All my great hopes!

SOL.

>   My father, my dear father,
> Thou call'dst me fondly, but some moments past,
> Thy gentle child.   I call my saint to witness
> I would be such.   To say I love this man
> Is shallow phrasing.   Since man's image first
> Flung its wild shadow on my virgin soul,
> It has borne no other reflex.   I know well
> Thou deemest he was forgotten; this day's passion
> Passed as unused confrontment, and so transient
> As it was turbulent.   No, no, full oft,
> When thinking on him, I have been the same.
> Fruitless or barren, this same form is his,

Or it is God's. My father, my dear father,
Remember he was mine, and thou didst pour
Thy blessing on our heads! O God, O God!
When I recall the passages of love
That have ensued between me and this man,
And with thy sanction, and then just bethink
He is another's, O, it makes me mad!
Talk not to me of sceptres: can she rule
Whose mind is anarchy? King of Castille,
Give me the heart that thou didst rob me of!
The penal hour's at hand. Thou didst destroy
My love, and I will end thy line — thy line
That is thy life.

KING.

Solisa, I will do all
A father can,—a father and a King.

SOL.

Give me Alarcos!

KING.

Hush, disturb me not;
I'm in the throes of some imaginings
A human voice might scare.

END OF THE FIRST ACT.

ACT II.

Scene I.

A Street in Burgos.

Enter the Count of Sidonia *and the* Count of Leon.

Sido.

IS SHE not fair?

Leon.

What then? She but fulfills
Her office as a woman. For
to be
A woman and not fair, is, in
my creed,
To be a thing unsexed.

Sido.

Happy Alarcos!
They say she was of Aquitaine, a daughter
Of the De Foix. I would I had been banished.

Leon.

Go and plot then. They cannot take your head,
For that is gone.

Sido.

But banishment from Burgos
Were worse than fifty deaths. O, my good Leon,

Didst ever see, didst ever dream could be,
Such dazzling beauty?

LEON.

Dream! I never dream;
Save when I've revelled over late, and then
My visions are most villainous; but you,
You dream when you're awake.

SIDO.

Wert ever, Leon,
In pleasant Aquitaine?

LEON.

O talk of Burgos;
It is my only subject — matchless town,
Where all I ask are patriarchal years
To feel satiety like my sad friend.

SIDO.

'Tis not satiety now makes me sad;
So check thy mocking tongue, or cure my cares.

LEON.

Absence cures love. Be off to Aquitaine.

SIDO.

I chose a jester for my friend, and feel
His value now.

LEON.

You share the lover's lot
When you desire and you despair. What then?
You know right well that woman is but one,
Though she take many forms, and can confound
The young with subtle aspects. Vanity
Is her sole being. Make the myriad vows
That passionate fancy prompts. At the next
tourney

Maintain her colours 'gainst the two Castilles
And Aragon to boot. You'll have her!

SIDO.

Why!

This was the way I woo'd the haughty Lara,
But I'll not hold such passages approach
The gentle lady of this morn.

LEON.

Well, then,

Try silence, only sighs and hasty glances
Withdrawn as soon as met. Could'st thou but
    blush:
But there's no hope. In time our sighs become
A sort of plaintive hint what hopeless rogues
Our stars have made us. Would we had but
    met
Earlier, yet still we hope she'll spare a tear
To one she met too late. Trust me, she'll spare
    it;
She'll save this sinner who reveres a saint.
Pity or admiration gains them all.
You'll have her!

SIDO.

Well, whate'er the course pursued,
Be thou a prophet!

Enter ORAN.

ORAN.

Stand, Señors, in God's name.

LEON.

Or the devil's.

Well, what do you want?

ORAN.

Many things, but one

Most principal.

SIDO.

And that's —

ORAN.

A friend.

LEON.

You're right

To seek one in the street, he'll prove as true
As any that you're fostered with.

ORAN.

In brief,

I'm, as you see, a Moor; and I have slain
One of our princes. Peace exists between
Our kingdom and Castille; they track my steps.
You're young, you should be brave, generous you
     may be.
I shall be impaled. Save me!

LEON.

Frankly spoken.

Will you turn Christian?

ORAN.

Show me Christian acts,

And they may prompt to Christian thoughts.

SIDO.

Although

The slain's an infidel, thou art the same.
The cause of this rash deed?

ORAN.

I am a soldier,

And my sword's notched, sirs. This said Emir struck
     me,

Before the people, too, in the great square
Of our chief place, Granada, and forsooth,
Because I would not yield the way at mosque.
His life has soothed my honour: if I die,
I die content; but with your gracious aid
I would live happy.

LEON.

You love life?

ORAN.

Most dearly.

LEON.

Sensible Moor, although he be impaled
For mobbing in a mosque. I like this fellow;
His bearing suits my humour. He shall live
To do more murders. Come, bold infidel,
Follow to the Leon Palace; and, sir, prithee
Don't stab us in the back.

[Exeunt omnes.

————

SCENE 2.

Chamber in the Palace of COUNT ALARCOS. At the
back of the Scene the Curtains of a large
jalousie withdrawn.

Enter COUNT ALARCOS.

ALAR.

'Tis circumstance makes conduct; life's a ship,
The sport of every wind. And yet men tack

Against the adverse blast. How shall I steer,
Who am the pilot of Necessity?
But whether it be fair or foul, I know not;
Sunny or terrible. Why, let her wed him?
What care I if the pageant's weight may fall
On Hungary's ermined shoulders, if the spring
Of all her life be mine? The tiar'd brow
Alone makes not a king. Would that my wife
Confessed a worldlier mood! Her recluse fancy
Haunts still our castled bowers. Thou civic air,
Inflame her thoughts! Teach her to vie and revel,
Find sport in peerless robes, the pomp of feasts
And ambling of a genet —   [*A serenade is heard.*
      Hah! that voice
Should not be strange. A tribute to her charms.
'Tis music sweeter to a spouse's ear
Than gallants dream of. Ay, she'll find adorers,
Or Burgos is right changed.   [*Enter the* COUNTESS.
      Listen, child.
     [*Again the serenade is heard.*

COUN.

'Tis very sweet.

ALAR.

It is inspired by thee.

COUN.

Alarcos!

ALAR.

  Why dost look so grave? Nay, now,
There's not a dame in Burgos would not give
Her jewels for such songs.

COUN.

Inspired by me!

ALAR.

And who so fit to fire a lover's breast?
He's clearly captive.

COUN.

O! thou knowest I love not
Such jests, Alarcos.

ALAR.

Jest! I do not jest.
I am right proud the partner of my state
Should count the chief of our Castillian knights
Among her train.

COUN.

I pray thee let me close
These blinds.

ALAR.

Poh, poh! what, baulk a serenade!
'Twould be an outrage to the courtesies
Of this great city. Faith! his voice *is* sweet.

COUN.

Would that he had not sung! It is a sport
In which I find no pastime.

ALAR.

Marry, come,
It gives me great delight. 'Tis well for thee,
On thy first entrance to our world to find
So high a follower.

COUN.

Wherefore should I need
His following?

ALAR.

Naught's more excellent for woman,
Than to be fixed on as the cynosure

Of one whom all do gaze on. 'Tis a stamp
Whose currency, not wealth, rank, blood, can match;
These are raw ingots, till they are impressed
With fashion's picture.

COUN.

Would I were once more
Within our Castle!

ALAR.

Nursery days! The world
Is now our home, and we must worldly be,
Like its bold stirrers. I sup with the King.
There is no feast, and yet to do me honour,
Some chiefs will meet. I stand right well at Court,
And with thine aid will stand e'en better.

COUN.

Mine!

I have no joy but in thy joy, no thought
But for thy honour, and yet, how to aid
Thee in these plans or hopes, indeed, Alarcos?
Indeed, I am perplexed.

ALAR.

Art not my wife?
Is not this Burgos? And this pile, the palace
Of my great fathers? They did raise these halls
To be the symbols of their high estate,
The fit and haught metropolis of all
Their force and faction. Fill them, fill them, wife,
With those who'll serve me well. Make this the centre
Of all that's great in Burgos. Let it be
The eye of the town, whereby we may perceive

What passes in his heart: the clustering point
Of all convergence. Here be troops of friends
And ready instruments. Wear that sweet smile,
That wins a partisan quicker than power;
Speak in that tone gives each a special share
In thy regard, and what is general
Let all deem private. O! thou'lt play it rarely.

COUN.

I would do all that may become thy wife.

ALAR.

I know it, I know it. Thou art a treasure, Florimonde!
And this same singer—thou hast not asked his name.
Didst guess it? Ah! upon thy gentle cheek
I see a smile.

COUN.

My lord—indeed—

ALAR.

                              Thou playest
Thy game less like a novice than I deemed.
Thou canst not say thou didst not catch the voice
Of the Sidonia?

COUN.

            My good lord, indeed
His voice to me is as unknown as mine
Must be to him.

ALAR.

            Whose should the voice but his,
Whose stricken sight left not thy face an instant,
But gazed as if some new-born star had risen
To light his way to paradise? I tell thee,
Among my strict confederates I would count

This same young noble.   He is a paramount chief;
Perchance his vassals might outnumber mine;
Conjoined we're adamant.   No monarch's breath
Makes me again an exile.   Florimonde,
Smile on him; smiles cost nothing; should he judge
They mean more than they say, why, smile again;
And what he deems affection, registered,
Is but chaste mockery.   I must to the citadel.
Sweet wife, good-night.   [*Exit* ALARCOS.

COUN.

                    O! misery, misery, misery!
Must we do this?   I fear there's need we must,
For he is wise in all things, and well learned
In this same world that to my simple sense
Seems very fearful.   Why should men rejoice,
They can escape from the pure breath of heaven
And the sweet franchise of their natural will,
To such a prison-house?   To be confined
In body and in soul; to breathe the air
Of dark close streets, and never use one's tongue
But for some measured phrase that hath its bent
Well gauged and chartered; to find ready smiles
When one is sorrowful, or looks demure
When one would laugh outright.   Never to be
Exact but when dissembling.   Is this life?
I dread this city.   As I passed its gates
My litter stumbled, and the children shrieked
And clung unto my bosom.   Pretty babes!
I'll go to them.   O! there is innocence
Even in Burgos.
                              [*Exit* COUNTESS.

SCENE 3.

A Chamber in the Royal Palace.   The INFANTA
SOLISA *alone.*

SOL.

I can but think my father will be just
And see us righted.   O 'tis only honest,
The hand that did this wrong should now supply
The sovereign remedy, and balm the wound
Itself inflicted.   He is with him now;
Would I were there, unseen, yet seeing all!
But ah! no cunning arras could conceal
This throbbing heart.   I've sent my little Page,
To mingle with the minions of the Court,
And get me news.   How he doth look, how eat.
What says he and what does, and all the haps
Of this same night, that yet to me may bring
A cloudless morrow.   See, even now he comes.

                              [*Enter the* PAGE.

Prithee what news?   Now tell me all, my child;
When thou'rt a knight, will I not work the scarf
For thy first tourney!   Prithee tell me all.

PAGE.

O lady mine, the royal Seneschal
He was so crabbed, I did scarcely deem
I could have entered.

SOL.

                    Cross-grained Seneschal!
He shall repent of this, my pretty Page;
But thou didst enter?

PAGE.

  I did so contrive.

SOL.

Rare imp! And then?

PAGE.

    Well, as you told me, then
I mingled with the Pages of the King.
They're not so very tall; I might have passed
I think for one upon a holiday.

SOL.

O thou shalt pass for better than a Page;
But tell me, child, didst see my gallant Count?

PAGE.

On the right hand —

SOL.

    Upon the King's right hand?

PAGE.

Upon the King's right hand, and there were also —

SOL.

Mind not the rest; thou'rt sure on the right hand?

PAGE.

Most sure; and on the left —

SOL.

    Ne'er mind the left.
Speak only of the right. How did he seem?
Did there pass words between him and the King?
Often or scant? Did he seem gay or grave?
Or was his aspect of a middle tint,
As if he deemed that there were other joys
Not found within that chamber?

PAGE.

               Sooth to say,
He did seem what he is, a gallant knight.
Would I were such! For talking with the King,
He spoke, yet not so much but he could spare
Words to the other lords. He often smiled,
Yet not so often, that a limner might
Describe his mien as jovial.

SOL.

          'Tis himself!
What next? Will they sit long?

PAGE.

               I should not like
Myself to quit such company. In truth,
The Count of Leon is a merry lord.
There were some tilting jests, I warrant you,
Between him and your knight.

SOL.

          O tell it me!

PAGE.

The Count Alarcos, as I chanced to hear,
For tiptoe even would not let me see,
And that same Pedro, who has lately come
To Court, the Señor of Montilla's son,
He is so rough, and says a lady's page
Should only be where there are petticoats.

SOL.

Is he so rough? He shall be soundly whipped.
But tell me, child, the Count Alarcos —

PAGE.

               Well,
The Count Alarcos — but indeed, sweet lady,
I do not wish that Pedro should be whipped.

SOL.

He shall not then be whipped — speak of the Count.

PAGE.

The Count was showing how your Saracen
Doth take your lion captive, thus and thus:
And fashioned with his scarf a dexterous noose
Made of a tiger's skin: your unicorn,
They say, is just as good.

SOL.

      Well, then Sir Leon —

PAGE.

Why then, your Count of Leon — but just then
Sancho, the Viscount of Toledo's son,
The King's chief Page, takes me his handkerchief
And binds it on my eyes, he whispering round
Unto his fellows, Here you see I've caught
A most ferocious cub. Whereat they kicked,
And pinched, and cuffed me till I nearly roared
As fierce as any lion, you be sure.

SOL.

Rude Sancho, he shall sure be sent from Court!
My little Ferdinand — thou hast incurred
Great perils for thy mistress. Go again
And show this signet to the Seneschal,
And tell him that no greater courtesy
Be shown to any guest than to my Page.
This from myself — or I perchance will send,
Shall school their pranks. Away, my faithful imp,
And tell me how the Count Alarcos seems.

PAGE.

I go, sweet lady, but I humbly beg
Sancho may not be sent from Court this time.

SOL.

Sancho shall stay.

[*Exit* PAGE.

I hope, ere long, sweet child,
Thou too shalt be a page unto a king.
I'm glad Alarcos smiled not overmuch;
Your smilers please me not. I love a face
Pensive, not sad; for where the mood is thought-
    ful,
The passion is most deep and most refined.
Gay tempers bear light hearts — are soonest gained
And soonest lost; but he who meditates
On his own nature, will as deeply scan
The mind he meets, and when he loves, he casts
His anchor deep.

[*Re-enter* PAGE.

Give me the news.

PAGE.

The news!
I could not see the Seneschal, but gave
Your message to the Pages. Whereupon
Sancho, the Viscount of Toledo's son,
Pedro, the Señor of Montilla's son,
The young Count of Almeira, and —

SOL.

My child,
What ails thee?

PAGE.

O the Viscount of Jodar,
I think he was the very worst of all;
But Sancho of Toledo was the first.

SOL.

What did they?

PAGE.

       'Las, no sooner did I say
All that you told me, than he gives the word,
'A guest, a guest, a very potent guest,'
Takes me a goblet brimful of strong wine
And hands it to me, mocking, on his knee.
This I decline, when on his back they lay
Your faithful Page, nor set me on my legs
Till they had drenched me with this fiery stuff,
That I could scarcely see, or reel my way
Back to your presence.

SOL.

       Marry, 'tis too much
E'en for a page's license. Ne'er you mind,
They shall to prison by to-morrow's dawn.
I'll bind this kerchief round your brow, its scent
Will much revive you. Go, child, lie you down
On yonder couch.

PAGE.

       I'm sure I ne'er can sleep
If Sancho of Toledo shall be sent
To-morrow's dawn to prison.

SOL.

       Well, he's pardoned.

PAGE.

Also the Señor of Montilla's son.

SOL.

He shall be pardoned too. Now prithee sleep.

PAGE.

The young Count of Almeira—

SOL.

O! no more.
They all are pardoned.

PAGE.

I do humbly pray
The Viscount of Jodar be pardoned too.

[*Exit* SOLISA.

———

SCENE 4.

A Banquet; the KING *seated; on his right* ALARCOS.
SIDONIA, LEON, *the* ADMIRAL OF CASTILLE, *and other*
LORDS. *Groups of* PAGES, CHAMBERLAINS, *and* SERVING-
MEN.

The KING.

Would'st match them, cousin, 'gainst our barbs?

ALAR.

Against
Our barbs, Sir!

KING.

Eh, Lord Leon, you can scan
A courser's points?

LEON.

O, Sir, your travellers
Need fleeter steeds than we poor shambling folks
Who stay at home. To my unskilful sense,
Speed for the chase and vigour for the tilt,
Meseems enough.

ALAR.

If riders be as prompt.

LEON.

Our tourney is put off, or please your Grace,
I'd try conclusions with this marvellous beast,
This Pegasus, this courser of the sun,
That is to blind us all with his bright rays
And cloud our chivalry.

KING.

My Lord Sidonia,
You're a famed judge: try me this Cyprus wine;
An English prince did give it me, returning
From the holy sepulchre.

SIDO.

Most rare, my liege,
And glitters like a gem!

KING.

It doth content
Me much, your Cyprus wine. Lord Admiral,
Hast heard the news? The Saracens have fled
Before the Italian galleys.

THE ADMIRAL OF CASTILLE.

No one guides
A galley like your Pisan.

ALAR.

The great Doge
Of Venice, sooth, would barely veil his flag
To Pisa.

ADM.

Your Venetian hath his craft.
This Saracenic rout will surely touch
Our turbaned neighbors?

KING.

> To the very core,
> Granada's all a-mourning. Good, my Lords,
> One goblet more. We'll give our cousin's health.
> Here's to the Count Alarcos.

OMNES.

> To the Count
> Alarcos!

(*The guests rise, pay their homage to the* KING, *and are retiring.*)

KING.

> Good night, Lord Admiral; my Lord of Leon,
> My Lord Sidonia, and my Lord of Lara,
> Gentle adieus: to you, my Lord, and you,
> To all and each. Cousin, good night — and yet
> A moment rest awhile; since your return
> I've looked on you in crowds, it may become us
> To say farewell alone.

[*The* KING *waves his hand to the* SENESCHAL — *the Chamber is cleared.*

ALAR.

> Most gracious Sire,
> You honour your poor servant.

KING.

> Prithee, sit.
> This scattering of the Saracen, methinks,
> Will hold the Moor to his truce?

ALAR.

> It would appear
> To have that import.

KING.

Should he pass the mountains,
We can receive him.

ALAR.

Where's the crown in Spain
More prompt and more prepared?

KING.

Cousin, you're right.
We flourish. By St. James, I feel a glow
Of the heart to see you here once more, my
    cousin;
I'm low in the vale of years, and yet I think
I could defend my crown with such a knight
On my right hand.

ALAR.

Such liege and land would raise
Our lances high.

KING.

We carry all before us.
Leon reduced, the crescent paled in Cordova;
Why, if she gain Valencia, Aragon
Must kick the beam. And shall she gain Valencia?
It cheers my blood to find thee by my side;
Old days, old days return, when thou to me
Wert as the apple of mine eye.

ALAR.

My liege,
This is indeed most gracious.

KING.

Gentle cousin,
Thou shalt have cause to say that I am gracious.
O! I did ever love thee; and for that

Some passages occurred between us once,
That touch my memory to the quick; I would
Even pray thee to forget them, and to hold
I was most vilely practised on, my mind
Poisoned, and from a fountain that to deem
Tainted were frenzy.

ALAR.

(*Falling on his knee, and taking the* KING'S *hand.*)

My most gracious liege,
This morn to thee I did my fealty pledge.
Believe me, Sire, I did so with clear breast,
And with no thought to thee and to thy line
But fit devotion.

KING.

O, I know it well,
I know thou art right true.   Mine eyes are moist
To see thee here again.

ALAR.

It is my post,
Nor could I seek another.

KING.

Thou dost know
That Hungary leaves us?

ALAR.

I was grieved to hear
There were some crosses.

KING.

Truth, I am not grieved.
Is it such joy this fair Castillian realm,
This glowing flower of Spain, be rudely plucked
By a strange hand?   To see our chambers filled

With foreign losels; our rich fiefs and abbeys
The prey of each bold scatterling, that finds
No heirship in his country? Have I lived
And laboured for this end, to swell the sails
Of alien fortunes? O my gentle cousin,
There was a time we had far other hopes!
I suffer for my deeds.

ALAR.

We must forget,
We must forget, my liege.

KING.

Is't then so easy?
Thou hast no daughter. Ah! thou canst not tell
What 'tis to feel a father's policy
Hath dimmed a child's career. A child so peerless!
Our race, though ever comely, vailed to her.
A palm tree in its pride of sunny youth
Mates not her symmetry; her step was noticed
As strangely stately by her nurse. Dost know,
I ever deemed that winning smile of hers
Mournful, with all its mirth? But ah! no more
A father gossips; nay, my weakness 'tis not.
'Tis not with all that I would prattle thus;
But you, my cousin, know Solisa well,
And once you loved her.

ALAR. (*rising*).

Once! O God!
Such passions are eternity.

KING (*advancing*).

What then,
Shall this excelling creature, on a throne
As high as her deserts, shall she become

A spoil for strangers? Have I cause to grieve
That Hungary quit us? O that I could find
Some noble of our land might dare to mix
His equal blood with our Castillian seed!
Art thou more learnèd in our pedigrees?
Hast thou no friend, no kinsman? Must this realm
Fall to the spoiler, and a foreign graft
Be nourished by our sap?

ALAR.

Alas! alas!

KING.

Four crowns; our paramount Castille, and Leon,
Seviglia, Cordova, the future hope
Of Murcia, and the inevitable doom
That waits the Saracen; all, all, all;
And with my daughter!

ALAR.

Ah! ye should have blasted
My homeward path, ye lightnings!

KING.

Such a son
Should grudge his sire no days. I would not live
To whet ambition's appetite. I'm old;
And fit for little else than hermit thoughts.
The day that gives my daughter, gives my crown:
A cell's my home.

ALAR.

O, life, I will not curse thee!
Let bald and shaven crowns denounce thee vain;
To me thou wert no shade! I loved thy stir
And panting struggle. Power, and pomp, and
     beauty,

Cities and courts, the palace and the fane,
The chase, the revel, and the battle-field,
Man's fiery glance, and woman's thrilling smile,
I loved ye all. I curse not thee, O life!
But on my stars confusion. May they fall
From out their spheres, and blast our earth no
    more
With their malignant rays, that mocking placed
All the delights of life within my reach,
And chained me from fruition.

            KING.

                Gentle cousin,
Thou art disturbed; I fear these words of mine,
Chance words ere I did say to thee good night,—
For O, 'twas joy to see thee here again,
Who art my kinsman, and my only one,—
Have touched on some old cares for both of us.
And yet the world has many charms for thee;
Thou'rt not like us, and thy unhappy child
The world esteems so favoured.

            ALAR.

                Ah, the world
Ill estimates the truth of any lot.
Their speculation is too far and reaches
Only externals; they are ever fair.
There are vile cankers in your gaudiest flowers,
But you must pluck and peer within the leaves
To catch the pest.

            KING.

              Alas! my gentle cousin,
To hear thou hast thy sorrows too, like us,
It pains me much and yet I'll not believe it;
For with so fair a wife ——

ALAR.

Torture me not,
Although thou art a King.

KING.

My gentle cousin,
I spoke to solace thee. We all do hear
Thou art most favoured in a right fair wife.
We do desire to see her; can she find
A friend becomes her better than our child?

ALAR.

My wife? would she were not!

KING.

I say so too,
Would she were not!

ALAR.

Ah me! why did I marry?

KING.

Truth, it was very rash.

ALAR.

Who made me rash?
Who drove me from my hearth, and sent me forth
On the unkindred earth? With the dark spleen
Goading injustice, that 'tis vain to quell,
Entails on restless spirits. Yes, I married,
As men do oft, from very wantonness;
To tamper with a destiny that's cross,
To spite my fate, to put the seal upon
A balked career, in high and proud defiance
Of hopes that yet might mock me, to beat down
False expectation and its damnèd lures,
And fix a bar betwixt me and defeat.

KING.

These bitter words would rob me of my hope,
That thou at least wert happy.

ALAR.

Would I slept
With my grey fathers!

KING.

And my daughter too!
O most unhappy pair!

ALAR.

There is a way.
To cure such woes, one only.

KING.

'Tis my thought.

ALAR.

No cloister shall entomb this life; the grave
Shall be my refuge.

KING.

Yet to die were witless,
When Death, who with his fatal finger taps
At princely doors, as freely as he gives
His summons to the serf, may at this instant
Have sealed the only life that throws a shade
Between us and the sun.

ALAR.

She's very young.

KING.

And may live long, as I do hope she will;
Yet have I known as blooming as she die,
And that most suddenly. The air of cities
To unaccustomed lungs is very fatal;

Perchance the absence of her accustomed sports,
The presence of strange faces, and a longing
For those she had been bred among: I've known
This most pernicious: she might droop and pine;
And when they fail, they sink most rapidly.
God grant she may not; yet I do remind thee
Of this wild chance, when speaking of thy lot.
In truth 'tis sharp, and yet I would not die
When Time, the great enchanter, may change all,
By bringing somewhat earlier to thy gate
A doom that must arrive.

ALAR.

Would it were there!

KING.

'Twould be the day thy hand should clasp my
daughter's,
That thou hast loved so long; 'twould be the day
My crown, the crown of all my realms, Alarcos,
Should bind thy royal brow. Is this the morn
Breaks in our chamber? Why, I did but mean
To say good night unto my gentle cousin
So long unseen. O, we have gossipped, coz,
So cheering dreams!

[*Exeunt.*

END OF THE SECOND ACT.

ACT III.

Scene 1.

Interior of the Cathedral of Burgos. The High Altar illuminated; in the distance, various Chapels lighted, and in each of which Mass is celebrating: in all directions groups of kneeling Worshippers. Before the High Altar the Prior of Burgos officiates, attended by his Sacerdotal Retinue. In the front of the Stage, opposite to the Audience, a Confessional. The chanting of a solemn Mass here commences; as it ceases,

Enter ALARCOS.

ALAR.

WOULD it were done! and yet I dare not say
It should be done. O, that some natural cause,
Or superhuman agent, would step in,
And save me from its practice! Will no pest
Descend upon her blood? Must thousands die
Daily, and her charmed life be spared? As young
Are hourly plucked from out their hearts. A life!
Why, what's a life? A loan that must return
To a capricious creditor; recalled

Often as soon as lent. I'd wager mine
To-morrow like the dice, were my blood pricked.
Yet now,
When all that endows life with all its price,
Hangs on some flickering breath I could puff out,
I stand agape. I'll dream 'tis done: what then?
Mercy remains? For ever, not for ever
I charge my soul? Will no contrition ransom,
Or expiatory torments compensate
The awful penalty? Ye kneeling worshippers,
That gaze in silent ecstacy before
Yon flaming altar, you come here to bow
Before a God of mercy. Is't not so?

[ALARCOS *walks towards the High Altar and kneels.*

*A procession advances from the back of the Scene,
singing a solemn Mass, and preceding the Prior of
Burgos, who seats himself in the Confessional, his
Train filing off on each side of the Scene: the
lights of the High Altar are extinguished, but the
Chapels remain illuminated.*

THE PRIOR.

Within this chair I sit, and hold the keys
That open realms no conqueror can subdue,
And where the monarchs of the earth must fain
Solicit to be subjects: Heaven and Hades,
Lands of Immortal light and shores of gloom,
Eternal as the chorus of their wail,
And the dim isthmus of that middle space,
Where the compassioned soul may purge its sins
In pious expiation. Then advance,
Ye children of all sorrows, and all sins,

Doubts that perplex, and hopes that tantalize,
All the wild forms the fiend Temptation takes
To tamper with the soul! Come with the care
That eats your daily life; come with the thought
That is conceived in the noon of night,
And makes us stare around us though alone;
Come with the engendering sin, and with the crime
That is full-born. To counsel and to soothe,
I sit within this chair.

[ALARCOS *advances and kneels by the Confessional.*

ALAR.

O, holy father
My soul is burthened with a crime.

PRIOR.

My son,
The Church awaits thy sin.

ALAR.

It is a sin
Most black and terrible. Prepare thine ear
For what must make it tremble.

PRIOR.

Thou dost speak
To Power above all passion, not to man.

ALAR.

There was a lady, father, whom I loved,
And with a holy love, and she loved me
As holily. Our vows were blessed, if favour
Hang on a father's benediction.

PRIOR.

Her
Mother?

ALAR.

She had a mother, if to bear
Children be all that makes a mother: one
Who looked on me, about to be her child,
With eyes of lust.

PRIOR.

And thou?

ALAR.

O, if to trace
But with the memory's too veracious aid
This tale be anguish, what must be its life
And terrible action? Father, I abjured
This lewd she-wolf. But ah! her fatal vengeance
Struck to my heart. A banished scatterling
I wandered on the earth.

PRIOR.

Thou didst return?

ALAR.

And found the being that I loved, and found
Her faithful still.

PRIOR.

And thou, my son, wert happy?

ALAR.

Alas! I was no longer free. Strange ties
Had bound a hopeless exile. But she I had loved,
And never ceased to love, for in the form,
Not in the spirit was her faith more pure,
She looked upon me with a glance that told
Her death but in my love. I struggled—nay,

'Twas not a struggle, 'twas an agony.
Her agèd sire, her dark impending doom,
And the o'erwhelming passion of my soul: —
My wife died suddenly.

PRIOR.

And by a life
That should have shielded hers?

ALAR.

Is there hope of mercy?
Can prayers, can penances, can they avail?
What consecration of my wealth, for I'm rich,
Can aid me? Can it aid me? Can endowments?
Nay, set no bounds to thy unlimited schemes
Of saving charity. Can shrines, can chauntries,
Monastic piles, can they avail? What if
I raise a temple not less proud than this,
Enriched with all my wealth, with all, with all?
Will endless masses, will eternal prayers,
Redeem me from perdition?

PRIOR.

What, would gold
Redeem the sin it prompted?

ALAR.

No, by Heaven!
No, Fate had dowered me with wealth might feed
All but a royal hunger.

PRIOR.

And alone
Thy fatal passion urged thee?

ALAR.

Hah!

PRIOR.

Probe deep
Thy wounded soul.

ALAR.

'Tis torture: fathomless
I feel the fell incision.

PRIOR.

There is a lure
Thou dost not own, and yet its awful shade
Lowers in the background of thy soul: thy tongue
Trifles the Church's ear.   Beware, my son,
And tamper not with Paradise.

ALAR.

A breath,
A shadow, essence subtler far than love:
And yet I loved her, and for love had dared
All that I ventured for this twin-born lure
Cradled with love, for which I soiled my soul.
O, father, it was Power.

PRIOR.

And this dominion
Purchased by thy soul's mortgage, still is't thine?

ALAR.

Yea, thousands bow to him who bows to thee.

PRIOR.

Thine is a fearful deed.

ALAR.

O, is there mercy?

PRIOR.

Say, is there penitence?

ALAR.

How shall I gauge it?
What temper of contrition might the Church
Require from such a sinner?

PRIOR.

Is't thy wish,—
Nay, search the very caverns of thy thought,
Is it thy wish this deed were now undone?

ALAR.

Undone, undone! It is; O, say it were,
And what am I? O, father, wer't not done,
I should not be less tortured than I'm now;
My life less like a dream of haunting thoughts
Tempting to unknown enormities. The sun
Would rise as beamless on my darkened days,
Night proffer the same torments. Food would fly
My lips the same, and the same restless blood
Quicken my harassed limbs. Undone! undone!
I have no metaphysic faculty
To deem this deed undone.

PRIOR.

Thou must repent
This terrible deed. Look through thy heart. Thy
wife,—
There was a time thou lov'dst her?

ALAR.

I'll not think
There was a time.

PRIOR.

And was she fair?

ALAR.

A form
Dazzling all eyes but mine.

PRIOR.

And pure?

ALAR.

No saint
More chaste than she.　Her consecrated shape
She kept as 'twere a shrine, and just as full
Of holy thoughts; her very breath was incense
And all her gestures sacred as the forms
Of priestly offices!

PRIOR.

I'll save thy soul.
Thou must repent that one so fair and pure,
And loving thee so well——

ALAR.

Father, in vain.
There is a bar betwixt me and repentance.
And yet——

PRIOR.

Ay, yet——

ALAR.

The day may come, I'll kneel
In such a mood, and might there then be hope?

PRIOR.

We hold the keys that bind and loosen all:
But penitence alone is mercy's portal.
The obdurate soul is doomed.　Remorseful tears
Are sinners' sole ablution.　O, my son,
Bethink thee yet, to die in sin like thine;
Eternal masses profit not thy soul,
Thy consecrated wealth will but upraise
The monument of thy despair.　Once more,
Ere yet the vesper lights shall fade away,

I do adjure thee, on the Church's bosom
Pour forth thy contrite heart.

ALAR.

                     A contrite heart!
A stainless hand would count for more. I see
No drops on mine. My head is weak, my heart
A wilderness of passion. Prayers, thy prayers!

             [ALARCOS *rises suddenly, and exit.*

SCENE 2.

Chamber in the Royal Palace.

The INFANTA *seated in despondency; the* KING *standing by her side.*

KING.

Indeed, 'tis noticed.

SOL.

            Solitude is all
I ask; and is it then so great a boon?

KING.

Nay, solitude's no princely appanage.
Our state's a pedestal, which men have raised
That they may gaze on greatness.

SOL.

               A false idol,
And weaker than its worshippers. I've lived
To feel my station's vanity. O, Death,
Thou endest all!

KING.

Thou art too young to die,
And yet may be too happy. Moody youth
Toys in its talk with the dark thought of death,
As if to die were but to change a robe.
It is their present refuge for all cares
And each disaster. When the sere has touched
Their flowing locks, they prattle less of death,
Perchance think more of it.

SOL.

Why, what is greatness?
Will't give me love, or faith, or tranquil thoughts?
No, no, not even justice.

KING.

'Tis thyself
That does thyself injustice. Let the world
Have other speculation than the breach
Of our unfilled vows. They bear too near
And fine affinity to what we would,
Ay, what we will. I would not choose this mo-
    ment;
Men brood too curiously upon the cause
Of the late rupture, for the cause detected
May bar the consequence.

SOL.

A day, an hour
Sufficed to crush me. Weeks and weeks pass on
Since I was promised right.

KING.

Take thou my sceptre
And do thyself this right. Is't, then, so easy?

SOL.

Let him who did the wrong, contrive the means
Of his atonement.

KING.

All a father can,
I have performed.

SOL.

Ah! then there is no hope.
The Bishop of Ossuna, you did say
He was the learnedest clerk of Christendom,
And you would speak to him?

KING.

What says Alarcos?

SOL.

I spoke not to him since I first received
His princely pledge.

KING.

Call on him to fulfill it.

SOL.

Can he do more than kings?

KING.

Yes, he alone;
Alone it rests with him.   This learn from me.
There is no other let.

SOL.

I learn from thee
What other lips should tell me.

KING.

Girl, art sure
Of this same lover?

SOL.

O! I'll never doubt him.

KING.

And yet may be deceived.

SOL.

He is as true
As talismanic steel.

KING.

Why, then thou art,
At least thou should'st be, happy. Smile, Solisa;
For since the Count is true, there is no bar.
Why dost not smile?

SOL.

I marvel that Alarcos
Hath been so mute on this.

KING.

But thou art sure
He is most true.

SOL.

Why should I deem him true?
Have I found truth in any? Woe is me,
I feel as one quite doomed. I know not why
I ever was ill-omened.

KING.

Listen, girl;
Probe this same lover to the core; 'tmay be,
I think he is, most true; he should be so
If there be faith in vows, and men ne'er break
The pledge it profits them to keep. And yet——

SOL.

And what?

KING.

To be his Sovereign's cherished friend,
And smiled on by the daughter of his King,

Why that might profit him, and please so much,
His wife's ill humour might be borne withal.

SOL.

You think him false?

KING.

I think he might be true:
But when a man's well placed he loves not
change.

(*Enter at the back of the scene Count* ALARCOS *disguised. He advances, dropping his hat and cloak.*)

Ah, gentle cousin, all our thoughts were thine.

ALAR.

I marvel men should think. Lady, I'll hope
Thy thoughts are like thyself, most fair.

KING.

Her thoughts
Are like her fortunes, lofty, but around
The peaks cling vapours.

ALAR.

Eagles live in clouds,
And they draw royal breath.

KING.

I'd have her quit
This strange seclusion, cousin. Give thine aid
To festive purposes.

ALAR.

A root, an egg,
Why, there's a feast with a holy mind.

KING.

If ever
I find my seat within a hermitage,
I'll think the same.

ALAR.

You have built shrines, sweet lady?

SOL.

What then, my lord?

ALAR.

Why, then you might be worshipped,
If your image were in front; I'd bow down
To anything so fair.

KING.

Dost know, my cousin,
Who waits me now? The deputies from Murcia.
The realm is ours (*whispers him*), is thine.

ALAR.

The Church has realms
Wider than both Castilles. But which of them
Will be our lot; that's it.

KING.

Mine own Solisa,
They wait me in my cabinet; (*aside to her*)
Bethink thee
With whom all rests.

[*Exit the* KING.

SOL.

You had sport to-day, my lord?
The King was at the chase.

ALAR.

I breathed my barb.

SOL.

They say the chase hath charm to cheer the spirit.

ALAR.

'Tis better than prayers.

SOL.

        Indeed, I think I'll hunt.
You and my father seem so passing gay.

ALAR.

Why this is no confessional, no shrine
Haunted with presaged gloom. I should be gay
To look at thee and listen to thy voice;
For if fair pictures and sweet sounds enchant
The soul of man, that are but artifice,
How then am I entranced, this living picture
Bright by my side, and listening to this music
That nature gave thee. What's eternal life
To this inspired mortality! Let priests
And pontiffs thunder, still I feel that here
Is all my joy.

SOL.

        Ah! why not say thy woe?
Who stands between thee and thy rights but me?
Who stands between thee and thine ease but
    me?
Who bars thy progress, brings thee cares, but
    me?
Lures thee to impossible contracts, goads thy
    faith
To mad performance, welcomes thee with sighs,
And parts from thee with tears? Is this joy?
    No!
I am thine evil genius.

ALAR.

Say my star
Of inspiration.   This reality
Baffles their mystic threats.   Who talks of cares?
Why, what's a Prince, if his imperial will
Be bitted by a priest?   There's naught impossible.
Thy sighs are sighs of love, and all thy tears
But affluent tenderness.

SOL.

You sing as sweet
As did the syrens; is it from the heart,
Or from the lips, that voice?

ALAR.

Solisa!

SOL.

Ay!
My ear can catch each treacherous tone; 'tis trained
To perfidy.   My lord Alarcos, look me
Straight in the face.   He quails not.

ALAR.

O my soul,
Is this the being for whose love I've pledged
Even thy forfeit!

SOL.

Alarcos, dear Alarcos,
Look not so stern!   I'm mad; yes, yes, my life
Upon thy truth; I know thou'rt true: he said
It rested but with thee; I said it not,
Nor thought it.

ALAR.

Lady!

SOL.

Not that voice!

ALAR.

I'll know
Thy thought; the King hath spoken?

SOL.

Words of joy
And madness. With thyself alone he says
It rests.

ALAR.

Nor said he more?

SOL.

It had found me deaf,
For he touched hearings quick.

ALAR.

Thy faith in me
Hath gone.

SOL.

I'll doubt our shrinèd miracles
Before I doubt Alarcos.

ALAR.

He'll believe thee,
For at this moment he has much to endure,
And that he could not.

SOL.

And yet I must choose
This time to vex thee. O, I am the curse
And blight of the existence, which to bless
Is all my thought! Alarcos, dear Alarcos,
I pray thee pardon me. I am so wretched:
This fell suspense is like a frightful dream
Wherein we fall from heights, yet never reach
The bottomless abyss. It wastes my spirit,
Wears down my life, gnaws ever at my heart,

Makes my brain quick when others are asleep,
And dull when theirs is active.   O, Alarcos,
I could lie down and die.

ALAR.

(*Advancing in soliloquy.*)
Asleep, awake,
In dreams and in the musing moods that wait
On unfulfillèd purposes, I've done it;
And thought upon it afterwards, nor shrunk
From the fell retrospect.

SOL.

He's wrapped in thought;
Indeed his glance was wild when first he entered,
And his speech lacked completeness.

ALAR.
How is it then,
The body that should be the viler part,
And made for servile uses, should rebel
'Gainst the mind's mandate, and should hold
    its aid
Aloof from our adventure ?   Why, the sin
Is in the thought, not in the deed; 'tis not
The body pays the penalty, the soul
Must clear that awful scot.   What palls my arm ?
It is not pity; trumpet-tongued ambition
Stifles her plaintive voice; it is not love,
For that inspires the blow!   Art thou Solisa ?

SOL.

I am that luckless maiden whom you love.

ALAR.

You could lie down and die.   Who speaks of
    death ?

There is no absolution for self-murder.
Why, 'tis the greater sin of the two. There is
More peril in't. What, sleep upon your post
Because you are wearied? No, we must spy on
And watch occasions. Even now they are ripe.
I feel a turbulent throbbing at my heart
Will end in action: for these spiritual tumults
Herald great deeds.

SOL.

It is the Church's scheme
Ever to lengthen suits.

ALAR.

The Church?

SOL.

Ossuna

Leans much to Rome.

ALAR.

And how concerns us that?

SOL.

His Grace spoke to the Bishop, you must know?

ALAR.

Ah, yes! his Grace, the Church, it is our friend.
And truly should be so. It gave our griefs,
And it should bear their balm.

SOL.

Hast pardoned me
That I was querulous? But lovers crossed
Wrangle with those that love them, as it were,
To spite affection.

ALAR.

We are bound together
As the twin powers of the storm. Very love

Now makes me callous.   The great bond is sealed;
Look bright; if gloomy, mortgage future bliss
For present comfort.   Trust me 'tis good 'surance.
I'll to the King.

[Exeunt.

———

SCENE 3.

A Street in Burgos.

Enter the COUNT OF LEON, *followed by* ORAN.

LEON.

He has been sighing like a Sybarite
These six weeks past, and now he sends to me
To hire my bravo.   Well, that smacks of man-
hood.
He'll pierce at least one heart, if not the right one.
Murder and marriage! which the greater crime
A schoolman may decide.   All arts exhausted,
His death alone remains.   A clumsy course.
I care not.   Truth, I hate this same Alarcos;
I think it is the colour of his eyes,
But I do hate him; and the royal ear
Lists coldly to me since this same return.
The King leans wholly on him.   Sirrah Moor,
All is prepared?

ORAN.

And prompt.

LEON.

'Tis well; no boggling;
Let it be cleanly done.

ORAN.

A stab or two,
And the Arlanzon's wave shall know the rest.

LEON.

I'll have to kibo his heels at Court, if you fail.

ORAN.

There is no fear.   We have the choicest spirits
In Burgos.

LEON.

Goodly gentlemen! you wait
Their presence?

ORAN.

Here anon.

LEON.

Good night, dusk infidel,
They'll take me for an Alguazil.   At home
Your news will reach me.

[*Exit* LEON.

ORAN.

And were all your throats cut,
I would not weep.   O, Allah, let them spend
Their blood upon themselves!   My life he shielded,
And now exacts one at my hands: we're quits,
When this is closed.   That thought will grace a
     deed
Otherwise graceless.   I would break the chain
That binds me to this man.   His callous eye
Repels devotion, while his reckless vein
Demands prompt sacrifice.   Now is't wise this?
Methinks 'twere wise to touch the humblest heart
Of those that serve us?   In maturest plans
There lacks that finish, which alone can flow

From zealous instruments. But here are some
That have no hearts to touch.

(*Enter Four* BRAVOS.)

                    How now, good señors, —
I cannot call them comrades; you're exact,
As doubtless ye are brave. You know your duty?

1ST BRAVO.

And will perform it, or my name is changed,
And I'm not Guzman Jaca.

ORAN.

                    You well know
The arm you cross is potent?

2ND BRAVO.

                    All the steel
Of Calatrava's knights shall not protect it.

3RD BRAVO.

And all the knights to boot.

4TH BRAVO.

                    A river business.

ORAN.

The safest sepulchre.

4TH BRAVO.

                    A burial ground
Of which we are the priests, and take our fees;
I never cross a stream, but I do feel
A sense of property.

ORAN.

                    You know the signal:
And when I boast I've friends, they may appear,
To prove I am no braggart.

1ST BRAVO.

    To our posts.
It shall be cleanly done, and brief.

2ND BRAVO.

      No oaths,
No swagger.

3RD BRAVO.

   Not a word; but all as pleasant
As we were nobles like himself.

4TH BRAVO.

    'Tis true, sir;
You deal with gentlemen.

       [*Exeunt* BRAVOS.

  Enter COUNT ALARCOS.

ALAR.

   The moon's a sluggard,
I think, to-night. How now, the Moor that dodged
My steps at vespers. Hem! I like not this.
Friends beneath cloaks; they're wanted. Save
  you, sir!

ORAN.

 And you, sir!

ALAR.

   Not the first time we have met,
Or I've no eye for lurkers.

ORAN.

    I have tasted
Our common heritage, the air, to-day;
And if the selfsame beam warmed both our bloods,
What then?

ALAR.

Why, nothing; but the sun has set,
And honest men should seek their hearths.

ORAN.

I wait
My friends.

(*The* BRAVOS *rush in, and assault* COUNT ALARCOS, *who,
dropping his Cloak, shows his Sword already
drawn, and keeps them at bay.*)

ALAR.

So, so! who plays with princes' blood?
No sport for varlets.   Thus and thus, I'll teach ye
To know your station.

1ST BRAVO.

Ah!

2ND BRAVO.

Away!

3RD BRAVO.

Fly, fly!

4TH BRAVO.

No place for quiet men.

[*The* BRAVOS *run off*.

ALAR.

A little breath
Is all they have cost me, tho' their blood has stained
My damask blade.   And still the Moor!   What ho!
Why fliest not like thy mates?

ORAN.

Because I wait
To fight.

ALAR.

Rash caitiff! knowest thou who I am?

ORAN.

One whom I heard was brave, and now has
proved it.

ALAR.

Am I thy foe?

ORAN.

No more than all thy race.

ALAR.

Go, save thy life.

ORAN.

Look to thine own, proud lord.

ALAR.

Perdition catch thy base-born insolence.

(*They fight: after a long and severe encounter,* ALAR-
COS *disarms* ORAN, *who falls wounded.*)

ORAN.

Be brief, dispatch me.

ALAR.

Not a word for mercy?

ORAN.

Why should'st thou give it?

ALAR.

'Tis not merited,
Yet might be gained.   Who set thee on to this?
My sword is at thy throat.   Give me his name,
And thine shall live.

ORAN.

I cannot.

ALAR.

What, is life
So light a boon? It hangs upon this point,
Bold Moor, is't then thy love to him who fees
thee
Makes thee so faithful?

ORAN.

No; I hate him.

ALAR.

What
Restrains thee, then?

ORAN.

The feeling that restrained
My arm from joining stabbers — Honour.

ALAR.

Humph!
An overseer of stabbers for some ducats.
And is that honour?

ORAN.

Once he screened my life,
And this was my return.

ALAR.

What if I spare
Thy life even now? Wilt thou accord to me
The same devotion?

ORAN.

Yea; the life thou givest
Thou shouldst command.

ALAR.

If I, too, have a foe
Crossing my path and blighting all my life?

ORAN.

This sword should strive to reach him.

ALAR.

Him! thy bond
Shall know no sex or nation. Limitless
Shall be thy pledge. I'll claim from thee a life
For that I spare. How now, wilt live?

ORAN.

To pay

A life for that now spared.

ALAR.

Swear to thy truth;
Swear by Mahound, and swear by all thy gods,
If thou hast any; swear it by the stars,
In which we all believe; and by thy hopes
Of thy false paradise; swear it by thy soul,
And by thy sword!

ORAN.

I swear.

ALAR.

Arise and live.

THE END OF THE THIRD ACT.

ACT IV.

SCENE I.

Interior of a Posada frequented by BRAVOS, *in an obscure quarter of Burgos.* FLIX *at the fire, frying eggs. Men seated at small tables drinking; others lying on benches. At the side, but in the front of the Scene, some Beggars squatted on the ground, thrumming a Mandolin; a Gipsy Girl dancing.*

A BRAVO.

COME, mother, dost take us for Saracens? I say we are true Christians, and so must drink wine.

ANOTHER BRAVO.

Mother Flix is sour to-night. Keep the evil eye from the olla!

A 3RD BRAVO (*advancing to her*).

Thou beauty of Burgos, what are dimples unless seen? Smile! wench.

FLIX.

A frying egg will not wait for the King of Cordova.

1ST BRAVO.

Will have her way. Graus knows a pretty wife's worth. A handsome hostess is bad for the guest's purse.

A BRAVO (*rising*).

Good companions make good company. Graus, Graus, another flagon.

ANOTHER BRAVO.

Of the right Catalan.

3RD BRAVO.

Nay, for my omelette.

FLIX.

Hungry men think the cook lazy.

Enter GRAUS *with a Flagon of Wine.*

1ST BRAVO.

'Tis mine.

2ND BRAVO.

No, mine.

1ST BRAVO.

We'll share.

2ND BRAVO.

No, each man his own beaker; he who shares has the worst half.

3RD BRAVO (*to* FLIX, *who brings the omelette*).

An egg and to bed.

GRAUS.

Who drinks, first chinks.

1ST BRAVO.

The debtor is stoned every day. There will be water-work to-morrow, and that will wash it out. You know me?

GRAUS.

In a long journey and a small inn, one knows one's company.

2ND BRAVO.

Come, I'll give, but I won't share. Fill up.

GRAUS.

That's liberal; my way; full measure but prompt
pezos; I loathe your niggards.

1ST BRAVO.

As the little tailor of Campillo said, who worked
for nothing, and found thread.

(*To the other* BRAVO.)

Nay, I'll not refuse; we know each other.

2ND BRAVO.

We've seen the stars together.

AN OLD MAN.

Burgos is not what it was.

A 5TH BRAVO (*waking*).

Sleep ends and supper begins. The olla, the olla,
Mother Flix (*shaking a purse*); there's the dinner bell.

2ND BRAVO.

That will bring courses.

1ST BRAVO.

An ass covered with gold has more respect than a
horse with a pack-saddle.

5TH BRAVO.

How for that ass?

2ND BRAVO.

Nay, the sheep should have his belly full who
quarrels with his mate.

5TH BRAVO.

But how for that ass?

A Friar (*advancing*).

Peace be with ye, brethren! A meal, in God's name.

5TH BRAVO.

Who asks in God's name, asks for two. But how
for that ass?

FLIX (*bringing the olla*).

Nay, an ye must brawl, go fight the Moors. 'Tis
a peaceable house, and we sleep quiet o' nights.

5TH BRAVO.

Am I an ass?

FLIX.

He is an ass who talks when he might eat.

5TH BRAVO.

A Secadon sausage! Come, mother, I'm all peace;
thou'rt a rare hand. As in thy teeth, comrade,
and no more on't.

1ST BRAVO.

When I will not, two cannot quarrel.

OLD MAN.

Everything is changed for the worse.

FRIAR.

For the love of St. Jago, señors; for the love of St.
Jago!

5TH BRAVO.

When it pleases not God, the saint can do little.

2ND BRAVO.

Nay, supper for all, and drink's the best meat.
Some have sung for it, some danced. There is
no fishing for trout in dry breeches. You shall
preach.

FRIAR.

Benedicite, brethren —

1ST BRAVO.

Nay, no Latin, for the devil's not here.

2ND BRAVO.

And prithee let it be as full of meat as an egg; for we who do many deeds, love not many words.

FRIAR.

Thou shalt not steal.

1ST BRAVO.

He blasphemes.

FRIAR.

But what is theft?

2ND BRAVO.

Ay! there it is.

FRIAR.

The tailor he steals the cloth, and the miller he steals the meal; is either a thief? 'tis the way of trade. But what if our trade be to steal? Why then our work is to cut purses; to cut purses is to follow our business; and to follow our business is to obey the King; and so thieving is no theft. And that's *probatum*, and so, amen.

5TH BRAVO.

Shall put thy spoon in the olla for that.

2ND BRAVO.

And drink this health to our honest fraternity.

OLD MAN.

I have heard sermons by the hour; this is brief; everything falls off.

Enter a Personage *masked and cloaked.*

1st Bravo (*to his Companions*).

See'st yon mask?

2nd Bravo.

'Tis strange.

Graus (*to* Flix).

Who is this?

Flix.

The fool wonders, the wise man asks. Must have no masks here.

Graus.

An obedient wife commands her husband. Business with a stranger, title enough. (*Advancing and addressing the Mask.*) Most noble Señor Mask.

The Unknown.

Well, fellow!

Graus.

Hem; as it may be. D'ye see, most noble Señor Mask, that 'tis an orderly house this, frequented by certain honest gentlemen, that take their siesta, and eat a fried egg after their day's work, and so are not ashamed to show their faces. Ahem!

The Unknown.

As in truth I am in such villanous company.

Graus.

Wheugh! but 'tis not the first ill word that brings a blow. Would'st sup indifferently well here at a moderate rate, we are thy servants. My Flix hath reputation at the frying-pan, and my wine hath made lips smack; but here, señor, faces must be uncovered.

THE UNKNOWN.

Poh! poh!

GRAUS.

Nay, then, I will send some to you shall gain softer words.

1ST BRAVO.

Why, what's this?

2ND BRAVO.

Our host is an honest man, and has friends.

5TH BRAVO.

Let me finish my olla, and I will discourse with him.

THE UNKNOWN.

Courage is fire and bullying is smoke. I come here on business, and with you all.

1ST BRAVO.

Carraho! and who's this?

THE UNKNOWN.

One who knows you, though you know not him. One whom you have never seen, yet all fear. And who walks at night, and where he likes.

2ND BRAVO.

The devil himself!

THE UNKNOWN.

It may be so.

2ND BRAVO.

Sit by me, Friar, and speak Latin.

THE UNKNOWN.

There is a man missing in Burgos, and I will know where he is.

OLD MAN.

There were many men missing in my time.

THE UNKNOWN.

Dead or alive, I care not; but land or water, river or turf, I will know where the body is stowed. See (*shaking a purse*) here is eno' to point all the poniards of the city. You shall have it to drink his health.

A BRAVO.

How call you him?

THE UNKNOWN.

Oran, the Moor.

1ST BRAVO.

(*Jumping from his seat and approaching the stranger.*)

My name is Guzman Jaca; my hand was in that business.

THE UNKNOWN.

With the Moor and three of your comrades?

1ST BRAVO.

The same.

THE UNKNOWN.

And how came your quarry to fly next day?

1ST BRAVO.

Very true; 'twas a bad business for all of us. I fought like a lion; see, my arm is still bound up; but he had advice of our visit; and no sooner had we saluted him, than there suddenly appeared a goodly company of twelve serving-men, or say twelve to fifteen ——

THE UNKNOWN.

You lie; he walked alone.

1ST BRAVO.

Very true; and if I am forced to speak the whole truth, it was thus. I fought like a lion; see, my arm is still bound up; but I was not quite his match alone, for I had let blood the day before, and my comrades were taken with a panic, and so left me in the lurch. And now you have it all.

THE UNKNOWN.

And Oran?

1ST BRAVO.

He fled at once.

THE UNKNOWN.

Come, come, Oran did not fly.

1ST BRAVO.

Very true. We left him alone with the Count. And now you have it all.

THE UNKNOWN.

Had he slain him, the body would have been found.

1ST BRAVO.

Very true. That's the difference between us professional performers, and you mere amateurs; we never leave the bodies.

THE UNKNOWN.

And you can tell me nothing of him?

1ST BRAVO.

No, but I engage to finish the Count any night you like now, for I have found out his lure.

THE UNKNOWN.

How's that?

1ST BRAVO.

Every evening, about an hour after sunset, he enters by a private way the citadel.

THE UNKNOWN.

Hah! what more?

1ST BRAVO.

He is stagged; there is a game playing, but what I
know not.

THE UNKNOWN.

Your name is Guzman Jaca?

1ST BRAVO.

The same.

THE UNKNOWN.

Honest fellow! there's gold for you. You know
nothing of Oran?

1ST BRAVO.

Maybe he has crawled to some place wounded.

THE UNKNOWN.

To die like a bird. Look after him. If I wish more,
I know where to find you. What ho, Master
Host! I cannot wait to try your mistress's art to-
night; but here's my scot for our next supper.

[*Exit the* UNKNOWN.

SCENE 2.

A chamber in the Palace of Alarcos.

The COUNTESS *and* SIDONIA.

SIDO.

Lady, you're moved: nay, 'twas an idle word.

COUN.

But was it true?

SIDO.

And yet might little mean.

COUN.

That I should live to doubt!

SIDO.

But do not doubt;
Forget it, lady.   You should know him well;
Nay, do not credit it.

COUN.

He's very changed.
I would not own, no, not believe that change.
I've given it every gloss that might confirm
My sinking heart.   Time and your tale agree;
Alas! 'tis true.

SIDO.

I hope not; still believe
It is not true.   Would that I had not spoken!
It was unguarded prate.

COUN.

You have done me service:
Condemned, the headsman is no enemy,
But closes suffering.

SIDO.

Yet a bitter doom
To torture those you'd bless.   I have a thought.
What if this eve you visit this same spot,
That shrouds these meetings? If he's wanting then,
The rest might prove as false.

COUN.

He will be there,
I feel he will be there.

SIDO.

We should not think so,
Until our eyes defeat our hopes.

Coun.
O Burgos,
My heart misgave me when I saw thy walls!
To doubt is madness, yet 'tis not despair,
And that may be my lot.

Sido.
The palace gardens
Are closed, except to master-keys. Here's one;
My office gives it me, and it can count
Few brethren. You will be alone.

Coun.
Alas!
I dare not hope so.

Sido.
Well, well, think of this;
Yet take the key.

Coun.
O that it would unlock
The heart now closed to me! To watch his ways
Was once my being. Shall I prove the spy
Of joys I may not share? I will not take
That fatal key.

Sido.
'Tis well; I pray you, pardon
My ill-timed zeal.

Coun.
Indeed, I should be grateful
That one should wish to serve me. Can it be?
'Tis not two months, two little, little months,
You crossed this threshold first. Ah! gentle sir,
And we were all so gay! What have I done?
What is all this? so sudden and so strange?

It is not true, I feel it is not true;
'Tis factious care that clouds his brow, and calls
For all this timèd absence. His brain's busy
With the State. Is't not so? I prithee speak,
And say you think it.

SIDO.

You should know him well;
And if you deem it so, why, should I deem
The inference just.

COUN.

Yet if he were not there,
How happy I should sleep! there is no peril;
The garden's near; and is there shame? 'Tis love
Makes me a lawful spy. He'll not be there,
And then there is no prying.

SIDO.

Near at hand,
Crossing the way that bounds your palace court,
There is a private portal.

COUN.

If I go,
He will not miss me. Ah, I would he might!
So very near; no, no; I cannot go;
And yet I'll take the key.

[*Takes the key.*

Would thou could'st speak,
Thou little instrument, and tell me all
The secrets of thy office! My heart beats;
'Tis my first enterprise; I would it were
To do him service. No, I cannot go;
Farewell, kind sir; indeed I am so troubled,
I must retire.

[*Exit* COUNTESS.

SIDO.

Thy virtue makes me vile;
And what should move my heart inflames my
    soul.
O marvellous world, wherein I play the villain
From very love of excellence!   But for him,
I'd be the rival of her stainless thoughts
And mate her purity.   Hah!

Enter ORAN.

ORAN.

My noble lord!

SIDO.

The Moor!

ORAN.

Your servant.

SIDO.

Here! 'tis passing strange.
How's this?

ORAN.

The accident of war, my lord.
I am a prisoner.

SIDO.

But at large, it seems.
You have betrayed me?

ORAN.

Had I chosen that,
I had been free and you not here.   I fought,
And fell in single fight.   Why spared I know not,
But that the lion's generous.

SIDO.

Will you prove
Your faith?

ORAN.

Nay, doubt it not.

SIDO.

You still can aid me.

ORAN.

I am no traitor, and my friends shall find
I am not wanting.

SIDO.

Quit these liberal walls
Where you're not watched.   In brief, I've coined
    a tale
Has touched the Countess to the quick.   She
    seeks,
Alone or scantily tended, even now,
The palace gardens; eager to discover
A faithless husband, where she'll chance to find
One more devout.   My steeds and servants wait
At the right post; my distant castle soon
Shall hold this peerless wife.   Your resolute spirit
May aid me much.   How say you, is it well
That we have met?

ORAN.

Right well.   I will embark
Most heartily in this.

SIDO.

With me at once.

ORAN.

At once?

SIDO.

No faltering. You have learned and know
Too much to spare you from my sight, good Oran.
With me at once.

ORAN.

'Tis urgent; well, at once,
And I will do good service, or I'll die.
For what is life unless to aid the life
Has aided thine?

SIDO.

On then; with me no eye
Will look with jealousy upon thy step.

[*Exeunt.*

————

SCENE 3.

A retired spot in the Gardens of the Palace.

Enter the COUNTESS.

COUN.

Is't guilt, that I thus tremble? Why should I
Feel like a sinner? I'll not dare to meet
His flashing eye. O, with what scorn, what hate
His lightning glance will wither me. Away,
I will away. I care not whom he meets.
What if he loved me not, he shall not loathe
The form he once embraced. I'll be content
To live upon the past, and dream again
It may return. Alas! were I the false one,
I could not feel more humbled. Ah, he comes!
I'll lie, I'll vow I'm vile, that I came here

To meet another, anything but that
I dared to doubt him.   What, my Lord Sidonia!

[*Enter* SIDONIA.

SIDO.

Thy servant and thy friend.   Ah! gentle lady,
I deemed this unused scene and ill-timed hour
Might render solace welcome.   He'll not come;
He crossed the mountains, ere the set of sun,
Towards Briviesca.

COUN.

Holy Virgin, thanks!
Home, home!

SIDO.

And can a hearth neglected cause
Such raptures?

COUN.

I, and only I, neglect it;
My cheek is fire, that I should ever dare
To do this stealthy deed.

SIDO.

And yet I feel
I could do one as secret and more bold.
A moment, lady; do not turn away
With that cold look.

COUN.

My children wait me, sir;
Yet I would thank you, for you meant me kindness.

SIDO.

And mean it yet.   Ah! beauteous Florimonde,
It is the twilight hour, when hearts are soft,

And mine is like the quivering light of eve;
I love thee!

SIDE. COUN.

   And for this I'm here, and he,
He is not false! O happiness!

SIDO.

      Sweet lady——

COUN.

My Lord Sidonia, I can pardon thee,
I am so joyful.

SIDO.

Nay, then.

COUN.

   Unhand me, sir!

SIDO.

But to embrace this delicate waist. Thou art
   mine:
I've sighed and thou hast spurned. What is not
   yielded
In war we capture. Ere a flying hour,
Thy hated Burgos vanishes. That voice;
What, must I stifle it, who fain would listen
Forever to its song? In vain thy cry,
For none are here but mine.

Enter ORAN.

ORAN.

   Turn, robber, turn——

SIDO.

Ah! treason in the camp! Thus to thy heart.

[*They fight.* ORAN *beats off* SIDONIA, *they leave the scene fighting; the* COUNTESS *swoons.*

Enter a procession with lighted torches, attending the Infanta SOLISA *from Mass.*

1ST USH.

A woman!

2ND USH.

Does she live?

SOL.

What stops our course?

[*The Train ranging themselves on each side, the Infanta approaches the* COUNTESS.

SOL.

Most strange and lovely vision! Does she breathe?
I'll not believe 'tis death. Her hand is cold,
And her brow damp; Griselda, Julia, maidens
Hither, and yet stand off; give her free air.
How shall we bear her home? Now, good
    Lorenzo,
You, and Sir Miguel, raise her; gently, gently.
Still gently, sirs. By heavens, the fairest face
I yet did gaze on! Some one here should know
    her,
'Tis one that must be known. That's well; re-
    lieve
That kerchief from her neck; mind not our state;
I'll by her side; a swoon, methinks; no more,
Let's hope and pray!

[*They raise the body of the* COUNTESS, *and bear her away.*

Enter Count of LEON.

LEON.

I'll fathom this same mystery,
If there be wit in Burgos. I have heard,
Before I knew the Court, old Nunez Leon
Whisper strange things — and what if they prove
    true?
It is not exile twice would cure that scar.
I'll reach him yet. 'Tis likely he may pass
This way; 'tis lonely, and well suits a step
Would not be noticed. Ha! a man approaches;
I'll stand awhile aside.

Re-enter ORAN.

ORAN.

Gone, is she gone?
Yet safe I feel. O Allah! thou art great!
The arm she bound, and tended with that glance
Of sweet solicitude, has saved her life,
And more than life. The dark and reckless vil-
    lains!
O! I could curse them, but my heart is soft
With holy triumph. I'm no more an outcast.
And when she calls me, I'd not change my lot
To be an Emir. In their hall to-night
There will be joy, and Oran will have smiles.
This house has knit me to their fate by ties
Stronger than gyves of iron.

LEON.

Do I see
The man I seek? Oran!

ORAN *turns, and recognising Leon, rushes and seizes him.*

ORAN.

Incarnate fiend,
Give her me, give her me!

LEON.

Off, ruffian, off!

ORAN.

I have thee and I'll hold thee. If I spare
Thy damnèd life, and do not dash thee down,
And trample on thee, fiend, it is because
Thou art the gaoler of a pearl of price
I cannot gain without thee. Now, where is she?
Now by thy life!

LEON.

Why, thou outrageous Moor,
Hast broken thy false prophet's rule, and so
Fell into unused drink, that thus thou darest
To flout me with thy cloudy menaces?
What mean'st thou, sir? And what have I with-
held
From thy vile touch? By heavens, I pass my days
In seeking thy dusk corpse, I deemed well drilled
Ere this, but it awaits my vengeance.

ORAN.

Boy!
Licentious boy! Where is she? Now, by Allah!
This poniard to thy heart, unless thou tell'st me.

LEON.

Whom dost thou mean?

ORAN.

      Thy comrade and thy crew;
They all have fled. I left the Countess here.
She's gone. Thou fill'st place.

LEON.

        What Countess? Speak.

ORAN.

The Count Alarcos' wife.

LEON.

      The Count Alarcos!
I'd be right glad to see him; but his wife
Concerns the Lord Sidonia. If he have played
Some pranks here, 'tis a fool, and he has marred
More than he'll ever make. My time's worth
    gems;
My knightly word, dusk Moor, I tell thee truth.
I will forget these jests, but we must meet
This night at my palace.

ORAN.

      I'll see her first.

                [*Exit* ORAN.

LEON.

Is it the Carnival? What mummery's this?
What have I heard? One thing alone is clear.
We must be rid of Oran.

SCENE 4.

A Chamber in the Palace. The Countess ALARCOS
lying on a Couch, the Infanta kneeling at her side;
MAIDENS *grouped around. A* PHYSICIAN *and the*
PAGE.

SOL.

Didst ever see so fair a skin? Her bodice
Should still be loosened. Bring the Moorish water,
Griselda, you. They are the longest lashes!
They hang upon her cheek. Doctor, there's
    warmth;
The blood returns?

PHY.

But slowly.

SOL.

Beauteous creature!
She seems an angel fallen from some star.
'Twas well we passed. Untie that kerchief, Julia;
Teresa, wave the fan. There seems a glow
Upon her cheek, what but a moment since
Was like a sculptured saint's.

PHY.

She breathes.

SOL.

Hush, hush!

COUN.

And what is this? Where am I?

SOL.

With thy friends.

COUN.

It is not home.

SOL.

If kindness make a home,
Believe it such.

[*The* PHYSICIAN *signifies silence.*

Nay lady, not a word,
Those lips must now be closed. I've seen such eyes
In pictures, girls.

PHY.

Methinks she'll sleep.

SOL.

'Tis well.

Maidens, away. I'll be her nurse; and, doctor,
Remain within.

[*Exeunt* PHYSICIAN *and* MAIDENS.

Know you this beauteous dame?

PAGE.

I have heard minstrels tell that fays are found
In lonely places.

SOL.

Well, she's magical,
She draws me charm-like to her. Vanish, imp,
And see our chamber still.   [*Exit* PAGE.

It is the hour
Alarcos should be here. Ah! happy hour,
That custom only makes more strangely sweet!
His brow has lost its cloud. The bar's removed
To our felicity; time makes amends
To patient sufferers.

[*Enter* COUNT ALARCOS.

Hush, my own love, hush!

[SOLISA *takes his hand and leads him aside.*
So strange an incident! the fairest lady!
Found in our gardens; it would seem a swoon;
Myself then passing; hither we have brought her;
She is so beautiful, you'll almost deem
She bears some charmèd life. You know that fays
Are found in lonely places.

ALAR.

In thy garden!
Indeed 'tis strange! The Virgin guard thee, love.
I am right glad I'm here. Alone to tend her,
'Tis scarcely wise.

SOL.

I think when she recovers,
She'll wave her wings and fly.

ALAR.

Nay, for one glance!
In truth you paint her bright.

SOL.

E'en now she sleeps.
Tread lightly, love; I'll lead you.

[SOLISA *cautiously leads* ALARCOS *to the couch; as they
approach it, the* COUNTESS *opens her eyes and
shrieks.*

COUN.

Ah! 'tis true,
Alarcos!   [*Relapses into a swoon.*
ALAR.

Florimonde!

SOL.

Who is this lady?

ALAR.

It is my wife.

SOL. (*flings away his arms and rushes forward*).

——— Not mad!
Virgin and Saints be merciful; not mad!
O spare my brain one moment; 'tis his wife.
I'm lost: she is too fair.   The secret's out
Of sick delays.   He's feigned; he has but feigned.

[*Rushing to Alarcos.*

Is that thy wife? and I? and what am I?
A trifled toy, a humoured instrument?
To guide with glozing words, vilely cajole
With petty perjuries?   Is that thy wife?
Thou said'st she was not fair, thou did'st not
    love her:
Thou lied'st.   O, anguish, anguish!

ALAR.

              By the cross,
My soul is pure to thee.   I'm wildered quite.
How came she here?

SOL.

          And she shall ne'er return.
Now, Count Alarcos, by the cross thou swearest
Thy faith is true to me.

ALAR.

         Ay, by the cross.

SOL.

Give me thy daggar.

ALAR.

        Not that hand or mine.

Sol.

Is this thy passion!   [*Takes his dagger.*
     Thus I gain the heart
I should despise.   [*Rushes to the couch.*

Coun.

What's this I see?

Alar. (*seizing the Infanta's upraised arm*).
        A dream;
A horrid dream, yet but a dream.

THE END OF THE FOURTH ACT.

ACT V.

Scene 1.

Exterior of Castle of Alarcos in the valley of Arlanɀon.

Enter the Countess.

Coun.

I WOULD recall the days gone by, and live
A moment in the past; if but to fly
The dreary present pressing on my brain,
Woe's omened harbinger. In ex-iled love
The scene he drew so fair! Ye castled crags,
The sunbeam plays on your embattled cliffs,
And softens your stern visage, as his love
Softened our early sorrows. But my sun
Has set for ever! Once we talked of cares
And deemed that we were sad. Men fancy sorrows
Until time brings the substance of despair,
And then their griefs are shadows. Give me exile!
It brought me love. Ah! days of gentle joy,
When pastime only parted us, and he
Returned with tales to make our children stare;
Or called my lute, while, round my waist entwined,

His hand kept chorus to my lay. No more!
O, we were happier than the happy birds;
And sweeter were our lives than the sweet flowers;
The stars were not more tranquil in their course,
Yet not more bright! The fountains in their play
Did most resemble us, that as they flow
Still sparkle!

> [*Enter* ORAN.

Oran, I am very sad.

ORAN.

Cheer up, sweet lady, for the God of all
Will guard the innocent.

COUN.

Think you he'll come
To visit us? Methinks he'll never come.

ORAN.

He's but four leagues away. This vicinage.
Argues a frequent presence.

COUN.

But three nights——
Have only three nights passed? It is an epoch
Distant and dim with passion. There are seasons
Feelings crowd on so, time not flies but staggers;
And memory poises on her burthened plumes
To gloat upon her prey. Spoke he of coming?

ORAN.

His words were scant and wild, and yet he murmured
That I should see him.

COUN.

I've not seen him since
That fatal night, yet even that glance of terror——
I'd hail it now. O, Oran, Oran, think you

He ever more will love me? Can I do
Aught to regain his love? They say your people
Are learnèd in these questions. Once I thought
There was no spell like duty—that devotion
Would bulwark love forever. Now, I'd distil
Philtres, converse with moonlit hags, defile
My soul with talismans, bow down to spirits,
And frequent accursèd places, all, yea all—
I'd forfeit all——but to regain his love.

ORAN.

There is a cloud now rising in the west,
In shape a hand, and scarcely would its grasp
Exceed mine own, it is so small; a spot.
A speck; see now again its colour flits!
A lurid tint; they call it on our coast
'The hand of God;' for when its finger rises
From out the horizon, there are storms abroad
And awful judgments.

COUN.

Ah! it beckons me.

ORAN.

Lady!

COUN.

Yes, yes, see now the finger moves
And points to me. I feel it on my spirit.

ORAN.

Methinks it points to me—

COUN.

To both of us.
It may be so. And what would it portend?
My heart's grown strangely calm. If there be chance
Of storms, my children should be safe. Let's home.

SCENE 2.

*An illuminated Hall in the Royal Palace at Burgos; in
the background Dancers.*

Groups of GUESTS *passing.*

1ST GUEST.

Radiant!

2ND GUEST.

Recalls old days.

3RD GUEST.

The Queen herself

Ne'er revelled it so high!

4TH GUEST.

The Infanta beams

Like some bright star!

5TH GUEST.

And brighter for the cloud

A moment screened her.

6TH GUEST.

Is it true 'tis over

Between the Count Sidonia and the Lara?

1ST GUEST.

A musty tale.   The fair Alarcos wins him.
Where's she to-night?

2ND GUEST.

All on the watch to view

Her entrance to our world.

3RD GUEST.

The Count is here.

4TH GUEST.

Where?

3RD GUEST.

With the King; at least a moment since.

2ND GUEST.

They say she's ravishing.

4TH GUEST.

Beyond belief!

3RD GUEST.

The King affects him much.

5TH GUEST.

He's all in all.

6TH GUEST.

Yon Knight of Calatrava, who is he?

1ST GUEST.

Young Mendola.

2ND GUEST.

What, he so rich?

1ST GUEST.

The same.

2ND GUEST.

The Lara smiles on him.

1ST GUEST.

No worthier quarry!

3RD GUEST.

Who has the vacant Mastership?

4TH GUEST.

I'll back

The Count of Leon.

3RD GUEST.
                    Likely; he stands well
With the Lord Admiral.

                              [*They move away.*

(*The Counts of* SIDONIA *and* LEON *come forward.*)

LEON.
            Doubt as you like,
Credulity will come, and in good season.

SIDO.
She is not here that would confirm your tale.

LEON.
'Tis history, my Sidonia.   Strange events
Have happened, stranger come.

SIDO.
                        I'll not believe it.
And favoured by the King!   What can it mean?

LEON.
What no one dares to say.

SIDO.
            A clear divorce.
O that accursèd garden!   But for that—

LEON.
'Twas not my counsel.   Now I'd give a purse
To wash good Oran in Arlanzon's wave;
The dusk dog needs a cleansing.

SIDO.
                        Hush! here comes
Alarcos and the King.

(They retire: the KING *and* COUNT ALARCOS *advance.)*

KING.

Solisa looks

A Queen.

ALAR.

The mirror of her earliest youth
Ne'er shadowed her so fair!

KING.

I am young again,
Myself to-night. It quickens my old blood
To see my nobles round me. This goes well.
'Tis Courts like these that make a King feel proud.
Thy future subjects, cousin.

ALAR.

Gracious Sire,

I would be one.

KING.

Our past seclusion lends

A lustre to this revel.

(The KING *approaches the Count of* LEON; SOLISA *advances to* ALARCOS.)*

SOL.

Why art thou grave?
I came to bid thee smile. In truth, to-night
I feel a lightness of the heart to me
Hath long been strange.

ALAR.

'Tis passion makes me grave.
I muse upon thy beauty. Thus I'd read
My oppressed spirit, for in truth these sounds
Jar on my humour.

SOL.

              Now my brain is vivid
With wild and blissful images. Canst guess
What laughing thought unbidden, but resistless,
Plays o'er my mind to-night? Thou canst not guess:
Meseems it is our bridal night.

ALAR.

                   Thy fancy
Outruns the truth but scantly.

SOL.

                  Not a breath.
Our long-vexed destinies — even now their streams
Blend in one tide. It is the hour, Alarcos:
There is a spirit whispering in my ear,
The hour is come. I would I were a man
But for a rapid hour. Should I rest here,
Prattling with gladsome revellers, when time,
Steered by my hand, might bring me to a port
I long had sighed to enter? But, alas!
These are a woman's thoughts.

ALAR.

             And yet I share them.

SOL.

Why not to-night? Now, when our hearts are high,
Our fancies glowing, pulses fit for kings,
And the whole frame and spirit of the man
Prepared for daring deeds?

ALAR.

                 And were it done —
Why, then, 'twere not to do.

SOL.

               The mind grows dull,
Dwelling on method of its deeds too long.

Our schemes should brood as gradual as the storm;
Their acting should be lightning.   How far is't?

ALAR.

An hour.

SOL.

Why, it wants two to midnight yet.
O could I see thee but re-enter here,
Ere yet the midnight clock strikes on my heart
The languish of new hours — I'd not ask thee
Why I had missed the mien, that draws to it ever
My constant glance.   There'd need no speech between
  us;
For I should meet —— my husband.

ALAR.

'Tis the burthen
Of this unfilled doom weighs on my spirit.
Why am I here?   My heart and face but mar
This festive hall.   To-night, why not to-night?
The night will soon have past: then 'twill be done.
We'll meet again to-night.

[Exit ALARCOS.

SCENE 3.

A Hall in the Castle of ALARCOS; in the back of the
Scene a door leading to another Apartment.

ORAN.

Reveal the future, lightnings!   Then I'd hail
That arrowy flash.   O darker than the storm
Cowed as the beasts now crouching in their caves,

Is my sad soul. Impending o'er this house,
I feel some bursting fate, my doomed arm
In vain would ward.

[Enter a Man-at-Arms.

How now, hast left thy post?

Man.

O worthy Castellan, the lightnings play
Upon our turrets, that no human step
Can keep the watch. Each forky flash seems mis-
sioned
To scathe our roof, and the whole platform flows
With a blue sea of flame.

Oran.

It is thy post.
No peril clears desertion. To thy post.
Mark me, my step will be as prompt as thine;
I will relieve thee. *[Exit* Man-at-Arms.
Let the mischievous fire
Wither this head. O Allah! grant no fate
More dire awaits me.

[Enter the Count Alarcos.

Hah! the Count! My lord,
In such a night!

Alar.

A night that's not so wild
As this tempestuous breast. How is she, Oran?

Oran.

Well.

Alar.

Ever well.

Oran.

The children —

ALAR.

Wine, I'm wearied.
The lightning scared my horse; he's galled my arm.
Get me some wine. [*Exit* ORAN.

The storm was not to stop me.
The mind intent construes each natural act.
To a personal bias, and so catches judgments
In every common course. In truth the flash,
Though it seemed opening hell, was not so
    dreadful
As that wild, glaring hall.

[*Re-enter* ORAN *with a goblet and flagon.*

Ah! this re-mans me!
I think the storm has lulled. Another cup.
Go see, good Oran, how the tempest speeds.

[*Exit* ORAN.

An hour ago I did not dare to think
I'd drink wine more.

Re-enter ORAN.

ORAN.

The storm indeed has lulled
As by a miracle; the sky is clear,
There's not a breath of air; and from the turret
I heard the bell of Huelgas.

ALAR.

Then 'twas nothing.
My spirit vaults! Oran, thou dost remember
The night that we first met?

ORAN.

'Tis graven deep
Upon my heart.

ALAR.

I think thou lov'st me, Oran?

ORAN.

And all thy house.

ALAR.

Nay, thou shalt love but me.
I'll no divisions in the hearts that are mine.

ORAN.

I have no love but that which knits me to thee
With deeper love.

ALAR.

I found thee, Oran, what—
I will not say. And now thou art, good Oran,
A Prince's Castellan.

ORAN.

I feel thy bounty.

ALAR.

Thou shalt be more. But serve me as I would,
And thou shalt name thy meed.

ORAN.

To serve my lord
Is my sufficient meed.

ALAR.

Come hither, Oran.
Were there a life between me and my life,
And all that makes that life a thing to cling to,
Love, Honour, Power, ay, what I will not name
Nor thou canst image—yet enough to stir
Ambition in the dead——I think, good Oran,
Thou would'st not see me foiled?

ORAN.

Thy glory's dearer
Than life to me.

ALAR.

I knew it, I knew it.
Thou shalt share all; thy alien blood shall be
No bar to thy preferment. Hast thou brothers?
I'll send for them. An aged sire, perchance?
Here's gold for him. Count it thyself. Contrive
All means of self-enjoyment. To the full
They shall lap up fruition. Thou hast, all have,
Some master wish which still eludes thy grasp,
And still's the secret idol of thy soul;
'Tis gained. And only if thou dost, good Oran,
What love and duty prompt.

ORAN.

Count on my faith,
I stand prepared to prove it.

ALAR.

Good, good, Oran.
It is an hour to midnight?

ORAN.

The moon is not
Within her midnight bower, yet near.

ALAR.

So late!
The Countess sleeps?

ORAN.

She has long retired.

ALAR.

She sleeps.
O, she must wake no more!

ORAN.

Thy wife!

ALAR.

It must
Be done, ere yet the Castle chime shall tell
Night wanes.

ORAN.

Thy wife! God of my fathers! none
Can do this deed!

ALAR.

Upon thy hand it rests.
The deed must fall on thee.

ORAN.

I will not do it.

ALAR.

Thine oath, thine oath! Hast thou forgot thine oath?
Thou owest me a life, and now I claim it.
What, hast thou trifled with me? Hast thou fooled
With one whose point was at thy throat? Beware!
Thou art my slave, and I have branded thee
With this infernal ransom!

ORAN.

I am thy slave,
And I will be thy slave, and all my days
Devoted to perdition. Not for gold
Or worldly worth; to cheer no agèd parent,
Though I have one, a mother; not to bask
My seed within thy beams; to feed no passions
And gorge no craving vanity; but because
Thou gavest me life, and led to that which made
That life for once delicious. O, great sir,
The King's thy foe? Surrounded by his guards

I would waylay him.   Hast thou some fierce
    rival?
I'll pluck his heart out.   Yea! there is no peril
I'd not confront, no rack I'll not endure,
No great offence commit, to do thee service —
So thou wilt spare me this, and spare thy soul
This unmatched sin.

             ALAR.

             I had exhausted suffering
Ere I could speak to thee.   I claim thine oath.

             ORAN.

One moment, yet one moment.   This is sudden
As it is terrible.

             ALAR.

        The womb is ripe,
And thou art but the midwife of the birth
I have engendered.

             ORAN.

        Think how fair she is,
How gracious, how devoted!

             ALAR.

             Need I thee
To tell me what she is!

             ORAN.

          Thy children's mother.

             ALAR.

Would she were not!   Another breast should bear
My children.

             ORAN.

        Thou inhuman bloody man —
It shall not be, it cannot, cannot be.

I tell thee, tyrant, there's a power abroad
E'en now that crushes thee. The storm that raged
Blows from a mystic quarter. 'Tis the hand
Of Allah guides the tempest of this night.

ALAR.

Thine oath, thine oath!

ORAN.

Accursèd be the hour
Thou sparedst my life!

ALAR.

Thine oath, I claim thine oath,
Nay, Moor, what is it? 'Tis a life, and thou
Hast learnt to rate existence at its worth.
A life, a woman's life! Why, sack a town,
And thousands die like her. My faithful Oran,
Come let me love thee, let me find a friend
When friends can prove themselves. It's not an
oath
Vowed in our sunshine ease, that shows a friend;
'Tis the tempestuous mood like this, that calls
For faithful service.

ORAN.

Hah! the Emir's blood
Cries for this judgment. It was sacred seed.

ALAR.

It flowed to clear thine honour. Art thou he
That honour loved so dearly, that he scorned
Betrayal of a foe, although that foe
Had changed him to a bravo?

ORAN.

Let me kiss
Thy garment's hem, and grovel at thy feet —

I pray, I supplicate — my lord, my lord —
Absolve me from that oath!

ALAR.

I had not thought
To claim it twice. It seems I lacked some judgment
In man, to deem that honour might be found
In hired stabbers.

ORAN.

Hah! I vowed to thee
A life for that which thou didst spare — 'tis well.
The debt is paid.   *[Stabs himself and falls.*

Enter the COUNTESS *from the inner Chamber.*

COUN.

I cannot sleep — my dreams are full of woe!
Alarcos! my Alarcos! Hah! dread sight!
Oran!

ORAN.

O, spare her; 'tis no sacrifice
If she be spared.

COUN.

Wild words! Thou dost not speak.
O, speak, Alarcos! speak!

ORAN.

His voice is death.

COUN.

Ye Saints uphold me now, for I am weak
And lost. What means this? Oran dying! Nay —
Alarcos! I'm a woman. Aid me, aid me.
Why's Oran thus? O, save him, my Alarcos!
Blood! And why shed? Why, let us staunch his
    wounds.

Why are there wounds? He will not speak. Alar-
   cos,
A word, a single word! Unhappy Moor!
Where is thy hurt?   [*Kneels by* ORAN.

ORAN.

      That hand! This is not death;
'Tis Paradise.   [*Dies.*

ALAR. (*advancing in soliloquy*).

He sets me great examples.
'Tis easier than I deemed; a single blow
And his bold soul has fled. His lavish life
Enlists me in quick service. Quit that dark corpse;
He died as did become a perjured traitor.

COUN.

To whom, my lord?

ALAR.

     To all Castille perchance.
Come hither, wife. Before the morning breaks
A lengthened journey waits thee. Art prepared?

COUN. (*springing to* ALARCOS).

I will not go. Alarcos, dear Alarcos,
Thy look is terrible! What mean these words?
Why should'st thou spare me? Why should Oran
   die?
The veil that clouds thy mind—I'll rend it. Tell
   me—
Yea! I'll know all. A power supports me now—
Defies even thee.

ALAR.

     A traitor's troubled tongue
Disturbs thy mind. I tell thee, thou must leave
This castle promptly.

COUN.

Not to Burgos — say
But that. I will not go. That fatal woman —
Her shadow's on thy soul.

ALAR.

No, not to Burgos.
'Tis not to Burgos that thy journey tends.
The children sleep?

COUN.

Spite of the storm.

ALAR.

Go — kiss them.
Thou canst not take them with thee. To thy chamber —
Quick to thy chamber.

[*The* COUNTESS *as if about to speak, but* ALARCOS
    stops her.

Nay, time presses, wife.

[*The* COUNTESS *slowly re-enters her Chamber.*

ALAR.

I am alone — with Death. And will she look
Serene as this? The visage of a hero
Stamped with a martyred end! Thou noble Moor!
What if thy fate were mine! Thou art at rest:
No dark fulfilment waits o'er thee. The tomb
Hath many charms.

(*The* COUNTESS *calls.*)

Alarcos!

ALAR.

Ay, anon.
Why did she tell me that she lived? Methought
It was all past. I came to confront death;

And we have met. This sacrificial blood —
What, bears it no atonement? 'Twas an offering
Fit for the Gods.

                                   [The midnight bell.

                She waits me now; her hand
Extends a diadem; my achieveless arm
Would wither at her scorn. 'Tis thus, Solisa,
I gain thy heart and realm!

[ALARCOS *moves hastily to the Chamber, which he en-*
ters; the stage for some seconds is empty; a shriek
is then heard; ALARCOS *re-appears, very pale, and*
slowly advances to the front of the stage.

'Tis over and I live. I heard a sound,
Was't Oran's spirit?
I'll not rest here, and yet I dare not back.
The bodies? Nay, 'tis done — I'll not shrink now.
I have seen death before. But is this death?
Methinks a deeper mystery. Well, 'tis done.
There'll be no hour so dark as this. I would
I had not caught her eye.

                             [A trumpet sounds.

                 The Warder's note!

Shall I meet life again?

                     [Another trumpet sounds.

                Enter the SENESCHAL.

                    SEN.

                Horsemen from Court.

              ALAR.

The Court! I'm sick at heart.   Perchance she's eager,
And cannot wait my coming.   *[Enter two* COURTIERS.
                                Well, good sirs!

1ST COURT.
Alas, my lord.

ALAR.
I live upon thy words.

What now?

1ST COURT.
We have rode post, my lord.

ALAR.
Bad news

Flies ever. 'Tis the King?

1ST COURT.
Alas!

ALAR.
She's ill.

My horse, my horse there!

1ST COURT.
Nay, my lord, not so.

ALAR.
Why, then, I care for naught.

1ST COURT.
Unheard-of horror!

The storm, the storm ——

ALAR.
I rode in it.

1ST COURT.
Methought

Each flash would fire the Citadel; the flame
Wreathed round its pinnacles, and poured in streams
Adown the pallid battlements. Our revellers
Forgot their festival, and stopped to gaze
On the portentous vision. When behold!

The curtained clouds re-opened, and a bolt
Came winged from the startling blue of heaven,
And struck ——— the Infanta!

ALAR.

There's a God of Vengeance!

1ST COURT.

She fell a blighted corpse. Amid the shrieks
Of women, prayers of hurrying multitudes,
The panic and the stir — we sought for thee;
The King's overwhelmed.

ALAR.

My wife's at least a Queen;
She reigns in Heaven. The King's o'erwhelmed —
poor man!
Go tell him, sirs, the Count Alarcos lived
To find a hell on earth; yet thus he sought
A deeper and a darker.   [*Falls.*

THE END

POPANILLA

ADVERTISEMENT.

This narrative of an imaginary voyage was first published
in 1827.

POPANILLA

CHAPTER I.

THE ISLE OF FANTAISIE.

HERE is an island in the Indian Ocean, so unfortunate as not yet to have been visited either by discovery ships or missionary societies. It is a place where all those things are constantly found which men most desire to see, and with the sight of which they are seldom favoured. It abounds in flowers, and fruit, and sunshine. Lofty mountains, covered with green and mighty forests, except where the red rocks catch the fierce beams of the blazing sun, bowery valleys, broad lakes, gigantic trees, and gushing rivers bursting from rocky gorges, are crowned with a purple and ever cloudless sky. Summer, in its most unctuous state and most mellow majesty, is here perpetual. So intense and overpowering, in the daytime, is the rich union of heat and perfume, that living animal or creature is never visible; and were you and I to pluck, before sunset, the huge fruit from yonder teeming tree, we might fancy ourselves for the moment the

future sinners of another Eden. Yet a solitude it
is not.

The island is surrounded by a calm and blue lagoon, formed by a ridge of coral rocks, which break
the swell of the ocean, and prevent the noxious spray
from banishing the rich shrubs which grow even to
the water's edge. It is a few minutes before sunset,
that the first intimation of animal existence in this
seeming solitude is given, by the appearance of mermaids, who, floating on the rosy sea, congregate
about these rocks. They sound a loud but melodious
chorus from their sea-shells, and a faint and distant
chorus soon answers from the island. The mermaidens
immediately repeat their salutations, and are greeted
with a nearer and a louder answer. As the red and
rayless sun drops into the glowing waters, the cho-
ruses simultaneously join; and rushing from the woods,
and down the mountain steeps to the nearest shore,
crowds of human beings, at the same moment, appear and collect.

The inhabitants of this island, in form and face, do
not misbecome the clime and the country. With the
vivacity of a faun, the men combine the strength of
a Hercules and the beauty of an Adonis; and, as their
more interesting companions flash upon his presence,
the least classical of poets might be excused for im-
agining that, like their blessed goddess, the women
had magically sprung from the brilliant foam of that
ocean which is gradually subsiding before them.

But sunset in this land is not the signal merely for
the evidence of human existence. At the moment
that the islanders, crowned with flowers, and waving goblets and garlands, burst from their retreats,
upon each mountain peak a lion starts forward,

stretches his proud tail, and, bellowing to the sun, scours back exulting to his forest; immense bodies, which before would have been mistaken for the trunks of trees, now move into life, and serpents, untwining their green and glittering folds, and slowly bending their crested heads around, seem proudly conscious of a voluptuous existence; troops of monkeys leap from tree to tree; panthers start forward, and alarmed, not alarming, instantly vanish; a herd of milk-white elephants tramples over the background of the scene; and instead of gloomy owls and noxious beetles, to hail the long-enduring twilight, from the bell of every opening flower beautiful birds, radiant with every rainbow tint, rush with a long and living melody into the cool air.

The twilight in this island is not that transient moment of unearthly bliss, which, in our less favoured regions, always leaves us so thoughtful and so sad; on the contrary, it lasts many hours, and consequently the islanders are neither moody nor sorrowful. As they sleep during the day, four or five hours of 'tipsy dance and revelry' are exercise and not fatigue. At length, even in this delightful region, the rosy tint fades into purple, and the purple into blue; the white moon gleams, and at length glitters; and the invisible stars first creep into light, and then blaze into radiancy. But no hateful dews discolour their loveliness! and so clear is the air, that instead of the false appearance of a studded vault, the celestial bodies may be seen floating in æther, at various distances and of various tints. Ere the showery fireflies have ceased to shine, and the blue lights to play about the tremulous horizon, amid the voices of a thousand birds, the dancers solace themselves with the rarest fruits, the most delicate fish, and the most delicious wines; but flesh they love not. They are an innocent and a happy, though a voluptuous and ignorant race. They have no manufactures, no commerce, no agriculture, and no printing-presses; but for their slight clothing they wear the bright skins of serpents; for corn, Nature gives them the bread-fruit; and for intellectual amusement, they have a pregnant fancy and a ready wit; tell inexhaustible stories, and always laugh at each other's jokes. A natural instinct gave them the art of making wine; and it was the same benevolent Nature that blessed them also with the knowledge of the art of making love. But time flies even here. The lovely companions have danced, and sung, and banqueted, and laughed; what further bliss remains for man? They rise, and in pairs wander about the island, and then to their bowers; their life ends with the night they love so well; and ere day, the everlasting conqueror, wave his flaming standard in the luminous East, solitude and silence will again reign in the ISLE OF FANTAISIE.

CHAPTER II.

HE last and loudest chorus had died away, and the islanders were pouring forth their libation to their great enemy the sun, when suddenly a vast obscurity spread over the glowing West. They looked at each other, and turned pale, and the wine from their trembling goblets fell useless on the shore. The women were too frightened to scream, and, for the first time in the Isle of Fantàisie, silence existed after sunset. They were encouraged when they observed that the darkness ceased at that point in the heavens which overlooked their coral rocks; and perceiving that their hitherto unsullied sky was pure, even at this moment of otherwise universal gloom, the men regained their colour, touched the goblets with their lips, further to reanimate themselves, and the women, now less discomposed, uttered loud shrieks.

Suddenly the wind roared with unaccustomed rage, the sea rose into large billows, and a ship was seen tossing in the offing. The islanders, whose experience of navigation extended only to a slight paddling in their lagoon, in the half of a hollow trunk of a tree, for the purpose of fishing, mistook the tight little frigate for a great fish; and being now aware of the cause of this disturbance, and at the same time feeling confident that the monster could never make way through the shallow waters to the island, they recovered their courage, and gazed upon the labouring leviathan with the same interested nonchalance with which students at a modern lecture observe an expounding philosopher.

'What a shadow he casts over the sky!' said the King, a young man, whose divine right was never questioned by his female subjects. 'What a commotion in the waters, and what a wind he snorts forth! It certainly must be the largest fish that exists. I remember my father telling me that a monstrous fish once got entangled among our rocks, and this part of the island really smelt for a month; I cannot help fancying that there is a rather odd smell now; pah!'

A favourite Queen flew to the suffering monarch, and pressing her aromatic lips upon his offended nostrils, his Majesty recovered.

The unhappy crew of the frigate, who, with the aid of their telescopes, had detected the crowds upon the shore, now fired their signal guns of distress, which came sullenly booming through the wind.

'Oh! the great fish is speaking!' was the universal exclamation.

'I begin to get frightened,' said the favourite Queen. 'I am sure the monster is coming here!' So saying, her Majesty grasped up a handful of pearls from the shore, to defend herself.

As screaming was now the fashion, all the women of course screamed; and animated by the example of their sovereign, and armed with the marine gems, the Amazons assumed an imposing attitude.

Just at the moment that they had worked up their enthusiasm to the highest pitch, and were actually desirous of dying for their country, the ship sunk.

CHAPTER III.

T IS the flush of noon; and, strange
to say, a human figure is seen
wandering on the shore of the
Isle of Fantaisie.

'One of the crew of the
wrecked frigate, of course? What
an escape! Fortunate creature! interesting man!
Probably the indefatigable Captain Parry; possibly the
undaunted Captain Franklin; perhaps the adventurous
Captain Lyon!'

No! sweet blue-eyed girl! my plots are not of
that extremely guessable nature so admired by your
adorable sex. Indeed, this book is so constructed
that if you were even, according to custom, to commence its perusal by reading the last page, you
would not gain the slightest assistance in finding out
'how the story ends.'

The wanderer belongs to no frigate-building nation. He is a true Fantaisian; who having, in his
fright during yesterday's storm, lost the lock of hair
which, in a moment of glorious favour, he had rav-
ished from his fair mistress's brow, is now, after a

sleepless night, tracing every remembered haunt of yesterday, with the fond hope of regaining his most precious treasure. Ye gentlemen of England, who live at home at ease, know full well the anxiety and exertion, the days of management, and the nights of meditation which the rape of a lock requires, and you can consequently sympathize with the agitated feelings of the handsome and the hapless Popanilla.

The favourite of all the women, the envy of all the men, Popanilla passed a pleasant life. No one was a better judge of wine, no one had a better taste for fruit, no one danced with more elegant vivacity, and no one whispered compliments in a more meaning tone. His stories ever had a point, his repartees were never ill-natured. What a pity that such an amiable fellow should have got into such a scrape!

In spite of his grief, however, Popanilla soon found that the ardency of his passion evaporated under a smoking sun; and, exhausted, he was about to return home from his fruitless search, when his attention was attracted by a singular appearance. He observed before him, on the shore, a square and hitherto unseen form. He watched it for some minutes, but it was motionless. He drew nearer, and observed it with intense attention; but, if it were a being, it certainly was fast asleep. He approached close to its side, but it neither moved nor breathed. He applied his nose to the mysterious body, and the elegant Fantaisian drew back immediately from a most villanous smell of pitch. Not to excite too much, in this calm age, the reader's curiosity, let him know at once that this strange substance was a sea-chest. Upon it was marked, in large black letters, S. D. K. No. 1.

For the first time in his life Popanilla experienced a feeling of overwhelming curiosity. His fatigue, his loss, the scorching hour, and the possible danger were all forgotten in an indefinite feeling that the body possessed contents more interesting than its unpromising exterior, and in a resolute determination that the development of the mystery should be reserved only for himself.

Although he felt assured that he must be unseen, he could not refrain from throwing a rapid glance of anxiety around him. It was a moment of perfect stillness: the island slept in sunshine, and even the waves had ceased to break over the opposing rocks. A thousand strange and singular thoughts rushed into his mind, but his first purpose was ever uppermost; and at length, unfolding his girdle of skin, he tied the tough cincture round the chest, and, exerting all his powers, dragged his mysterious waif into the nearest wood.

But during this operation the top fell off, and revealed the neatest collection of little packages that ever pleased the eye of the admirer of spruce arrangement. Popanilla took up packets upon all possible subjects; smelt them, but they were not savoury; he was sorely puzzled. At last, he lighted on a slender volume bound in brown calf, which, with the confined but sensual notions of a savage, he mistook for gingerbread, at least. It was 'The Universal Linguist, by Mr. Hamilton; or, the Art of Dreaming in Languages.'

No sooner had Popanilla passed that well-formed nose, which had been so often admired by the lady whose lock of hair he had unfortunately lost, a few times over a few pages of the Hamiltonian System than he sank upon his bed of flowers, and, in spite of his curiosity, was instantly overcome by a profound slumber. But his slumber, though deep, was not peaceful, and he was the actor in an agitating drama.

He found himself alone in a gay and glorious garden. In the centre of it grew a pomegranate tree of prodigious size; its top was lost in the sky, and its innumerable branches sprang out in all directions, covered with large fruit of a rich golden hue. Beautiful birds were perched upon all parts of the tree, and chanted with perpetual melody the beauties of their bower. Tempted by the delicious sight, Popanilla stretched forward his ready hand to pluck; but no sooner had he grasped the fruit than the music immediately ceased, the birds rushed away, the sky darkened, the tree fell under the wind, the garden vanished, and Popanilla found himself in the midst of a raging sea, buffeting the waves.

He would certainly have been drowned had he not been immediately swallowed up by the huge monster which had not only been the occasion of the storm of yesterday, but, ah! most unhappy business! been the occasion also of his losing that lock of hair.

Ere he could congratulate himself on his escape he found fresh cause for anxiety, for he perceived that he was no longer alone. No friends were near him; but, on the contrary, he was surrounded by strangers of a far different aspect. They were men certainly; that is to say, they had legs and arms, and heads, and bodies as himself; but instead of that bloom of

youth, that regularity of feature, that amiable joy-
ousness of countenance, which he had ever been
accustomed to meet and to love in his former companions, he recoiled in horror from the swarthy com-
plexions, the sad visages, and the haggard features of
his present ones. They spoke to him in a harsh and
guttural accent. He would have fled from their advances; but then he was in the belly of a whale!
When he had become a little used to their tones he
was gratified by finding that their attentions were far
from hostile; and, after having received from them a
few compliments, he began to think that they were
not quite so ugly. He discovered that the object of
their inquiries was the fatal pomegranate which still
remained in his hand. They admired its beauty, and
told him that they greatly esteemed an individual who
possessed such a mass of precious ore. Popanilla
begged to undeceive them, and courteously presented
the fruit. No sooner, however, had he parted with
this apple of discord, than the countenances of his
companions changed. Immediately discovering its real
nature, they loudly accused Popanilla of having deceived them; he remonstrated, and they recriminated;
and the great fish, irritated by their clamour, lashed
its huge tail, and with one efficacious vomit spouted
the innocent Popanilla high in the air. He fell with
such a dash into the waves that he was awakened by
the sound of his own fall.

The dreamer awoke amidst real chattering, and
scuffling, and clamour. A troop of green monkeys
had been aroused by his unusual occupation, and had
taken the opportunity of his slumber to become acquainted with some of the first principles of science.

What progress they had made it is difficult to ascertain; because, each one throwing a tract at Popanilla's head, they immediately disappeared. It is said, however, that some monkeys have been since seen skipping about the island, with their tails cut off; and that they have even succeeded in passing themselves off for human beings among those people who do not read novels, and are consequently unacquainted with mankind.

The morning's adventure immediately rushed into Popanilla's mind, and he proceeded forthwith to examine the contents of his chest; but with advantages which had not been yet enjoyed by those who had previously peeped into it. The monkeys had not been composed to sleep by the 'Universal Linguist' of Mr. Hamilton. As for Popanilla, he took up a treatise on hydrostatics, and read it straight through on the spot. For the rest of the day he was hydrostatically mad; nor could the commonest incident connected with the action or conveyance of water take place without his speculating on its cause and consequence.

So enraptured was Popanilla with his new accomplishments and acquirements that by degrees he avoided attendance on the usual evening assemblages, and devoted himself solely to the acquirement of useful knowledge. After a short time his absence was remarked; but the greatest and the most gifted has only to leave his coterie, called the world, for a few days, to be fully convinced of what slight importance he really is. And so Popanilla, the delight of society and the especial favourite of the women, was in a very short time not even inquired after. At first, of course, they supposed that he was in love, or that he had a slight cold, or that he was writing his memoirs; and as these suppositions, in due course, take their place in the annals of society as circumstantial histories, in about a week one knew the lady, another had heard him sneeze, and a third had seen the manuscript. At the end of another week Popanilla was forgotten.

CHAPTER IV.

POPANILLA BECOMES A PHILOSOPHER.

IX months had elapsed since the first chest of the cargo of Useful Knowledge destined for the fortunate Maldives had been digested by the recluse Popanilla; for a recluse he had now become. Great students are rather dull companions. Our Fantaisian friend, during his first studies, was as moody, absent, and querulous as are most men of genius during that mystical period of life. He was consequently avoided by the men and quizzed by the women, and consoled himself for the neglect of the first and the taunts of the second by the indefinite sensation that he should, some day or other, turn out that little being called a great man. As for his mistress, she considered herself insulted by being addressed by a man who had lost her lock of hair. When the chest was exhausted Popanilla was seized with a profound melancholy. Nothing depresses a man's spirits more completely than a self-conviction of self-conceit; and Popanilla, who had been accustomed to consider himself and his companions as the most elegant portion of the visible creation, now discovered, with dismay, that he and his fellow-islanders were nothing more than a horde of useless savages.

This mortification, however, was soon succeeded by a proud consciousness that he, at any rate, was now civilised; and that proud consciousness by a fond hope that in a short time he might become a civiliser. Like all projectors, he was not of a sanguine temperament; but he did trust that in the course of another season the Isle of Fantaisie might take its station among the nations. He was determined, however, not to be too rapid. It cannot be expected that ancient prejudices can in a moment be eradicated, and new modes of conduct instantaneously substituted and established. Popanilla, like a wise man, determined to conciliate. His views were to be as liberal, as his principles were enlightened. Men should be forced to do nothing. Bigotry, and intolerance, and persecution were the objects of his decided disapprobation; resembling, in this particular, all the great and good men who have ever existed, who have invariably maintained this opinion so long as they have been in the minority.

Popanilla appeared once more in the world.

'Dear me! is that you, Pop?' exclaimed the ladies. 'What have you been doing with yourself all this time? Travelling, I suppose. Every one travels now. Really you travelled men get quite bores. And where did you get that coat, if it be a coat?'

Such was the style in which the Fantaisian females saluted the long absent Popanilla; and really, when a man shuts himself up from the world for a considerable time, and fancies that in condescending to re-enter it he has surely the right to expect the homage due to a superior being, these salutations are awkward. The ladies of England peculiarly excel in this species of annihilation; and while they continue to drown puppies, as they daily do, in a sea of sarcasm, I think no true Englishman will hesitate one moment in giving them the preference for tact and manner over all the vivacious French, all the self-possessing Italian, and all the tolerant German women. This is a claptrap, and I have no doubt will sell the book.

Popanilla, however, had not re-entered society with the intention of subsiding into a nonentity; and he therefore took the opportunity, a few minutes after sunset, just as his companions were falling into the dance, to beg the favour of being allowed to address his sovereign only for one single moment.

'Sire!' said he, in that mild tone of subdued superciliousness with which we should always address kings, and which, while it vindicates our dignity, satisfactorily proves that we are above the vulgar passion of envy, 'Sire!' but let us not encourage that fatal faculty of oratory so dangerous to free states, and therefore let us give only the 'substance of Popanilla's speech.'* He commenced his address in a manner somewhat resembling the initial observations of those pleasing pamphlets which are the fashion of the present hour; and which, being intended to diffuse information among those who have not enjoyed

---

* *Substance of a speech*, in Parliamentary language, means a printed edition of an harangue which contains all that was uttered in the House, and about as much again.

the opportunity and advantages of study, and are consequently of a gay and cheerful disposition, treat of light subjects in a light and polished style. Popanilla, therefore, spoke of man in a savage state, the origin of society, and the elements of the social compact, in sentences which would not have disgraced the mellifluous pen of Bentham. From these he naturally digressed into an agreeable disquisition on the Anglo-Saxons; and, after a little badinage on the Bill of Rights, flew off to an airy *aperçu* of the French Revolution. When he had arrived at the Isle of Fantaisie he begged to inform his Majesty that man was born for something else besides enjoying himself. It was, doubtless, extremely pleasant to dance and sing, to crown themselves with chaplets, and to drink wine; but he was 'free to confess' that he did not imagine that the most barefaced hireling of corruption could for a moment presume to maintain that there was any utility in pleasure. If there were no utility in pleasure, it was quite clear that pleasure could profit no one. If, therefore, it were unprofitable, it was injurious; because that which does not produce a profit is equivalent to a loss; therefore pleasure is a losing business; consequently pleasure is not pleasant.

He also showed that man was not born for himself, but for society; that the interests of the body are alone to be considered, and not those of the individual; and that a nation might be extremely happy, extremely powerful, and extremely rich, although every individual member of it might at the same time be miserable, dependent, and in debt. He regretted to observe that no one in the island seemed in the slightest degree conscious of the object of his

being. Man is created for a purpose; the object of
his existence is to perfect himself. Man is imperfect
by nature, because if nature had made him perfect
he would have had no wants; and it is only by
supplying his wants that utility can be developed.
The development of utility is therefore the object of
our being, and the attainment of this great end the
cause of our existence. This principle clears all
doubts, and rationally accounts for a state of existence which has puzzled many pseudo-philosophers.

Popanilla then went on to show that the hitherto
received definitions of man were all erroneous; that
man is neither a walking animal, nor a talking animal, nor a cooking animal, nor a lounging animal, nor a debt-incurring animal, nor a tax-paying
animal, nor a printing animal, nor a puffing animal,
but a *developing animal*. Development is the discovery of utility. By developing the water we get
fish; by developing the earth we get corn, and cash,
and cotton; by developing the air we get breath; by
developing the fire we get heat. Thus, the use of
the elements is demonstrated to the meanest capacity. But it was not merely a material development
to which he alluded; a moral development was
equally indispensable. He showed that it was impossible for a nation either to think too much or to
do too much. The life of man was therefore to be
passed in a moral and material development until he
had consummated his perfection. It was the opinion
of Popanilla that this great result was by no means
so near at hand as some philosophers flattered themselves; and that it might possibly require another
half-century before even the most civilised nation
could be said to have completed the destiny of the

human race. At the same time, he intimated that there were various extraordinary means by which this rather desirable result might be facilitated; and there was no saying what the building of a new University might do, of which, when built, he had no objection to be appointed Principal.

In answer to those who affect to admire that deficient system of existence which they style simplicity of manners, and who are perpetually committing the blunder of supposing that every advance towards perfection only withdraws man further from his primitive. and proper condition, Popanilla triumphantly demonstrated that no such order as that which they associated with the phrase 'state of nature' ever existed. 'Man,' said he, 'is called the masterpiece of nature; and man. is also, as we all know, the most curious of machines; now, a machine is a work of art, consequently, the masterpiece of nature is. the masterpiece of art. The object of all mechanism is the attainment of utility; the object of man, who is the most perfect machine, is utility in the highest degree. Can we believe, therefore, that this machine was ever intended for a state which never could have called forth its powers, a state in which no utility could ever have been attained, a state in which there are no wants; consequently, no demand; consequently, no supply; consequently, no competition; consequently, no invention; consequently, no profits; only one great pernicious monopoly of comfort and ease? Society without wants is like a world without winds. It is quite clear, therefore, that there is no such thing as Nature; Nature is Art, or Art is Nature; that which is most useful is most natural, because utility is the test of nature; therefore a steam-engine is in fact a much more natural production than a mountain.*

'You are convinced, therefore,' he continued, 'by these observations, that it is impossible for an individual or a nation to be too artificial in their manners, their ideas, their laws, or their general policy; because, in fact, the more artificial you become the nearer you approach that state of nature of which you are so perpetually talking.' Here observing that some of his audience appeared to be a little sceptical, perhaps only surprised, he told them that what he said must be true, because it entirely consisted of first principles.†

After having thus preliminarily descanted for about two hours, Popanilla informed his Majesty that he was unused to public speaking, and then proceeded to show that the grand characteristic of the social action‡ of the Isle of Fantaisie was a total want of development. This he observed with equal sorrow and surprise; he respected the wisdom of their ances-

---

* The age seems as anti-mountainous as it is anti-monarchical. A late writer insinuates that if the English had spent their millions in levelling the Andes, instead of excavating the table-lands, society might have been benefited. These monstrosities are decidedly useless, and therefore can neither be sublime nor beautiful, as has been unanswerably demonstrated by another recent writer on political æsthetics.— See also a personal attack on Mont Blanc, in the second number of the *Foreign Quarterly Review*, 1828.

† First principles are the ingredients of positive truth. They are immutable, as may be seen by comparing the first principles of the eighteenth century with the first principles of the nineteenth.

‡ This simple and definite phrase we derive from the nation to whom we were indebted during the last century for some other phrases about as definite, but rather more dangerous.

tors; at the same time, no one could deny that they
were both barbarous and ignorant; he highly esteemed
also the constitution, but regretted that it was not in
the slightest degree adapted to the existing want of
society: he was not for destroying any establishments,
but, on the contrary, was for courteously affording
them the opportunity of self-dissolution. He finished
by re-urging, in strong terms, the immediate development of the island. In the first place, a great
metropolis must be instantly built, because a great
metropolis always produces a great demand; and,
moreover, Popanilla had some legal doubts whether
a country without a capital could in fact be considered a State. Apologising for having so long tres-
passed upon the attention of the assembly, he begged
distinctly to state * that he had no wish to see his
Majesty and his fellow-subjects adopt these new
principles without examination and without experience. They might commence on a small scale; let
them cut down their forests, and by turning them
into ships and houses discover the utility of timber;
let the whole island be dug up; let canals be cut,
docks be built, and all the elephants be killed
directly, that their teeth might yield an immediate
article for exportation. A short time would afford a
sufficient trial. In the meanwhile, they would not be
pledged to further measures, and these might be
considered 'only as an experiment.' † Taking for

* Another phrase of Parliament, which, I need not observe, is always made use of in oratory when the orator can see his meaning
about as distinctly as Sancho perceived the charms of Dulcinea.

† A very famous and convenient phrase this — but in politics *experiments* mean *revolutions*. 1828.

granted that these principles would be acted on, and taking into consideration the site of the island in the map of the world, the nature and extent of its resources, its magnificent race of human beings, its varieties of the animal creation, its wonderfully fine timber, its undeveloped mineral treasures, the spaciousness of its harbours, and its various facilities for extended international communication, Popanilla had no hesitation in saying that a short time could not elapse ere, instead of passing their lives in a state of unprofitable ease and useless enjoyment, they might reasonably expect to be the terror and astonishment of the universe, and to be able to annoy every nation of any consequence.

Here, observing a smile upon his Majesty's countenance, Popanilla told the King that he was only a chief magistrate, and he had no more right to laugh at him than a parish constable. He concluded by observing that although what he at present urged might appear strange, nevertheless, if the listeners had been acquainted with the characters and cases of Galileo and Turgot, they would then have seen, as a necessary consequence, that his system was perfectly correct, and he himself a man of extraordinary merit.

Here the chief magistrate, no longer daring to smile, burst into a fit of laughter; and turning to his courtiers said, 'I have not an idea what this man is talking about, but I know that he makes my head ache: give me a cup of wine, and let us have a dance.'

All applauded the royal proposition: and pushing Popanilla from one to another, until he was fairly hustled to the brink of the lagoon, they soon forgot the existence of this bore: in one word, he was cut.

When Popanilla found himself standing alone, and looking grave while all the rest were gay, he began to suspect that he was not so influential a personage as he previously imagined. Rather crest-fallen, he sneaked home; and consoled himself for having nobody to speak to by reading some amusing 'Conversations on Political Economy.'

CHAPTER V.

THE DANGER OF KNOWING TOO MUCH.

POPANILLA was discomposed, but he was not discomfited. He consoled himself for the Royal neglect by the recollection of the many illustrious men who had been despised, banished, imprisoned, and burnt for the maintenance of opinions which, centuries afterwards, had been discovered to be truth. He did not forget that in still further centuries the lately recognised truth had been re-discovered to be falsehood; but then these men were not less illustrious; and what wonder that their opinions were really erroneous, since they were not his present ones? The reasoning was equally conclusive and consolatory. Popanilla, therefore, was not discouraged; and although he deemed it more prudent not to go out of his way to seek another audience of his sovereign, or to be too anxious again to address a public meeting, he nevertheless determined to proceed cautiously, but constantly, propagating his doctrines and proselytizing in private.

Unfortunately for Popanilla, he did not enjoy one advantage which all founders of sects have duly appreciated, and by which they have been materially

assisted.   It is a great and an unanswerable argument
in favour of a Providence that we constantly perceive
that the most beneficial results are brought about by
the least worthy and most insignificant agents.   The
purest religions would never have been established
had they not been supported by sinners who felt the
burthen of the old faith; and the most free and enlightened governments are often generated by the discontented, the disappointed, and the dissolute.   Now,
in the Isle of Fantaisie, unfortunately for our revolu-
tionizer, there was not a single grumbler.

Unable, therefore, to make the bad passions of his
fellow-creatures the unconscious instruments of his
good purposes, Popanilla must have been contented
to have monopolised all the wisdom of the moderns,
had not he, with the unbaffled wit of an inventor,
hit upon a new expedient.   Like Socrates, our philosopher began to cultivate with sedulousness the society of youth.

In a short time the ladies of Fantaisie were forced
to observe that the fair sex most unfashionably pre-
dominated in their evening assemblages; for the young
gentlemen of the island had suddenly ceased to pay
their graceful homage at the altar of Terpsichore.   In
an Indian isle not to dance was as bad as heresy.
The ladies rallied the recreants, but their playful sar-
casms failed of their wonted effect.   In the natural
course of things they had recourse to remonstrances,
but their appeals were equally fruitless.   The delicate
creatures tried reproaches, but the boyish cynics received them with a scowl and answered them with a
sneer.

The women fled in indignation to their friendly
monarch; but the voluptuary of nature only shrugged

his shoulders and smiled. He kissed away their tears, and their frowns vanished as he crowned their long hair with roses.

'If the lads really show such bad taste,' said his Majesty, 'why I and my lords must do double duty, and dance with a couple of you at once.' Consoled and complimented, and crowned by a King, who could look sad? The women forgot their anger in their increasing loyalty.

But the pupils of Popanilla had no sooner mastered the first principles of science than they began to throw off their retired habits and uncommunicative manners. Being not utterly ignorant of some of the rudiments of knowledge, and consequently having completed their education, it was now their duty, as members of society, to instruct and not to study. They therefore courted, instead of shunned, their fellow-creatures; and on all occasions seized all opportunities of assisting the spread of knowledge. The voices of lecturing boys resounded in every part of the island. Their tones were so shrill, their manners so presuming, their knowledge so crude, and their general demeanour so completely unamiable, that it was impossible to hear them without delight, advantage, and admiration.

The women were not now the only sufferers and the only complainants. Dinned to death, the men looked gloomy; and even the King, for the first time in his life, looked grave. Could this Babel, he thought, be that empire of bliss, that delightful Fantaisie, where to be ruler only proved that you were the most skilful in making others happy! His brow ached under his light flowery crown, as if it were bound by the barbarous circle of a tyrant, heavy with gems and gold. In his despair he had some thoughts of leaving his kingdom and betaking himself to the mermaids.

The determination of the most precious portion of his subjects saved his empire. As the disciples of the new school were daily demanding, 'What is the use of dancing? what is the use of drinking wine? what is the use of smelling flowers?' the women, like prescient politicians, began to entertain a nervous suspicion that in time these sages might even presume to question the utility of that homage which, in spite of the Grecian Philosophers and the British Essayists, we have been in the habit of conceding to them ever since Eden; and they rushed again to the King like frightened deer. Something now was to be done; and the monarch, with an expression of countenance which almost amounted to energy, whispered consolation.

The King sent for Popanilla; the message produced a great sensation; the enlightened introducer of the new principles had not been at Court since he was cut. No doubt his Majesty was at last impregnated with the liberal spirit of the age; and Popanilla was assuredly to be Premier. In fact, it must be so; he was 'sent for;' there was no precedent in Fantaisie, though there might be in other islands, for a person being 'sent for' and not being Premier. His disciples were in high spirits; the world was now to be regulated upon right principles, and they were to be installed into their right places.

'Illustrious Popanilla!' said the King, 'you once did me the honour of making me a speech which, unfortunately for myself, I candidly confess, I was then incapable of understanding; no wonder, as it was the first I ever heard. I shall not, however, easily forget the effect which it produced upon me. I have since considered it my duty, as a monarch, to pay particular attention to your suggestions. I now understand them with sufficient clearness to be fully convinced of their excellence, and in future I intend to act upon them, without any exception or deviation. To prove my sincerity, I have determined to commence the new system at once; and as I think that, without some extension of our international relations, the commercial interest of this island will be incapable of furnishing the taxes which I intend to levy, I have determined, therefore, to fit out an expedition for the purpose of discovering new islands and forming relations with new islanders. It is but due to your merit that you should be appointed to the command of it; and further to testify my infinite esteem for your character, and my complete confidence in your abilities, I make you post-captain on the spot. As the axiom of your school seems to be that everything can be made perfect at once, without time, without experience, without practice, and without preparation, I have no doubt, with the aid of a treatise or two, you will make a consummate naval commander, although you have never been at sea in the whole course of your life. Farewell, Captain Popanilla!'

No sooner was this adieu uttered than four brawny lords of the bedchamber seized the Turgot of Fantaisie by the shoulders, and carried him with inconceivable rapidity to the shore. His pupils, who would have fled to his rescue, were stifled with the embraces of their former partners, and their utilitarianism dissolved in the arms of those they once so rudely rejected.   As for their tutor, he was thrust into one of the canoes, with some fresh water, bread-fruit, dried fish, and a basket of alligator-pears.   A band of mermaids carried the canoe with exquisite management through the shallows and over the breakers, and poor Popanilla in a few minutes found himself out at sea.   Tremendously frightened, he offered to recant all his opinions, and denounce as traitors any individuals whom the Court might select.   But his former companions did not exactly detect the utility of his return.   His offers, his supplications, were equally fruitless; and the only answer which floated to him on the wind was, 'Farewell, Captain Popanilla!'

CHAPTER VI.

A City of Surprises.

NIGHT fell upon the waters, dark and drear, and thick and misty. How unlike those brilliant hours that once summoned him to revelry and love! Unhappy Popanilla! Thy delicious Fantaisie has vanished! Ah, pitiable youth! What could possibly have induced you to be so very rash? And all from that unlucky lock of hair!

After a few natural paroxysms of rage, terror, anguish, and remorse, the Captain as naturally subsided into despair, and awaited with sullen apathy that fate which could not be far distant. The only thing which puzzled the philosophical navigator was his inability to detect what useful end could be attained by his death. At length, remembering that fish must be fed, his theory and his desperation were at the same time confirmed.

A clear, dry morning succeeded the wet, gloomy night, and Popanilla had not yet gone down. This extraordinary suspension of his fate roused him from his stupor, and between the consequent excitement and the morning air he acquired an appetite. Philosophical physicians appear to have agreed that sorrow, to a certain extent, is not unfavourable to digestion; and as Popanilla began to entertain some indefinite and unreasonable hopes, the alligator-pears quickly disappeared. In the meantime the little canoe cut her way as if she were chasing a smuggler; and had it not been for a shark or two who, in anticipation of their services being required, never left her side for a second, Popanilla really might have made some ingenious observations on the nature of tides. He was rather surprised, certainly, as he watched his frail bark cresting the waves; but he soon supposed that this was all in the natural course of things; and he now ascribed his previous fright, not to the peril of his situation, but to his inexperience of it.

Although his apprehension of being drowned was now removed, yet when he gazed on the boundless vacancy before him, and also observed that his provisions rapidly decreased, he began to fear that he was destined for a still more horrible fate, and that, after having eaten his own shoes, he must submit to be starved. In this state of despondency, with infinite delight and exultation he clearly observed, on the second day, at twenty-seven minutes past three P. M., though at a considerable distance, a mountain and an island. His joy and his pride were equal, and excessive: he called the first Alligator Mountain, in gratitude to the pears; and christened the second after his mistress, that unlucky mistress! The swift canoe soon reached the discoveries, and the happy discoverer further found, to his mortification, that the mountain was a mist and the island a sea-weed. Popanilla now grew sulky, and threw himself down in the bottom of his boat.

On the third morning he was awakened by a tremendous roar; on looking around him he perceived that he was in a valley formed by two waves, each several hundred feet high. This seemed the crisis of his fate; he shut his eyes, as people do when they are touched by a dentist, and in a few minutes was still bounding on the ocean in the eternal canoe, safe but senseless. Some tremendous peals of thunder, a roaring wind, and a scathing lightning confirmed his indisposition; and had not the tempest subsided, Popanilla would probably have been an idiot for life. The dead and soothing calm which succeeded this tornado called him back again gradually to existence. He opened his eyes, and, scarcely daring to try a sense, immediately shut them; then heaving a deep sigh, he shrugged his shoulders, and looked as pitiable as a prime minister with a rebellious cabinet. At length he ventured to lift up his head; there was not a wrinkle on the face of ocean; a halcyon fluttered over him, and then scudded before his canoe, and gamesome porpoises were tumbling at his side. The sky was cloudless, except in the direction to which he was driving; but even as Popanilla observed, with some misgivings, the mass of vapours which had there congregated, the great square and solid black clouds drew off like curtains, and revealed to his entranced vision a magnificent city rising out of the sea.

Tower, and dome, and arch, column, and spire, and obelisk, and lofty terraces, and many-windowed palaces, rose in all directions from a mass of building which appeared to him each instant to grow more huge, till at length it seemed to occupy the whole horizon. The sun lent additional lustre to

the dazzling quays of white marble which apparently
surrounded this mighty city, and which rose immediately from the dark blue waters.　As the navigator
drew nearer, he observed that in most parts the quays
were crowded with beings who, he trusted, were
human, and already the hum of multitudes broke upon
his inexperienced ear: to him a sound far more mysterious and far more exciting than the most poetical of winds to the most windy of poets.　On the
right of this vast city rose what was mistaken by
Popanilla for an immense but leafless forest; but more
practical men than the Fantaisian Captain have been
equally confounded by the first sight of a million of
masts.

The canoe cut its way with increased rapidity, and
ere Popanilla had recovered himself sufficiently to
make even an ejaculation, he found himself at the
side of a quay.　Some amphibious creatures, whom
he supposed to be mermen, immediately came to his
assistance, rather stared at his serpent-skin coat, and
then helped him up the steps.　Popanilla was instantly surrounded.

'Who are you?' said one.

'What are you?' asked another.

'Who is it?' exclaimed a third.

'What is it?' screamed a fourth.

'My friends, I am a man!'

'A man!' said the women; 'are you sure you are
a real man?'

'He must be a sea-god!' said the females.

'She must be a sea-goddess!' said the males.

'A Triton!' maintained the women.

'A Nereid!' argued the men.

'It is a great fish!' said the boys.

Thanks to the Universal Linguist, Captain Popanilla, under these peculiar circumstances, was more
loquacious than could have been Captain Parry.

'Good people! you see before you the most in-
.`-ed of human beings.'

ouncement inspired general enthusiasm.
ept, the men shook hands with him,
s huzzaed. Popanilla proceeded:—
y the most pure, the most patriotic, the
ne most enlightened, and the most use-
, I aspired to ameliorate the condition
-men. To this grand object I have sac-
at makes life delightful: I have lost my
society, my taste for dancing, my popu-
the men, my favour with the women;
but oh! not least (excuse this emotion), I
st a very particular lock of hair. In one
my friends, you see before you, banished,
, and unhappy, the victim of a despotic sov-
, a corrupt aristocracy, and a misguided peo-

o sooner had he ceased speaking than Popanilla
y imagined that he had only escaped the dangers
sedition and the sea to expire by less hostile,
ugh not less effective, means. To be strangled
as not much better than to be starved: and cer-
inly, with half-a-dozen highly respectable females
clinging round his neck, he was reminded for not
the first time in his life what a domestic bowstring
is an affectionate woman. In an agony of suffoca-
tion he thought very little of his arms, although the
admiration of the men had already, in his imagination, separated these useful members from his miserable body; and had it not been for some justifiable

kicking and plunging, the veneration of the ingenuous
and surrounding youth, which manifested itself by
their active exertions to divide his singular garment
into relics of a martyr of liberty, would soon have
effectually prevented the ill-starred Popanilla from
being again mistaken for a Nereid. Order was at
length restored, and a committee of eight appointed
to regulate the visits of the increasing mob.

The arrangements were judicious; the whole populace was marshalled into ranks; classes of twelve
persons were allowed consecutively to walk past the
victim of tyranny, corruption, and ignorance; and
each person had the honour to touch his finger.
During this proceeding, which lasted a few hours,
an influential personage generously offered to receive
the eager subscriptions of the assembled thousands.
Even the boys subscribed, and ere six hours had
passed since his arrival as a coatless vagabond in
this liberal city, Captain Popanilla found himself a
person of considerable means.

The receiver of the subscriptions, while he crammed
Popanilla's serpent-skin pockets full of gold pieces, at
the same time kindly offered the stranger to introduce him to an hotel.   Popanilla, who was quite
beside himself, could only bow his assent, and me-
chanically accompanied his conductor.   When he had
regained his faculty of speech, he endeavoured, in
wandering sentences of grateful incoherency, to express his deep sense of this unparalleled liberality.
'It was an excess of generosity in which mankind
could never have before indulged!'

'By no means!' said his companion, with great
coolness; 'far from this being an unparalleled affair, I
assure you it is a matter of hourly occurrence: make

your mind quite easy. You are probably not aware
that you are now living in the richest and most
charitable country in the world?'

'Wonderful!' said Popanilla; 'and what is the
name, may I ask, of this charitable city?'

'Is it possible,' said his companion, with a faint
smile, 'that you are ignorant of the great city of
Hubbabub; the largest city not only that exists, but
that ever did exist, and the capital of the island of
Vraibleusia, the most famous island not only that is
known, but that ever was known?'

While he was speaking they were accosted by
a man upon crutches, who, telling them in a broken
voice that he had a wife and twelve infant children
dependent on his support, supplicated a little charity.
Popanilla was about to empty part of his pocketfuls
into the mendicant's cap, but his companion re-
pressed his unphilosophical facility. 'By no means!'
said his friend, who, turning round to the beggar,
advised him, in a mild voice, to *work*; calmly adding,
that if he presumed to ask charity again he should
certainly have him bastinadoed. Then they walked
on.

Popanilla's attention was so distracted by the
variety, the number, the novelty, and the noise of
the objects which were incessantly hurried upon his
observation, that he found no time to speak; and as
his companion, though exceedingly polite, was a
man of few words, conversation rather flagged.

At last, overwhelmed by the magnificence of the
streets, the splendour of the shops, the number of
human beings, the rattling of the vehicles, the dashing of the horses, and a thousand other sounds and
objects, Popanilla gave loose to a loud and fervent

wish that his hotel might have the good fortune of being situated in this interesting quarter.

'By no means!' said his companion; 'we have yet much further to go. Far from this being a desirable situation for you, my friend, no civilised person is even seen here; and had not the cause of civil and religious liberty fortunately called me to the water-side to-day, I should have lost the opportunity of showing how greatly I esteem a gentleman who has suffered so severely in the cause of national amelioration.'

'Sir!' said Popanilla, 'your approbation is the only reward which I ever shall desire for my exertions. You will excuse me for not quite keeping up with you; but the fact is, my pockets are so stuffed with cash that the action of my legs is greatly impeded.'

'Credit me, my friend, that you are suffering from an inconvenience which you will not long experience in Hubbabub. Nevertheless, to remedy it at present, I think the best thing we can do is to buy a purse.'

They accordingly entered a shop where such an article might be found, and taking up a small sack, for Popanilla was very rich, his companion inquired its price, which he was informed was four crowns. No sooner had the desired information been given than the proprietor of the opposite shop rushed in, and offered him the same article for three crowns. The original merchant, not at all surprised at the intrusion, and not the least apologising for his former extortion, then demanded two. His rival, being more than his match, he courteously dropped upon his knee, and requested his customer to accept the article gratis, for his sake. The generous dealer would infallibly have carried the day, had not his rival humbly supplicated the purchaser not only to receive his article as a gift, but also the compliment of a crown inside.

'What a terrible cheat the first merchant must have been!' said the puzzled Popanilla, as they proceeded on their way.

'By no means!' said his calm companion; 'the purse was sufficiently cheap even at four crowns. This is not cheatery; this is competition!'

'What a wonderful nation, then, this must be, where you not only get purses gratis but even well loaded! What use, then, is all this heavy gold? It is a tremendous trouble to carry; I will empty the bag into this kennel, for money surely can be of no use in a city where, when in want of cash, you have only to go into a shop and buy a purse!'

'Your pardon!' said his companion; 'far from this being the case, Vraibleusia is, without doubt, the dearest country in the world.'

'If, then,' said the inquisitive Popanilla, with great animation, 'if, then, this country be the dearest in the world; if, how ——'

'My good friend!' said his companion; 'I really am the last person in the world to answer questions. All that I know is, that this country is extremely dear, and that the only way to get things cheap is to encourage competition.'

Here the progress of his companion was impeded for some time by a great crowd, which had assembled to catch a glimpse of a man who was to fly off a steeple, but who had not yet arrived. A chimney-sweeper observed to a scientific friend that probably the density of the atmosphere might prevent the intended volitation; and Popanilla, who, having read almost as many pamphlets as the observer, now felt quite at home, exceedingly admired the observation.

'He must be a very superior man, this gentleman in black!' said Popanilla to his companion.

'By no means! he is of the lowest class in society. But you are probably not aware that you are in the most educated country in the world.'

'Delightful!' said Popanilla.

The Captain was exceedingly desirous of witnessing the flight of the Vraibleusian Dædalus, but his friend advised their progress. This, however, was not easy; and Popanilla, animated for the moment by his natural aristocratic disposition, and emboldened by his superior size and strength, began to clear his way in a manner which was more cogent than logical. The chimney-sweeper and his comrades were soon in arms, and Popanilla would certainly have been killed or ducked by this superior man and his friends, had it not been for the mild remonstrance of his conductor and the singular appearance of his costume.

'What could have induced you to be so imprudent?' said his rescuer, when they had escaped from the crowd.

'Truly,' said Popanilla, 'I thought that in a country where you may bastinado the wretch who presumes to ask you for alms, there could surely be no objection to my knocking down the scoundrel who dared to stand in my way.'

'By no means!' said his friend, slightly elevating his eyebrows. 'Here all men are equal. You are probably not aware that you are at present in the freest country in the world.'

'I do not exactly understand you; what is this freedom?'

'My good friend, I really am the last person in the world to answer questions. Freedom is, in one word, Liberty: a kind of thing which you foreigners never can understand, and which mere theory can make no man understand. When you have been in the island a few weeks all will be quite clear to you. In the meantime, do as others do, and never knock men. down!'

CHAPTER VII.

THE GREAT SHELL QUESTION.

LTHOUGH we are yet some way from our hotel,' remarked Popanilla's conductor, 'we have now arrived at a part of the city where I can ease you, without difficulty, from your troublesome burthen; let us enter here!'

As he spoke, they stopped before a splendid palace, and proceeding through various halls full of individuals apparently intently busied, the companions were at last ushered into an apartment of smaller size, but of more elegant character. A personage of prepossessing appearance was lolling on a couch of an appearance equally prepossessing. Before him, on a table, were some papers, exquisite fruits, and some liqueurs. Popanilla was presented, and received with fascinating complaisance. His friend stated the object of their visit, and handed the sackful of gold to the gentleman on the sofa. The gentleman on the sofa ordered a couple of attendants to ascertain its contents. While this computation was going on he amused his guests by his lively conversation, and charmed Popanilla by his polished manners and easy civility. He offered him, during his stay in Vraibleusia, the use of a couple of equipages, a villa, and an opera-box; insisted on sending to his hotel some pine-apples and some rare wine, and gave him a perpetual ticket to his picture-gallery. When his attendants had concluded their calculation, he ordered them to place Popanilla's precious metal in his treasury; and then, presenting the Captain with a small packet of pink shells, he kindly enquired whether he could be of any further use to him. Popanilla was loth to retire without his gold, of the utility of which, in spite of the conveniency of competition, he seemed to possess an instinctive conception; but as his friend rose and withdrew, he could do nothing less than accompany him; for, having now known him nearly half a day, his confidence in his honour and integrity was naturally unbounded.

'That was the King, of course?' said Popanilla, when they were fairly out of the palace.

'The King!' said the unknown, nearly surprised into an exclamation; 'by no means!'

'And what then?'

'My good friend! is it possible that you have no bankers in your country?'

'Yes, it is very possible; but we have mermaids, who also give us shells which are pretty. What then are your bankers?'

'Really, my good friend, that is a question which I never remember having been asked before; but a banker is a man who — keeps our money for us.'

'Ah! and he is bound, I suppose, to return your money when you choose?'

'Most assuredly!'

'He is, then, in fact your servant: you must pay him handsomely, for him to live so well?'

'By no means! we pay him nothing.'

'That is droll; he must be very rich then?'

'Really, my dear friend, I cannot say. Why, yes! I—I suppose he may be very rich!'

''Tis singular that a rich man should take so much trouble for others!'

'My good friend! of course he lives by his trouble.'

'Ah! How, then,' continued the inquisitive Fantaisian, 'if you do not pay him for his services, and he yet lives by them; how, I pray, does he acquire these immense riches?'

'Really, my good sir, I am, in truth, the very last man in the world to answer questions: he is a banker; bankers are always rich; but why they are, or how they are, I really never had time to inquire. But I suppose, if the truth were known, they must have very great opportunities.'

'Ah! I begin to see,' said Popanilla. 'It was really very kind of him,' continued the Captain, 'to make me a present of these little pink shells: what would I not give to turn them into a necklace, and send it to a certain person at Fantaisie!'

'It would be a very expensive necklace,' observed his companion, almost surprised. 'I had no idea, I confess, from your appearance, that in your country they indulged in such expensive tastes in costume.'

'Expensive!' said Popanilla. 'We certainly have no such shells as these in Fantaisie; but we have much more beautiful ones. I should think, from their look, they must be rather common.'

His conductor for the first time nearly laughed. 'I forgot,' said he, 'that you could not be aware that these pink shells are the most precious coin of the land, compared with which those bits of gold with which

you have recently parted are nothing; your whole
fortune is now in that little packet. The fact is,'
continued the unknown, making an effort to com-
municate, 'although we possess in this country more
of the precious metals than all the rest of the world
together, the quantity is nevertheless utterly dispro-
portioned to the magnitude of our wealth and our
wants. We have been, therefore, under the necessity
of resorting to other means of representing the first
and supplying the second; and, taking advantage of
our insular situation, we have introduced these small
pink shells, which abound all round the coast. Being much more convenient to carry, they are in general circulation, and no genteel person has ever
anything else in his pocket.'

'Wonderful! But surely, then, it is no very difficult thing in this country to accumulate a fortune,
since all that is necessary to give you every luxury
of life is a stroll one morning of your existence along
the beach?'

'By no means, my friend! you are really too rapid.
The fact is, that no one has the power of originally
circulating these shells but our Government; and if
any one, by any chance, choose to violate this arrangement, we make up for depriving him of his
solitary walks on the shore by instant submersion in
the sea.'

'Then the whole circulation of the country is at
the mercy of your Government?' remarked Popanilla,
summoning to his recollection the contents of one of
those shipwrecked *brochures* which had exercised so
strange an influence on his destiny. 'Suppose they
do not choose to issue?'

'That is always guarded against. The mere quarterly payments of interest upon our national debt will secure an ample supply.'

'Debt! I thought you were the richest nation in the world?'

''Tis true; nevertheless, if there were a golden pyramid with a base as big as the whole earth and an apex touching the heavens, it would not supply us with sufficient metal to satisfy our creditors.'

'But, my dear sir,' exclaimed the perplexed Popanilla, 'if this really be true, how then can you be said to be the richest nation in the world?'

'It is very simple. The annual interest upon our debt exceeds the whole wealth of the rest of the world; therefore we must be the richest nation in the world.'

''Tis true,' said Popanilla; 'I see I have yet much to learn. But with regard to these pink shells, how can you possibly create for them a certain standard of value? It is merely agreement among yourselves that fixes any value to them.'

'By no means! you are so rapid! Each shell is immediately convertible into gold; of which metal, let me again remind you, we possess more than any other nation; but which, indeed, we only keep as a sort of dress coin, chiefly to indulge the prejudices of foreigners.'

'But,' said the perpetual Popanilla, 'suppose every man who held a shell on the same day were to——'

'My good friend! I really am the last person in the world to give explanations. In Vraibleusia, we have so much to do that we have no time to think; a habit which only becomes nations who are not employed. You are now fast approaching the Great Shell Question; a question which, I confess, affects the interests of every man in this island more than any other; but of which, I must candidly own, every man in this island is more ignorant than of any other. No one, however, can deny that the system works well; and if anything at any time go wrong, why, really, Mr. Secretary Periwinkle is a wonderful man, and our most eminent conchologist. He, no doubt, will set it right; and if, by any chance, things are past even his management, why then, I suppose, to use our national motto, *something will turn up.*'

Here they arrived at the hotel. Having made every arrangement for the comfort and convenience of the Fantaisian stranger, Popanilla's conductor took his leave, previously informing him that his name was Skindeep; that he was a member of one of the largest families in the island; that, had he not been engaged to attend a lecture, he would have stayed and dined with him; but that he would certainly call upon him on the morrow.

Compared with his hotel the palace of his banker was a dungeon; even the sunset voluptuousness of Fantaisie was now remembered without regret in the blaze of artificial light and in the artificial gratification of desires which art had alone created. After a magnificent repast, his host politely inquired of Popanilla whether he would like to go to the opera, the comedy, or a concert; but the Fantaisian philosopher was not yet quite corrupted; and, still inspired with a desire to acquire useful knowledge, he begged his landlord to procure him immediately a pamphlet on the Shell Question.

While his host was engaged in procuring this luxury a man entered the room and told Popanilla that he had walked that day two thousand five hun-

dred paces, and that the tax due to the Excise upon
this promenade was fifty crowns. The Captain
stared, and remarked to the excise-officer that he
thought a man's paces were a strange article to tax.
The excise-officer, with great civility, answered that
no doubt at first sight it might appear rather strange,
but that it was the only article left untaxed in Vraibleusia; that there was a slight deficiency in the last
quarter's revenue, and that therefore the Government
had no alternative; that it was a tax which did not
press heavily upon the individual, because the Vraibleusians were of a sedentary habit; that, besides, it
was an opinion every day more received among the
best judges that the more a man was taxed the
richer he ultimately would prove; and he concluded
by saying that Popanilla need not make himself
uneasy about these demands, because, if he were
ruined to-morrow, being a foreigner, he was entitled
by the law of the land to five thousand a-year;
whereas he, the excise-man, being a native-born
Vraibleusian, had no claims whatever upon the Government; therefore he hoped his honour would give
him something to drink.

His host now entered with the 'Novum Organon'
of the great Periwinkle. While Popanilla devoured
the lively pages of this treatise, he discovered that the
system which had been so subtilely introduced by the
Government, and which had so surprised him in
the morning, had soon been adopted in private life;
and although it was drowning matter to pick up pink
shells, still there was nothing to prevent the whole
commerce of the country from being carried on by
means of a system equally conchological. He found
that the social action in every part of the island was

regulated and assisted by this process. Oyster-shells were first introduced; muscle-shells speedily followed; and, as commerce became more complicate, they had even been obliged to have recourse to snail-shells. Popanilla retired to rest with admiration of the people who thus converted to the most useful purposes things apparently so useless. There was no saying now what might not be done even with a nutshell. It was evident that the nation who contrived to be the richest people in the world while they were over head and ears in debt must be fast approaching to a state of perfection. Finally, sinking to sleep in a bed of eiderdown, Popanilla was confirmed in his prejudices against a state of nature.

CHAPTER VIII.

KINDEEP called upon Popanilla on the following morning in an elegant equipage, and with great politeness proposed to attend him in a drive about the city.

The island of Vraibleusia is one hundred and fifty miles in circumference, two-thirds of which are covered by the city of Hubbabub. It contains no other city, town, or village. The rest of the island consists of rivers, canals, and railroads. Popanilla was surprised when he was informed that Hubbabub did not contain more than five millions of inhabitants; but his surprise was decreased when their journey occasionally lay through tracts of streets, consisting often of capacious mansions entirely tenantless. On seeking an explanation of this seeming desolation, he was told that the Hubbabubians were possessed by a frenzy of always moving westward; and that consequently great quarters of the city are perpetually deserted. Even as Skindeep was speaking their passage was stopped by a large caravan of carriages and waggons heavily laden with human creatures and their children and chattels. On Skindeep inquiring the cause of this great movement, he was informed by one on horseback, who

(52)

seemed to be the leader of the horde, that they were the late dwellers in sundry squares and streets situated far to the east; that their houses having been ridiculed by an itinerant ballad-singer, the female part of the tribe had insisted upon immediately quitting their unfashionable fatherland; and that now, after three days' journey, they had succeeded in reaching the late settlement of a horde who had migrated to the extreme west.

Quitting regions so subject to revolutions and vicissitudes, the travellers once more emerged into quarters of a less transitory reputation; and in the magnificent parks, the broad streets, the ample squares, the palaces, the triumphal arches, and the theatres of occidental Hubbabub, Popanilla lost those sad and mournful feelings which are ever engendered by contemplating the gloomy relics of departed greatness. It was impossible to admire too much the architecture of this part of the city. The elevations were indeed imposing. In general, the massy Egyptian appropriately graced the attic-stories; while the finer and more elaborate architecture of Corinth was placed on a level with the eye, so that its beauties might be more easily discovered. Spacious colonnades were flanked by porticoes, surmounted by domes; nor was the number of columns at all limited, for you occasionally met with porticoes of two tiers, the lower one of which consisted of three, the higher one of thirty columns. Pedestals of the purest Ionic Gothic were ingeniously intermixed with Palladian pediments; and the surging spire exquisitely harmonised with the horizontal architecture of the ancients. But perhaps, after all, the most charming effect was produced by the pyramids, surmounted by weathercocks.

Popanilla was particularly pleased by some chimneys of Caryatides, and did not for a moment hesitate in assenting to the assertion of Skindeep that the Vraibleusians were the most architectural nation in the world.   True it was, they had begun late; their attention as a people having been, for a considerable time, attracted to much more important affairs; but they had compensated for their tardy attention by their speedy excellence.*

Before they returned home Skindeep led Popanillo to the top of a tower, from whence they had a complete view of the whole island.   Skindeep particularly directed the Captain's attention to one spot, where flourished, as he said, the only corn-fields in the country, which supplied the whole nation, and were the property of one individual.   So unrivalled was his agricultural science that the vulgar only accounted for his admirable produce by a miraculous fecundity! The proprietor of these hundred golden acres was a rather mysterious sort of personage.   He was an aboriginal inhabitant, and, though the only one of the aborigines in existence, had lived many centuries, and, to the consternation of some of the Vraibleusians and the exultation of others, exhibited no signs of decay. This awful being was without a name.   When spoken of by his admirers he was generally described by such panegyrical periphrases as 'soul of the country,' 'foundation of the State,' 'the only real, and true, and substantial being;' while, on the other hand, those who presumed to differ from those sentiments were in the

---

*See a work which will be shortly published, entitled, 'The difference detected between *Architecture* and *Parchitecture*, by Sansovino the Second.'

habit of styling him 'the dead weight,' 'the vampire,' 'the night-mare,' and other titles equally complimentary. They also maintained that, instead of being either real or substantial, he was, in fact, the most flimsy and fictitious personage in the whole island; and then, lashing themselves up into metaphor, they would call him a meteor, or a vapour, or a great windy bubble, that would some day burst.

The aboriginal insisted that it was the common law of the land that the islanders should purchase their corn only of him. They grumbled, but he growled; he swore that it was the constitution of the country; that there was an uninterrupted line of precedents to confirm the claim; and that, if they did not approve of the arrangement, they and their fathers should not have elected to have settled, or presumed to have been spawned, upon his island. Then, as if he were not desirous of resting his claim on its mere legal merits, he would remind them of the superiority of his grain, and the impossibility of a scarcity, in the event of which calamity an insular people could always find a plentiful though temporary resource in sea-weed. He then clearly proved to them that, if ever they had the imprudence to change any of their old laws, they would necessarily never have more than one meal a day as long as they lived. Finally, he recalled to their recollection that he had made the island what it was, that he was their mainstay, and that his counsel and exertions had rendered them the wonder of the world. Thus, between force, and fear, and flattery, the Vraibleusians paid for their corn nearly its weight in gold; but what did that signify to a nation with so many pink shells!

CHAPTER IX.

THE third day after his drive with his friend Skindeep, Popanilla was waited upon by the most eminent bookseller in Hubbabub, who begged to have the honour of introducing to the public a Narrative of Captain Popanilla's Voyage. This gentleman assured Popanilla that the Vraibleusian public were nervously alive to anything connected with discovery; that so ardent was their attachment to science and natural philosophy that voyages and travels were sure to be read with eagerness, particularly if they had coloured plates. Popanilla was charmed with the proposition, but blushingly informed the mercantile Mæcenas that he did not know how to write. The publisher told him that this circumstance was not of the slightest importance; that he had never for a moment supposed that so sublime a savage could possess such a vulgar accomplishment; and that it was by no means difficult for a man to publish his travels without writing a line of them.

Popanilla having consented to become an author upon these terms, the publisher asked him to dine with him, and introduced him to an intelligent individual. This intelligent individual listened attentively to all Popanilla's adventures. The Captain concealed nothing. He began with the eternal lock of hair, and showed how wonderfully this world was constituted, that even the loss of a thing was not useless; from which it was clear that utility was Providence. After drinking some capital wine, the intelligent individual told Popanilla that he was wrong in supposing Fantaisie to be an island; that, on the contrary, it was a great continent; that this was proved by the probable action of the tides in the part of the island which had not yet been visited; that the consequence of these tides would be that, in the course of a season or two, Fantaisie would become a great receptacle for icebergs, and be turned into the North Pole; that, therefore, the seasons throughout the world would be changed; that this year, in Vraibleusia, the usual winter would be omitted, and that when the present summer was finished the dog-days would again commence. Popanilla took his leave highly delighted with this intelligent individual and with the bookseller's wine.

Owing to the competition which existed between the publishers, the printers, and the engravers of the city of Hubbabub, and the great exertions of the intelligent individual, the Narrative of Captain Popanilla's Voyage was brought out in less than a week, and was immediately in everybody's hand. The work contained a detailed account of everything which took place during the whole of the three days, and formed a quarto volume. The plates were numerous and highly interesting. There was a line engraving of Alligator Mountain and a mezzotint of Seaweed Is-

land; a view of the canoe N.E.; a view of the canoe
N.W.; a view of the canoe S.E.; a view of the canoe
S.W. There were highly-finished coloured drawings
of the dried fish and the bread-fruit, and an exquisitely tinted representation of the latter in a mouldy
state. But the *chef-d'œuvre* was the portrait of the
author himself. He was represented trampling on
the body of a boa constrictor of the first quality, in
the skin of which he was dressed; at his back were
his bow and arrows; his right hand rested on an up-
rooted pine-tree; he stood in a desert between two
volcanoes; at his feet was a lake of magnitude; the
distance lowered with an approaching tornado; but a
lucky flash of lightning revealed the range of the
Andes and both oceans. Altogether he looked the
most dandified of savages, and the most savage of
dandies. It was a sublime lithograph, and produced
scarcely less important effects upon Popanilla's fortune than that lucky 'lock of hair;' for no sooner
was the portrait published than Popanilla received a
ticket for the receptions of a lady of quality. On
showing it to Skindeep, he was told that the honour
was immense, and therefore he must go by all means.
Skindeep regretted that he could not accompany him,
but he was engaged to a lecture on shoemaking; and a
lecture was a thing he made it a point never to miss,
because, as he very properly observed, 'By lectures
you may become extremely well informed without
any of the inconveniences of study. No fixity of attention, no continuity of meditation, no habits of reflec-
tion, no aptitude of combination, are the least requisite;
all which things only give you a nervous headache;
and yet you gain all the results of all these processes.
True it is that that which is so easily acquired is not

always so easily remembered; but what of that? Suppose you forget any subject, why then you go to another lecture.' 'Very true!' said Popanilla.

Popanilla failed not to remember his invitation from Lady Spirituelle; and at the proper hour his announcement produced a sensation throughout her crowded saloons. Spirituelle was a most enchanting lady; she asked Popanilla how tall he really was, and whether the women in Fantaisie were as handsome as the men. Then she said that the Vraibleusians were the most intellectual and the most scientific nation in the world, and that the society at her house was the most intellectual and the most scientific in Vraibleusia. She told him also that she had hoped by this season the world would have been completely regulated by mind; but that the subversion of matter was a more substantial business than she and the committee of management had imagined: she had no doubt, however, that in a short time mind must carry the day, because matter was mortal and mind eternal; therefore mind had the best chance. Finally, she also told him that the passions were the occasion of all the misery which had ever existed; and that it was impossible for mankind either to be happy or great until, like herself and her friends, they were 'all soul.'

Popanilla was charmed with his company. What a difference between the calm, smiling, easy, uninteresting, stupid, sunset countenances of Fantaisie and those around him. All looked so interested and so intelligent; their eyes were so anxious, their gestures so animated, their manners so earnest. They must be very clever! He drew nearer. If before he were charmed, now he was enchanted. What an universal acquisition of useful knowledge! Three or four dukes were earnestly imbibing a new theory of gas from a brilliant little gentleman in black, who looked like a Will-o'-the-wisp. The Prime Minister was anxious about pin-making; a Bishop equally interested in a dissertation on the escapements of watches; a Field-Marshal not less intent on a new specific from the concentrated essence of hellebore. But what most delighted Popanilla was hearing a lecture from the most eminent lawyer and statesman in Vraibleusia on his first and favourite study of hydrostatics. His associations quite overcame him: all Fantaisie rushed upon his memory, and he was obliged to retire to a less frequented part of the room to relieve his too excited feelings.

He was in a few minutes addressed by the identical little gentleman who had recently been speculating with the dukes.

The little gentleman told him that he had heard with great pleasure that in Fantaisie they had no historians, poets, or novelists. He proved to Popanilla that no such thing as experience existed; that, as the world was now to be regulated on quite different principles from those by which it had hitherto been conducted, similar events to those which had occurred could never again take place; and therefore it was absolutely useless to know anything about the past. With regard to literary fiction, he explained that, as it was absolutely necessary, from his nature, that man should experience a certain quantity of excitement, the false interest which these productions created prevented their readers from obtaining this excitement by methods which, by the discovery of the useful, might greatly benefit society.

'You are of opinion, then,' exclaimed the delighted Popanilla, 'that nothing is good which is not useful ?'

'Is it possible that an individual exists in this world who doubts this great first principle ?' said the little man, with great animation.

'Ah, my dear friend!' said Popanilla, 'if you only knew what an avowal of this great first principle has cost me; what I have suffered; what I have lost!'

'What have you lost?' asked the little gentleman.

'In the first place, a lock of hair ——'

'Poh, nonsense!'

'Ah! you may say Poh! but it was a particular lock of hair.'

'My friend, that word is odious. Nothing is *particular*, everything is *general*. Rules are general, feelings are general, and property should be general; and, sir, I tell you what, in a very short time it must be so. Why should Lady Spirituelle, for instance, receive me at her house, rather than I receive her at mine ?'

'Why don't you, then ?' asked the simple Popanilla.

'Because I have not got one, sir!' roared the little gentleman.

He would certainly have broken away had not Popanilla begged him to answer one question. The Captain, reiterating in the most solemn manner his firm belief in the dogma that nothing was good which was not useful, and again detailing the persecutions which this conviction had brought upon him, was delighted that an opportunity was now afforded to gain from the lips of a distinguished philosopher a definition of what *utility* really was. The distinguished philosopher could not refuse so trifling a favour.

'Utility,' said he, 'is —— '

At this critical moment there was a universal buzz throughout the rooms, and everybody looked so interested that the philosopher quite forgot to finish his answer. On inquiring the cause of this great sensation, Popanilla was informed that a rumour was about that a new element had been discovered that afternoon. The party speedily broke up, the principal philosophers immediately rushing to their clubs to ascertain the truth of this report. Popanilla was unfashionable enough to make his acknowledgments to his hostess before he left her house. As he gazed upon her ladyship's brilliant eyes and radiant complexion, he felt convinced of the truth of her theory of the passions; he could not refrain from pressing her hand in a manner which violated etiquette, and which a nativity in the Indian Ocean could alone excuse; the pressure was graciously returned. As Popanilla descended the staircase, he discovered a little note of pink satin paper entangled in his ruffle. He opened it with curiosity. It was 'All soul.' He did not return to his hotel quite so soon as he expected.

CHAPTER X.

OPANILLA breakfasted rather late the next morning, and on looking over the evening papers, which were just published, his eyes lighted on the following paragraph: —

'Arrived yesterday at the Hôtel Diplomatique, His Excellency Prince Popanilla, Ambassador Extraordinary and Minister Plenipotentiary from the newly-recognised State of Fantaisie.'

Before his Excellency could either recover from his astonishment or make any inquiries which might throw any illustration upon its cause, a loud shout in the street made him naturally look out of the window. He observed three or four magnificent equipages drawing up at the door of the hotel, and followed by a large crowd. Each carriage was drawn by four horses, and attended by footmen so radiant with gold and scarlet that, had Popanilla been the late ingenious Mr. Keats, he would have mistaken them for the natural children of Phœbus and Aurora. The ambassador forgot the irregularity of the paragraph in the splendour of the liveries. He felt triumphantly conscious that the most beautiful rose in the world must look extremely pale by the side of scarlet cloth; and this new example of the superiority of art over nature reminding him of the inferiority of bread-fruit to grilled muffin, he resolved to return to breakfast.

But it was his fate to be reminded of the inutility of the best resolutions, for ere the cup of coffee had touched his parched lips the door of his room flew open, and the Marquess of Moustache was announced.

His Lordship was a young gentleman with an expressive countenance; that is to say, his face was so covered with hair, and the back of his head cropped so bald, that you generally addressed him in the rear by mistake. He did not speak, but continued bowing for a considerable time, in that diplomatic manner which means so much. By the time he had finished bowing his suite had gained the apartment, and his private secretary, one of those uncommonly able men who only want an opportunity, seized the present one of addressing Popanilla.

Bowing to the late Captain with studied respect, he informed him that the Marquess Moustache was the nobleman appointed by the Government of Vraibleusia to attend upon his Excellency during the first few weeks of his mission, with the view of affording him all information upon those objects which might naturally be expected to engage the interest or attract the attention of so distinguished a personage. The 'ancien marin' and present ambassador had been so used to miracles since the loss of that lock of hair, that he did not think it supernatural, having during the last few days been in turn a Fantaisian nobleman, a post-captain, a fish, a goddess, and, above all,

an author, he should now be transformed into a plenipotentiary. Drinking, therefore, his cup of coffee,
he assumed an air as if he really were used to have
a Marquess for an attendant, and said that he was at
his Lordship's service.

The Marquess bowed low, and the private secretary remarked that the first thing to be done by his
Excellency was to be presented to the Government.
After that he was to visit all the manufactories in
Vraibleusia, subscribe to all the charities, and dine
with all the corporations, attend a *déjeûner à la four-
chette* at a palace they were at present building under
the sea, give a gold plate to be run for on the fashionable racecourse, be present at morning prayers at
the Government Chapel, hunt once or twice, give a
dinner or two himself, make one pun, and go to the
play, by which various means, he said, the good
understanding between the two countries would be
materially increased and, in a manner, established.

As the Fantaisian ambassador and his suite entered their carriages, the sky, if it had not been for
the smoke, would certainly have been rent by the acclamations of the mob. 'Popanilla for ever!' sounded
from all quarters, except where the shout was varied
by 'Vraibleusia and Fantaisie against the world!'
which perhaps was even the most popular sentiment
of the two. The ambassador was quite agitated, and
asked the Marquess what he was to do. The private
secretary told his Excellency to bow. Popanilla
bowed with such grace that in five minutes the
horses were taken out of his carriage, and that carriage dragged in triumph by the enthusiastic populace. He continued bowing, and their enthusiasm
continued increasing. In the meantime his Excel-

lency's portrait was sketched by an artist who hung
upon his wheel, and in less than half an hour a litho-
graphic likeness of the popular idol was worshipped
in every print-shop in Hubbabub.

As they drew nearer the hall of audience the
crowd kept increasing, till at length the whole city
seemed poured forth to meet him. Although now
feeling conscious that he was the greatest man in the
island, and therefore only thinking of himself, Popanilla's attention was nevertheless at this moment attracted by a singular figure. He was apparently a
man: in stature a Patagonian, and robust as a well-
fed ogre. His countenance was jolly, but conse-
quential; and his costume a curious mixture of a
hunting-dress and a court suit. He was on foot, and
in spite of the crowd, with the aid of a good whip
and his left fist made his way with great ease. On
inquiring who this extraordinary personage might be,
Popanilla was informed that it was THE ABORIGINAL
INHABITANT. As the giant passed the ambassador's
carriages, the whole suite, even Lord Moustache, rose
and bent low; and the secretary told Popanilla that
there was no person in the island for whom the
Government of Vraibleusia entertained so profound a
respect.

The crowd was now so immense that even the
progress of the Aboriginal Inhabitant was for a moment impeded. The great man got surrounded by a
large body of little mechanics. The contrast between
the pale perspiring visages and lean forms of these
emaciated and half-generated creatures, and the jolly
form and ruddy countenance, gigantic limbs and ample
frame, of the Aboriginal, was most striking; nor
could any one view the group for an instant without

feeling convinced that the latter was really a superior existence. The mechanics, who were worn by labour, not reduced by famine, far from being miserable, were impudent. They began rating the mighty one for the dearness of his corn. He received their attacks with mildness. He reminded them that the regulation by which they procured their bread was the aboriginal law of the island, under which they had all so greatly flourished. He explained to them that it was owing to this protecting principle that he and his ancestors, having nothing to do but to hunt and shoot, had so preserved their health that, unlike the rest of the human race, they had not degenerated from the original form and nature of man. He showed that it was owing to the vigour of mind and body consequent upon this fine health that Vraibleusia had become the wonder of the world, and that they themselves were so actively employed; and he inferred that they surely could not grudge him the income which he derived, since that income was, in fact, the foundation of their own profits. He then satisfactorily demonstrated to them that if by any circumstances he were to cease to exist, the whole island would immediately sink under the sea. Having thus condescended to hold a little parley with his fellow-subjects, though not fellow-creatures, he gave them all a good sound flogging, and departed amidst the enthusiastic cheering of those whom he had so briskly lashed.

By this time Popanilla had arrived at the hall of audience.

' It was a vast and venerable pile.'

His Excellency and suite quitted their carriages amidst the renewed acclamations of the mob. Proceeding through a number of courts and quadrangles, crowded with guards and officials, they stopped before a bronze gate of great height. Over it was written, in vast characters of living flame, this inscription:

TO

THE WISEST AND THE BEST,

THE RICHEST AND THE MIGHTIEST,

THE GLORY AND THE ADMIRATION,

THE DEFENCE AND THE CONSTERNATION.

On reading this mysterious inscription his Excellency experienced a sudden and awful shudder. Lord Moustache, however, who was more used to mysteries, taking up a silver trumpet, which was fixed to the portal by a crimson cord, gave a loud blast. The gates flew open with the sound of a whirlwind, and Popanilla found himself in what at first appeared an illimitable hall. It was crowded, but perfect order was preserved. The ambassador was conducted with great pomp to the upper end of the apartment, where, after an hour's walk, his Excellency arrived. At the extremity of the hall was a colossal and metallic Statue of extraordinary appearance. It represented an armed monarch. The head and bust were of gold, and the curling hair was crowned with an imperial diadem; the body and arms were of silver, worked in the semblance of a complete suit of enamelled armour of the feudal ages; and the thighs and legs were of iron, which the artist had clothed in the bandaged hose of the old Saxons. The figure bore the appearance of great antiquity, but had evidently been often repaired and renovated since its first formation. The workmanship was clearly of different eras, and the reparations, either from ignorance or intention, had often been effected with little deference to the original design. Part of the shoulders had been supplied by the other, though less precious, metal, and the Roman and imperial ornaments had unaccountably been succeeded by the less classic, though more picturesque, decorations of Gothic armour. On the other hand, a great portion of the chivalric and precious material of the body had been removed, and replaced by a style and substance resembling those of the lower limbs. In its right hand the Statue brandished a naked sword, and with its left leant upon a huge, though extremely rich and elaborately carved, crosier. It trampled upon a shivered lance and a broken chain.

'Your Excellency perceives,' said the secretary, pointing to the Statue, 'that ours is a mixed Government.'

Popanilla was informed that this extraordinary Statue enjoyed all the faculties of an intellectual being, with the additional advantage of some faculties which intellectual beings do not enjoy. It possessed not only the faculty of speech, but of speaking truth; not only the power of judgment, but of judging rightly; not only the habit of listening, but of listening attentively. Its antiquity was so remote that the most profound and acute antiquarians had failed in tracing back its origin. The Aboriginal Inhabitant, however, asserted that it was the work of one of his ancestors; and as his assertion was confirmed by all traditions, the allegation was received. Whatever might have been its origin, certain it was that it was now immortal, for it could never die; and to whomsoever it might have been originally indebted for its power, not less sure was it that it was now omnipotent, for it could do all things. Thus alleged and thus believed the Vraibleusians, marvellous and sublime people! who, with all the impotence of mortality, have created a Government which is both immortal and omnipotent!

Generally speaking, the Statue was held in great reverence and viewed with great admiration by the whole Vraibleusian people. There were a few persons, indeed, who asserted that the creation of such a Statue was by no means so mighty a business as it had been the fashion to suppose; and that it was more than probable that, with the advantages afforded by the scientific discoveries of modern times, they would succeed in making a more useful one. This, indeed, they offered to accomplish, provided the present Statue were preliminarily destroyed; but as they were well assured that this offer would never be accepted, it was generally treated by those who refused it as a braggadocio. There were many also who, though they in general greatly admired and respected the present Statue, affected to believe that, though the execution was wonderful, and the interior machinery indeed far beyond the powers of the present age, nevertheless the design was in many parts somewhat rude, and the figure altogether far from being well-proportioned. Some thought the head too big, some too small; some that the body was disproportionately little; others, on the contrary, that it was so much too large that it had the appearance of being dropsical; others maintained that the legs were too weak for the support of the whole, and that they should be rendered more important and prominent members of the figure; while, on the contrary, there were yet others who cried out that really these members were already so extravagantly huge, so coarse, and so ungenteel, that they quite marred the general effect of a beautiful piece of sculpture.

The same differences existed about the comparative excellence of the three metals and the portions of the body which they respectively formed. Some admired the gold, and maintained that if it were not for the head the Statue would be utterly useless; others preferred the silver, and would assert that the body, which contained all the machinery, must clearly be the most precious portion; while a third party triumphantly argued that the iron legs which supported both body and head must surely be the most valuable part, since without them the Statue must fall. The first party advised that in all future reparations gold only should be introduced; and the other parties, of course, recommended with equal zeal their own favourite metals. It is observable, however, that if, under these circumstances, the iron race chanced to fail in carrying their point, they invariably voted for gold in preference to silver. But the most contradictory opinions, perhaps, were those which were occasioned by the instruments with which the Statue was armed and supported. Some affected to be so frightened by the mere sight of the brandished sword, although it never moved, that they pretended it was dangerous to live even under the same sky with it; while others, treating very lightly the terrors of this warlike instrument, would observe that much more was really to be apprehended from the remarkable strength and thickness of the calm and peace-inspiring crosier; and that as long as the Government was supported by this huge pastoral staff nothing could prevail against it; that it could dare all things, and even stand without the help of its legs. All these various opinions at least proved that, although the present might not be the most miraculous Statue that could possibly be created, it was nevertheless quite impossible ever to form one which would please all parties.

The care of this wonderful Statue was entrusted to twelve 'Managers,' whose duty it was to wind up and regulate its complicated machinery, and who answered for its good management by their heads. It was their business to consult the oracle upon all occasions, and by its decisions to administer and regulate all the affairs of the State. They alone were permitted to hear its voice; for the Statue never spoke in public save on rare occasions, and its sentences were then really so extremely commonplace that, had it not been for the deep wisdom of its general conduct, the Vraibleusians would have been almost tempted to believe that they really might exist without the services of the capital member. The twelve Managers surrounded the Statue at a respectful distance; their posts were the most distinguished in the State; and indeed the duties attached to them were so numerous, so difficult, and so responsible, that it required no ordinary abilities to fulfil, and demanded no ordinary courage to aspire to, them.

The Fantaisian ambassador, having been presented, took his place on the right hand of the statue, next to the Aboriginal Inhabitant, and public business then commenced.

There came forward a messenger, who, knocking his nose three times with great reverence on the floor, a knock for each metal of the figure, thus spoke:

'O thou wisest and best! thou richest and mightiest! thou glory and admiration! thou defence and consternation! Lo! the King of the North is cutting all his subjects' heads off!'

This announcement produced a great sensation. The Marquess Moustache took snuff; the private secretary said he had long suspected that this would be the case; and the Aboriginal Inhabitant remarked to Popanilla that the corn in the North was of an exceedingly coarse grain. While they were making these observations the twelve Managers had assembled in deep consultation around the Statue, and in a very few minutes the oracle was prepared. The answer was very simple, but the exordium was sublime. It professed that the Vraibleusian nation was the saviour and champion of the world; that it was the first principle of its policy to maintain the cause of any people struggling for their rights as men; and it avowed itself to be the grand patron of civil and religious liberty in all quarters of the globe. Forty-seven battalions of infantry and eighteen regiments of cavalry, twenty-four sail of the line, seventy transports, and fifteen bombketches, were then ordered to leave Vraibleusia for the North in less than sixty minutes!

'What energy!' said Popanilla; 'what decision! what rapidity of execution!'

'Ay!' said the Aboriginal, smacking his thigh; 'let them say what they like about their proportions, and mixtures, and metals — abstract nonsense! No one can deny that our Government works well. But see! here comes another messenger!'

'O thou wisest and best! thou richest and mightiest! thou glory and admiration! thou defence and consternation! Lo! the people of the South have cut their king's head off!'

'Well! I suppose that is exactly what you all want,' said the innocent Popanilla.

The private secretary looked mysterious, and said that he was not prepared to answer; that his department never having been connected with this species of business, he was unable at the moment to give his Excellency the requisite information. At the same time, he begged to state that, provided anything he said should not commit him, he had no objection to answer the question hypothetically. The Aboriginal Inhabitant said that he would have no hypotheses or Jacobins; that he did not approve of cutting off kings' heads; and that the Vraibleusians were the most monarchical people in the world. So saying he walked up, without any ceremony, to the chief Manager, and taking him by the button, conversed with him some time in an earnest manner, which made the stocks fall two per cent.

The Statue ordered three divisions of the grand army and a battering-train of the first grade off to the South without the loss of a second. A palace and establishment were immediately directed to be prepared for the family of the murdered monarch, and the commander-in-chief was instructed to make every exertion to bring home the body of his Majesty embalmed. Such an immense issue of pink shells was occasioned by this last expedition that stocks not only recovered themselves, but rose considerably.

The excitement occasioned by this last announcement evaporated at the sight of a third messenger.

He informed the Statue that the Emperor of the East was unfortunately unable to pay the interest upon his national debt; that his treasury was quite empty and his resources utterly exhausted. He requested the assistance of the most wealthy and the most generous of nations; and he offered them as security for their advances his gold and silver mines, which, for the breadth of their veins and the richness of their ores, he said, were unequalled. He added, that the only reason they were unworked was the exquisite flavour of the water-melons in his empire, which was so delicious that his subjects of all classes, passing their whole day in devouring them, could be induced neither by force nor persuasion to do anything else. The cause was so reasonable, and the security so satisfactory, that the Vraibleusian Government felt themselves authorised in shipping off immediately all the gold in the island. Pink shells abounded, and stocks were still higher.

'You have no mines in Vraibleusia, I believe?' said Popanilla to the Aboriginal.

'No! but we have taxes.'

'Very true!' said Popanilla.

'I understand that a messenger has just arrived from the West,' said the secretary to the Fantaisian Plenipotentiary. 'He must bring interesting intelligence from such interesting countries. Next to ourselves, they are evidently the most happy, the most wealthy, the most enlightened, and the most powerful Governments in the world. Although founded only last week, they already rank in the first class of nations. I will send you a little pamphlet to-morrow, which I have just published upon this subject, in which you will see that I have combated, I trust not unsuccessfully, the ridiculous opinions of those cautious statesmen who insinuate that the stability of these Governments is even yet questionable.'

The messenger from the Republics of the West now prostrated himself before the Statue. He informed it that two parties had, unfortunately, broken out in these countries, and threatened their speedy dissolution; that one party maintained that all human government originated in the *wants* of man; while the other party asserted that it originated in the *desires* of man. That these factions had become so violent and so universal that public business was altogether stopped, trade quite extinct, and the instalments due to Vraibleusia not forthcoming. Finally, he entreated the wisest and the best of nations to send to these distracted lands some discreet and trusty personages, well instructed in the first principles of government, in order that they might draw up constitutions for the ignorant and irritated multitude.

The private secretary told Popanilla that this was no more than he had long expected; that all this would subside, and that he should publish a postscript to his pamphlet in a few days, which he begged to dedicate to him.

A whole *corps diplomatique* and another shipful of abstract philosophers, principally Scotchmen, were immediately ordered off to the West; and shortly after, to render their first principles still more effective and their administrative arrangements still more influential, some brigades of infantry and a detachment of the guards followed. Free constitutions are apt to be misunderstood until half of the nation are bayoneted and the rest imprisoned.

As this mighty Vraibleusian nation had, within the

last half-hour, received intelligence from all quarters
of the globe, and interfered in all possible affairs,
civil and military, abstract, administrative, diplomatic,
and financial, Popanilla supposed that the assembly
would now break up. Some petty business, however, remained. War was declared against the King
of Sneezeland, for presuming to buy pocket-handker-
chiefs of another nation; and the Emperor of Pastilles
was threatened with a bombardment for daring to
sell his peppers to another people. There were also
some dozen commercial treaties to be signed, or can-
vassed, or cancelled; and a report having got about
that there was a rumour that some disturbance had
broken out in some parts unknown, a flying expedition was despatched, with sealed orders, to circum-
navigate the globe and arrange affairs. By this time
Popanilla thoroughly understood the meaning of the
mysterious inscription.

Just as the assembly was about to be dissolved
another messenger, who, in his agitation, even forgot
the accustomed etiquette of salutation, rushed into the
presence.

'O most mighty! Sir Bombastes Furioso, who
commanded our last expedition, having sailed, in the
hurry, with wrong orders, has attacked our ancient
ally by mistake, and utterly destroyed him!'

Here was a pretty business for the Best and
Wisest! At first the Managers behaved in a manner
the most undiplomatic, and quite lost their temper;
they raved, they stormed, they contradicted each
other, they contradicted themselves, and swore that
Sir Bombastes' head should answer for it. Then they
subsided into sulkiness, and at length, beginning to
suspect that the fault might ultimately attach only to

themselves, they got frightened, and held frequent consultations with pale visages and quivering lips. After some time they thought they could do nothing wiser than put a good face upon the affair; whatever might be the result, it was, at any rate, a victory, and a victory would please the vainest of nations: and so these blundering and blustering gentlemen determined to adopt the conqueror, whom they were at first weak enough to disclaim, then vile enough to bully, and finally forced to reward. The Statue accordingly whispered a most elaborate panegyric on Furioso, which was of course duly delivered. The Admiral, who was neither a coward nor a fool, was made ridiculous by being described as the greatest commander that ever existed; one whom Nature, in a gracious freak, had made to shame us little men; a happy compound of the piety of Noah, the patriotism of Themistocles, the skill of Columbus, and the courage of Nelson; and his exploit styled the most glorious and unrivalled victory that was ever achieved, even by the Vraibleusians! Honours were decreed in profusion, a general illumination ordered for the next twenty nights, and an expedition immediately despatched to attack the right man.

All this time the conquerors were in waiting in an ante-room, in great trepidation, and fully prepared to be cashiered or cut in quarters. They were rather surprised when, bowing to the ground, they were saluted by some half-dozen lords-in-waiting as the heroes of the age, congratulated upon their famous achievements, and humbly requested to appear in the Presence.

The warriors accordingly walked up in procession to the Statue, who, opening its mighty mouth, vomited forth a flood of ribbons, stars, and crosses, which were divided among the valiant band. This oral discharge the Vraibleusians called the 'fountain of honour.'

Scarcely had the mighty Furioso and his crew disappeared than a body of individuals arrived at the top of the hall, and, placing themselves opposite the Managers, began rating them for their inefficient administration of the island, and expatiated on the inconsistency of their late conduct to the conquering Bombastes. The Managers defended themselves in a manner perfectly in character with their recent behaviour; but their opponents were not easily satisfied with their confused explanations and their explained confusions, and the speeches on both sides grew warmer. At'length the opposition proceeded to expel the administration from their places by force, and an eager scuffle between the two parties now commenced. The general body of spectators continued only to observe, and did not participate in the fray. At first, this *mêlée* only excited amusement; but as it lengthened some wisely observed that public business greatly suffered by these private squabbles; and some even ventured to imagine that the safety of the Statue might be implicated by their continuance. But this last fear was futile.

Popanilla asked the private secretary which party he thought would ultimately succeed. The private secretary said that, if the present Managers retained their places, he thought that they would not go out; but if, on the other hand, they were expelled by the present opposition, it was probable that the present opposition would become Managers. The Aboriginal thought both parties equally incompetent; and told

Popanilla some long stories about a person who was chief Manager in his youth, about five hundred years ago, to whom he said he was indebted for all his political principles, which did not surprise Popanilla.

At this moment a noise was heard throughout the hall which made his Excellency believe that something untoward had again happened, and that another conqueror by mistake had again arrived. A most wonderful being galloped up to the top of the apartment. It was half man and half horse. The secretary told Popanilla that this was the famous Centaur Chiron; that his Horseship, having wearied of his ardent locality in the constellations, had descended some years back to the island of Vraibleusia; that he had commanded the armies of the nation in all the great wars, and had gained every battle in which he had ever been engaged. Chiron was no less skilful, he said, in civil than in military affairs; but the Vraibleusians, being very jealous of allowing themselves to be governed by their warriors, the Centaur had lately been out of employ. While the secretary was giving him this information Popanilla perceived that the great Chiron was attacking the combatants on both sides. The tutor of Achilles, Hercules, and Æneas, of course, soon succeeded in kicking them all out, and constituted himself chief and sole Manager of the Statue. Some grumbled at this autocratic conduct 'upon principle,' but they were chiefly connections of the expelled. The great majority, wearied with public squabbles occasioned by private ends, rejoiced to see the public interest entrusted to an individual who had a reputation to lose. Intelligence of the appointment of the Centaur was speedily diffused throughout the island, and produced great and general satisfaction. There were a few, indeed, impartial personages, who had no great taste for Centaurs in civil capacities, from an apprehension that, if he could not succeed in persuading them by his eloquence, his Grace might chance to use his heels.

CHAPTER XI.

N THE evening of his presentation day his Excellency the Fantaisian Ambassador and suite honoured the national theatre with their presence. Such a house was never known! The pit was miraculously overflown before the doors were opened, although the proprietor did not permit a single private entrance. The enthusiasm was universal, and only twelve persons were killed. The private secretary told Popanilla, with an air of great complacency, that the Vraibleusian theatres were the largest in the world. Popanilla had little doubt of the truth of this information, as a long time elapsed before he could even discover the stage. He observed that every person in the theatre carried a long black glass, which he kept perpetually fixed to his eye. To sit in a huge room hotter than a glass-house, in a posture emulating the most sanctified faquir, with a throbbing head-ache, a breaking back, and twisted legs, with a heavy tube held over one eye, and the other covered with the unemployed hand, is in Vraibleusia called a public amusement.

(82)

The play was by the most famous dramatist that Vraibleusia ever produced; and certainly, when his Excellency witnessed the first scenes, it was easier to imagine that he was once more in his own sunset Isle of Fantaisie than in the railroad state of Vraibleusia; but, unfortunately, this evening the principal characters and scenes were omitted, to make room for a moving panorama, which lasted some hours, of the chief and most recent Vraibleusian victories. The audience fought their battles o'er again with great fervour. During the play one of the inferior actors was supposed to have saluted a female chorus-singer with an ardour which was more than theatrical, and every lady in the house immediately fainted; because, as the eternal secretary told Popanilla, the Vraibleusians are the most modest and most moral nation in the world. The male part of the audience insisted, in indignant terms, that the offending performer should immediately be dismissed. In a few minutes he appeared upon the stage to make a most humble apology for an offence which he was not conscious of having committed; but the most moral and the most modest of nations was implacable, and the wretch was expelled. Having a large family dependent upon his exertions, the actor, according to a custom prevalent in Vraibleusia, went immediately and drowned himself in the nearest river. Then the ballet commenced.

It was soon discovered that the chief dancer, a celebrated foreigner, who had been announced for this evening, was absent. The uproar was tremendous, and it was whispered that the house would be pulled down; because, as Popanilla was informed, the Vraibleusians are the most particular and the freest

people in the world, and never will permit themselves to be treated with disrespect. The principal
chandelier having been destroyed, the manager appeared, and regretted that Signor Zephyrino, being
engaged to dine with a grandee of the first class,
was unable to fulfil his engagement. The house became frantic, and the terrified manager sent immediately for the Signor. The artist, after a proper
time had elapsed, appeared with a napkin round his
neck and a fork in his hand, with which he stood
some moments, until the uproar had subsided, pick-
ing his teeth. At length, when silence was obtained,
he told them that he was surprised that the most
polished and liberal nation in the world should behave themselves in such a brutal and narrow-minded
manner. He threatened them that he would throw
up his engagement immediately, and announce to all
foreign parts that they were a horde of barbarians;
then, abusing them for a few seconds in round terms,
he retired, amidst the cheerings of the whole house,
to finish his wine.

When the performances were finished the audience rose and joined in chorus. On Popanilla enquiring the name and nature of this effusion, he was
told that it was the national air of the Isle of Fantaisie, sung in compliment to himself. His Excellency
shrugged his shoulders and bowed low.

The next morning, attended by his suite, Popanilla visited the most considerable public offices and
manufactories in Hubbabub. He was received in all
places with the greatest distinction. He was invariably
welcomed either by the chiefs of the department or
the proprietors themselves, and a sumptuous collation
was prepared for him in every place. His Excellency

evinced the liveliest interest in everything that was pointed out to him, and instantaneously perceived that the Vraibleusians exceeded the rest of the world in manufactures and public works as much as they did in arms, morals, modesty, philosophy, and politics. The private secretary being absent upon his postscript, Popanilla received the most satisfactory information upon all subjects from the Marquess himself. Whenever he addressed any question to his Lordship, his noble attendant, with the greatest politeness, begged him to take some refreshment. Popanilla returned to his hotel with a great admiration of the manner in which refined philosophy in Vraibleusia was applied to the common purposes of life; and found that he had that morning acquired a general knowledge of the chief arts and sciences, eaten some hundred sandwiches, and tasted as many bottles of sherry.

CHAPTER XII.

SOCIAL STRUGGLES IN VRAIBLEUSIA.

THE most commercial nation in the world was now busily preparing to diffuse the blessings of civilisation and competition throughout the native country of their newly-acquired friend. The greatest exporters that ever existed had never been acquainted with such a subject for exportation as the Isle of Fantaisie. There everything was wanted. It was not a partial demand which was to be satisfied, nor a particular deficiency which was to be supplied; but a vast population was thoroughly to be furnished with every article which a vast population must require. From the manufacturer of steam-engines to the manufacturer of stockings, all were alike employed. There was no branch of trade in Vraibleusia which did not equally rejoice at this new opening for commercial enterprise, and which was not equally interested in this new theatre for Vraibleusian industry, Vraibleusian invention, Vraibleusian activity, and, above all, Vraibleusian competition.

Day and night the whole island was employed in preparing for the great fleet and in huzzaing Popanilla. When at home, every ten minutes he was obliged to appear in the balcony, and then, with hand on heart and hat in hand, ah! that bow! that perpetual motion of popularity! If a man love ease, let him be most unpopular. The Managers did the impossible to assist and advance the intercourse between the two nations. They behaved in a liberal and enlightened manner, and a deputation of liberal and enlightened merchants consequently waited upon them with a vote of thanks. They issued so many pink shells that the price of the public funds was doubled, and affairs arranged so skilfully that money was universally declared to be worth nothing, so that every one in the island, from the Premier down to the Mendicant whom the lecture-loving Skindeep threatened with the bastinado, was enabled to participate in some degree, in the approaching venture, if we should use so dubious a term in speaking of profit so certain.

Compared with the Fantaisian connection, the whole commerce of the world appeared to the Vraibleusians a retail business. All other customers were neglected or discarded, and each individual seemed to concentrate his resources to supply the wants of a country where they dance by moonlight, live on fruit, and sleep on flowers. At length the first fleet of five hundred sail, laden with wonderful specimens of Vraibleusian mechanism, and innumerable bales of Vraibleusian manufactures; articles raw and refined, goods dry and damp, wholesale and retail; silks and woollen cloths; cottons, cutlery, and camlets; flannels and ladies' albums; under waistcoats, kid gloves, engravings, coats, cloaks, and ottomans; lamps and looking-glasses; sofas, round tables, equipages, and

scent-bottles; fans and tissue-flowers; porcelain, poetry, novels, newspapers, and cookery books; bear's-
grease, blue pills, and bijouterie; arms, beards,
poodles, pages, mustachios, court-guides, and bon-
bons; music, pictures, ladies' maids, scrap-books,
buckles, boxing-gloves, guitars, and snuff-boxes; together with a company of opera-singers, a band of
comedians, a popular preacher, some quacks, lecturers,
artists, and literary gentlemen, principally sketch-
book men, quitted, one day, with a favourable wind,
and amid the exultation of the inhabitants, the port
of Hubbabub!

When his Excellency Prince Popanilla heard of the
contents of this stupendous cargo, notwithstanding
his implicit confidence in the superior genius and
useful knowledge of the Vraibleusians, he could not
refrain from expressing a doubt whether, in the present undeveloped state of his native land, any returns
could be made proportionate to so curious and elaborate an importation; but whenever he ventured to
intimate his opinion to any of the most commercial
nation in the world he was only listened to with an
incredulous smile which seemed to pity his inexperience, or told, with an air of profound self-com-
placency, that in Fantaisie 'there must be great
resources.'

In the meantime, public companies were formed
for working the mines, colonising the waste lands,
and cutting the coral rocks of the Indian Isle, of all
which associations Popanilla was chosen director by
acclamation. These, however, it must be confessed,
were speculations of a somewhat doubtful nature; but
the Branch Bank Society of the Isle of Fantaisie really
held out flattering prospects.

When the fleet had sailed they gave Popanilla a public dinner. It was attended by all the principal men in the island, and he made a speech, which was received in a rather different manner than was his sunset oration by the monarch whom he now represented. Fantaisie and its accomplished envoy were at the same time the highest and the universal fashion. The ladies sang *à la Syrène,* dressed their hair *à la Mermède,* and themselves *à la Fantastique;* which, by-the-bye, was not new; and the gentlemen wore boa-constrictor cravats and waltzed *à la mer Indienne* — a title probably suggested by a remembrance of the dangers of the sea.

It was soon discovered that, without taking into consideration the average annual advantages which would necessarily spring from their new connection, the profits which must accrue upon the present expedition alone had already doubled the capital of the island. Everybody in Vraibleusia had either made a fortune, or laid the foundation of one. The penniless had become prosperous, and the principal merchants and manufacturers, having realised large capitals, retired from business. But the colossal fortunes were made by the gentlemen who had assisted the administration in raising the price of the public funds and in managing the issues of the pink shells. The effect of this immense increase of the national wealth and of this creation of new and powerful classes of society was speedily felt. Great moves to the westward were perpetual, and a variety of sumptuous squares and streets were immediately run up in that chosen land. Butlers were at a premium; coach-makers never slept; card-engravers, having exhausted copper, had recourse to steel; and the demand for arms at the

Heralds' College was so great that even the mystical genius of Garter was exhausted, and hostile meetings were commenced between the junior members of some ancient families, to whom the same crest had been unwittingly apportioned; but, the seconds interfering, they discovered themselves to be relations. All the eldest sons were immediately to get into Parliament, and all the younger ones as quickly into the Guards; and the simple Fantaisian Envoy, who had the peculiar felicity of taking everything *au pied de la lettre,* made a calculation that, if these arrangements were duly effected, in a short time the Vraibleusian representatives would exceed the Vraibleusian represented; and that there would be at least three officers in the Vraibleusian Guards to every private. Judging from the beards and mustachios which now abounded, this great result was near at hand. With the snub nose which is the characteristic of the millionaires, these appendages produce a pleasing effect.

When the excitement had a little subsided; when their mighty mansions were magnificently furnished; when their bright equipages were fairly launched, and the due complement of their liveried retainers perfected; when, in short, they had imitated the aristocracy in every point in which wealth could rival blood: then the new people discovered with dismay that one thing was yet wanting, which treasure could not purchase, and which the wit of others could not supply — manner. In homely phrase, the millionaires did not know how to behave themselves. Accustomed to the counting-house, the factory, or the exchange, they looked queer in saloons, and said 'Sir!' when they addressed you; and seemed stiff, and hard, and hot. Then the solecisms they committed in more

formal society, oh! they were outrageous; and a leading article in an eminent journal was actually written
upon the subject. I dare not write the deeds they
did; but it was whispered that when they drank
wine they filled their glasses to the very brim. All
this delighted the old class, who were as envious of
their riches as the new people were emulous of their
style.

In any other country except Vraibleusia persons
so situated would have consoled themselves for their
disagreeable position by a consciousness that their
posterity would not be annoyed by the same defi-
ciencies; but the wonderful Vraibleusian people re-
sembled no other, even in their failings. They
determined to acquire in a day that which had hitherto been deemed the gradual consequence of tedious
education.

A 'Society for the Diffusion of Fashionable Knowledge' was announced; the millionaires looked triumphantly mysterious, the aristocrats quizzed. The
object of the society is intimated by its title; and
the method by which its institutors proposed to attain this object was the periodical publication of
pamphlets, under the superintendence of a compe-
tent committee. The first treatise appeared: its subject was NONCHALANCE. It instructed its students ever
to appear inattentive in the society of men, and
heartless when they conversed with women. It
taught them not to understand a man if he were
witty; to misunderstand him if he were eloquent; to
yawn or stare if he chanced to elevate his voice, or
presumed to ruffle the placidity of the social calm by
addressing his fellow-creatures with teeth unparted.
Excellence was never to be recognised, but only dis-

paraged with a look: an opinion or a sentiment, and the *nonchalant* was lost for ever. For these, he was to substitute a smile like a damp sunbeam, a moderate curl of the upper lip, and the all-speaking and perpetual shrug of the shoulders. By a skilful management of these qualities it was shown to be easy to ruin another's reputation and ensure your own without ever opening your mouth. To woman, this exquisite treatise said much in few words: 'Listlessness, listlessness, listlessness,' was the edict by which the most beautiful works of nature were to be regulated, who are only truly charming when they make us feel and feel themselves. 'Listlessness, listlessness, listlessness;' for when you choose not to be listless, the contrast is so striking that the triumph must be complete.

The treatise said much more, which I shall omit. It forgot, however, to remark that this vaunted nonchalance may be the offspring of the most contemptible and the most odious of passions: and that while it may be exceedingly refined to appear uninterested when others are interested, to witness excellence without emotion, and to listen to genius without animation, the heart of the insensible may as often be inflamed by envy as inspired by fashion.

Dissertations 'On leaving cards,' 'On cutting intimate friends,' 'On cravats,' 'On dinner courses,' 'On poor relations,' 'On bores,' 'On lions,' were announced as speedily to appear. In the meantime, the essay on nonchalance produced the best effects. A *ci-devant* stock-broker cut a duke dead at his club the day after its publication; and his daughter yawned while his Grace's eldest son, the Marquess, made her an offer as she was singing 'Di tanti palpiti.' The aristocrats got a little frightened, and when an eminent hop-merchant and his lady had asked a dozen countesses to dinner, and forgot to be at home to receive them, the old class left off quizzing.

The pamphlets, however, continued issuing forth, and the new people advanced at a rate which was awful. They actually began to originate some ideas of their own, and there was a whisper among the leaders of voting the aristocrats old-fashioned. The Diffusion Society now caused these exalted personages great anxiety and uneasiness. They argued that fashion was a relative quality; that it was quite impossible, and not be expected, that all people were to aspire to be fashionable; that it was not in the nature of things, and that, if it were, society could not exist; that the more their imitators advanced the more they should baffle their imitations; that a first and fashionable class was a necessary consequence of the organisation of man; and that a line of demarcation would for ever be drawn between them and the other islanders. The warmth and eagerness with which they maintained and promulgated their opinions might have tempted, however, an impartial person to suspect that they secretly entertained some doubts of their truth and soundness.

On the other hand, the other party maintained that fashion was a positive quality; that the moment a person obtained a certain degree of refinement he or she became, in fact and essentially, fashionable; that the views of the old class were unphilosophical and illiberal, and unworthy of an enlightened age; that men are equal, and that everything is open to everybody; and that when we take into consideration the nature of man, the origin of society, and a few other things, and duly consider the constant inclination and progression towards perfection which mankind evinces, there was no reason why, in the course of time, the whole nation should not go to Almack's on the same night.

At this moment of doubt and dispute the Government of Vraibleusia, with that spirit of conciliation and liberality and that perfect wisdom for which it had been long celebrated, caring very little for the old class, whose interest, it well knew, was to support it, and being exceedingly desirous of engaging the affections of the new race, declared in their favour; and acting upon that sublime scale of measures for which this great nation has always been so famous, the Statue issued an edict that a new literature should be invented, in order at once to complete the education of the millionaires and the triumph of the romantic over the classic school of manners.

The most eminent writers were, as usual, in the pay of the Government, and BURLINGTON, A TALE OF FASHIONABLE LIFE, in three volumes post octavo, was sent forth. Two or three similar works, bearing titles equally euphonious and aristocratic, were published daily; and so exquisite was the style of these productions, so naturally artificial the construction of their plots, and so admirably inventive the conception of their characters, that many who had been repulsed by the somewhat abstract matter and arid style of the treatises, seduced by the interest of a story, and by the dazzling delicacies of a charming style, really now picked up a considerable quantity of very useful knowledge; so that when the delighted students had eaten some fifty or sixty imaginary dinners in my lord's dining-room, and whirled some fifty or sixty imaginary waltzes in my lady's dancing-room, there was scarcely a brute left among the whole million-aires. But what produced the most beneficial effects on the new people, and excited the greatest indigna-tion and despair among the old class, were some volumes which the Government, with shocking Machiavelism, bribed some needy scions of nobility to scribble, and which revealed certain secrets vainly believed to be quite sacred and inviolable.

CHAPTER XIII.

THE COLONIAL SYSTEM.

SHORTLY after the sailing of the great fleet the private secretary engaged in a speculation which was rather more successful than any one contained in his pamphlet on 'The Present State of the Western Republics.'

One morning, as he and Popanilla were walking on a quay, and deliberating on the clauses of the projected commercial treaty between Vraibleusia and Fantaisie, the secretary suddenly stopped, as if he had seen his father's ghost or lost the thread of his argument, and asked Popanilla, with an air of suppressed agitation, whether he observed anything in the distance. Popanilla, who, like all savages, was long-sighted, applying to his eye the glass which, in conformity to the custom of the country, he always wore round his neck, confessed that he saw nothing. The secretary, who had never unfixed his glass nor moved a step since he asked the question, at length, by pointing with his finger, attracted Popanilla's attention to what his Excellency conceived to be a porpoise bobbing up and down in the waves. The secretary, however, was not of the same opinion as the ambassador. He was not very communicative, indeed, as to his own opinion upon this grave subject, but he talked of making farther observations when the tide went down; and was so listless, abstracted, and absent, during the rest of their conversation, that it soon ceased, and they speedily parted.

The next day, when Popanilla read the morning papers, a feat which he regularly performed, for spelling the newspaper was quite delicious to one who had so recently learned to read, he found that they spoke of nothing but of the discovery of a new island, information of which had been received by the Government only the preceding night. The Fantaisian Ambassador turned quite pale, and for the first time in his life experienced the passion of jealousy, the green-eyed monster, so called from only being experienced by greenhorns. Already the prominent state he represented seemed to retire to the background. He did not doubt that the Vraibleusians were the most capricious as well as the most commercial nation in the world. His reign was evidently over. The new island would send forth a prince still more popular. His allowance of pink shells would be gradually reduced, and finally withdrawn. His doubts, also, as to the success of the recent expedition to Fantaisie began to revive. His rising reminiscences of his native land, which, with the joint assistance of popularity and philosophy, he had hitherto succeeded in stifling, were indeed awkward. He could not conceive his mistress with a page and a poodle. He feared much that the cargo was not well assorted. Popanilla determined to enquire after his canoe.

His courage, however, was greatly reassured when, on reading the second edition, he learned that the new island was not of considerable size, though most eligibly situate; and, moreover, that it was perfectly void of inhabitants. When the third edition was published he found, to his surprise, that the private secretary was the discoverer of this opposition island. This puzzled the plenipotentiary greatly. He read on; he found that this acquisition, upon which all Vraibleusia was congratulated in such glowing terms by all its journals, actually produced nothing. His Excellency began to breathe; another paragraph, and he found that the rival island was, a rock! He remembered the porpoise of yesterday. The island certainly could not be very large, even at low water. Popanilla once more felt like a prince: he defied all the discoverers that could ever exist. He thought of the great resources of the great country he represented with proud satisfaction. He waited with easy confidence the return of the fleet which had carried out the most judicious assortment with which he had ever been acquainted to the readiest market of which he had any knowledge. He had no doubt his mistress would look most charming in a barège. Popanilla determined to present his canoe to the National Museum.

Although his Excellency had existed in the highest state of astonishment during his whole mission to Vraibleusia, it must be confessed, now that he understood his companion's question of yesterday, he particularly stared. His wonder was not decreased in the evening, when the 'Government Gazette' appeared. It contained an order for the immediate fortification of the new island by the most skilful engineers, without estimates. A strong garrison was instantly embarked. A governor, and a deputy-governor, and storekeepers, more plentiful than stores, were to accompany them. The private secretary went out as president of council. A bishop was promised; and a complete Court of Judicature, Chancery, King's Bench, Common Pleas, and Exchequer, were to be off the next week. It is only due to the characters of courtiers, who are so often reproached with ingratitude to their patrons, to record that the private secretary, in the most delicate manner, placed at the disposal of his former employer, the Marquess Moustache, the important office of Agent for the Indemnity Claims of the original Inhabitants of the Island; the post being a sinecure, the income being considerable, and local attendance being unnecessary, the noble lord, in a manner equally delicate, appointed himself.

'Upon what system,' one day enquired that unwearied political student, the Fantaisian Ambassador, of his old friend Skindeep, 'does your Government surround a small rock in the middle of the sea with fortifications, and cram it full of clerks, soldiers, lawyers, and priests?'

'Why, really, your Excellency, I am the last man in the world to answer questions; but I believe we call it THE COLONIAL SYSTEM!'

Before the president, and governor, and deputy-governor, and storekeepers had embarked, the Vraibleusian journals, who thought that the public had been satiated with congratulations on the Colonial System, detected that the present colony was a job. Their reasoning was so convincing, and their denunciations so impressive, that the Managers got frightened, and cut off one of the deputy-storekeepers. The President of Council now got more frightened than the Managers. He was one of those men who think that the world can be saved by writing a pamphlet. A pamphlet accordingly appeared upon the subject of the new colony. The writer showed that the debatable land was the most valuable acquisition ever attained by a nation famous for their acquisitions; that there was a spring of water in the middle of the rock of a remarkable freshness, and which was never dry except during the summer and the earlier winter months; that all our outward-bound ships would experience infinite benefit from this fresh water; that the scurvy would therefore disappear from the service; and that the naval victories which the Vraibleusians would gain in future wars would consequently be occasioned by the present colony. No one could mistake the felicitous reasoning of the author of 'The Present State of the Western Republics!'

About this time Popanilla fell ill. He lost his appetite and his spirits, and his digestion was sadly disordered. His friends endeavoured to console him by telling him that dyspepsia was the national disease of Vraibleusia; that its connection with civil and religious liberty was indissoluble; that every man, woman, and child above fifteen in the island was a martyr to it; that it was occasioned by their rapid mode of despatching their meals, which again was occasioned by the little time which the most active nation in the world could afford to bestow upon such a losing business as eating.

All this was no consolation to a man who had lost his appetite; and so Popanilla sent for a gentleman who, he was told, was the most eminent phy-

sician in the island. The most eminent physician,
when he arrived, would not listen to a single syl-
lable that his patient wished to address to him. He
told Popanilla that his disorder was 'decidedly liver;'
that it was occasioned by his eating his meat before his bread instead of after it, and drinking at the
end of the first course instead of the beginning of the
second; that he had only to correct these ruinous
habits, and that he would then regain his tone.

Popanilla observed the instructions of the eminent
physician to the very letter. He invariably eat his
bread before his meat, and watched the placing of
the first dish of the second course upon the table ere
he ventured to refresh himself with any liquid. At
the end of a week he was infinitely worse.

He now called in a gentleman who was recommended to him as the most celebrated practitioner in
all Vraibleusia. The most celebrated practitioner listened with great attention to every particular that his
patient had to state, but never condescended to open
his own mouth. Popanilla was delighted, and revenged himself for the irritability of the eminent physician. After two more visits, the most celebrated
practitioner told Popanilla that his disorder was 'un-
questionably nervous;' that he had over-excited himself by talking too much; that in future he must count
five between each word he uttered, never ask any
questions, and avoid society; that is, never stay at
an evening party on any consideration later than
twenty-two minutes past two, and never be induced
by any persuasion to dine out more than once on the
same day. The most celebrated practitioner added
that he had only to observe these regulations, and
that he would speedily recover his energy.

Popanilla never asked a question for a whole week, and Skindeep never knew him more delightful. He not only counted five, but ten, between every word he uttered; and determining that his cure should not be delayed, whenever he had nobody to speak to he continued counting. In a few days this solitary computation brought on a slow fever.

He now determined to have a consultation between the most eminent physician and the most celebrated practitioner. It was delightful to witness the meeting of these great men. Not a shade of jealousy dimmed the sunshine of their countenances. After a consultation, they agreed that Popanilla's disorder was neither 'liver,' nor 'nervous,' but 'mind:' that he had done too much; that he had overworked his brain; that he must take more exercise; that he must breathe more air; that he must have relaxation; that he must have change of scene.

'Where shall I go?' was the first question which Popanilla had sent forth for a fortnight, and it was addressed to Skindeep.

'Really, your Excellency, I am the last man in the world to answer questions; but the place which is generally frequented by us when we are suffering from your complaint is Blunderland.'

'Well, then, to Blunderland let us go!'

Shortly before Popanilla's illness he had been elected a member of the Vraibleusian Horticultural Society, and one evening he had endeavoured to amuse himself by reading the following CHAPTER ON FRUIT.

CHAPTER XIV.

HAT a taste for fruit is inherent in man is an opinion which is sanctioned by the conduct of man in all ages and in all countries. While some nations have considered it profanation or pollution to nourish themselves with flesh or solace themselves with fish, while almost every member of the animal creation has in turn been considered either sacred or unclean, mankind, in all climes and in all countries, the Hindoo and the Hebrew, the Egyptian and the Greek, the Roman and the Frank, have, in some degree, made good their boastful claim to reason, by universally feeding upon those delightful productions of Nature which are nourished with the dews of heaven, and which live for ever in its breath.

And, indeed, when we consider how exceedingly refreshing at all times is the flavour of fruit; how very natural, and, in a manner, born in him, is man's inclination for it; how little it is calculated to pall upon his senses; and how conducive, when not eaten to excess, it is to his health, as well as to his pleasure; we must not be surprised that a conviction of its excellence should have been one of those few subjects on which men have never disagreed.

That some countries are more favoured in their fruit than others is a fact so notorious that its notice is unnecessary; but we are not therefore to suppose that their appetite for it is more keen than the appetite of other nations for their fruit who live in less genial climes. Indeed, if we were not led to believe that all nations are inspired by an equal love for this production, it might occasionally be suspected that some of those nations who are least skilful as horticulturists evince a greater passion for their inferior growths than more fortunate people for their choicer produce. The effects of bad fruit, however, upon the constitution, and consequently upon the national character, are so injurious that every liberal man must regret that any people, either from ignorance or obligation, should be forced to have recourse to anything so fatal, and must feel that it is the duty of everyone who professes to be a philanthropist to propagate and encourage a taste for good fruit throughout all countries of the globe.

A vast number of centuries before Popanilla had the fortune to lose his mistress's lock of hair, and consequently to become an ambassador to Vraibleusia, the inhabitants of that island, then scarcely more civilised than their new allies of Fantaisie were at present, suffered very considerably from the trash which they devoured, from that innate taste for fruit already noticed. In fact, although there are antiquaries who pretend that the Vraibleusians possessed some of the species of wild plums and apples even at that early period, the majority of enquirers are disposed to believe that their desserts were solely confined to the wildest berries, horse-chestnuts, and acorns.

A tradition runs, that while they were committing these abominations a ship, one of the first ships that had ever touched at the island, arrived at the present port of Hubbabub, then a spacious and shipless bay. The master of the vessel, on being brought before the King (for the story I am recording happened long before the construction of the miraculous Statue), presented, with his right hand, to his Majesty, a small pyramidal substance of a golden hue, which seemed to spring out of green and purple leaves. His Majesty did not exactly understand the intention of this ceremony; but of course, like a true legitimate, construed it into a symbol of homage. No sooner had the King brought the unknown substance near to his eyes, with the intention of scrutinising its nature, than the fragrance was so delightful that by mistake he applied it to his mouth. The King only took one mouthful, and then, with a cry of rapture, instantly handed the delicacy to his favourite, who, to the great mortification of the Secretary of State, finished it. The stranger, however, immediately supplied the surrounding courtiers from a basket which was slung on his left arm; and no sooner had they all tasted his gift than they fell upon their knees to worship him, vowing that the distributor of such delight must be more than man. If this avowal be considered absurd and extraordinary in this present age of philosophy, we must not forget to make due allowance for the palates of individuals who, having been so long accustomed merely to horse-chestnuts, and acorns, suddenly, for the first time in their lives, tasted pineapple.

The stranger, with an air of great humility, disclaimed their proffered adoration, and told them that, far from being superior to common mortals, he was, on the contrary, one of the lowliest of the human race; in fact, he did not wish to conceal it; in spite of his vessel and his attendants, he was merely a market-gardener on a great scale. This beautiful fruit he had recently discovered in the East, to which quarter of the world he annually travelled in order to obtain a sufficient quantity to supply the great Western hemisphere, of which he himself was a native. Accident had driven him, with one of his ships, into the Island of Vraibleusia; and, as the islanders appeared to be pleased with his cargo, he said that he should have great pleasure in supplying them at present and receiving their orders for the future.

The proposition was greeted with enthusiasm. The King immediately entered into a contract with the market-gardener on his own terms. The sale, or cultivation, or even the eating of all other fruits was declared high treason, and pine-apple, for weighty reasons duly recited in the royal proclamation, announced as the established fruit of the realm. The cargo, under the superintendence of some of the most trusty of the crew, was unshipped for the immediate supply of the island; and the merchant and his customers parted, mutually delighted and mutually profited.

Time flew on. The civilisation of Vraibleusia was progressive, as civilisation always is; and the taste for pine-apples ever on the increase, as the taste for pine-apples ever should be. The supply was regular and excellent, the prices reasonable, and the tradesmen civil. They, of course, had not failed to ad-

vance in fair proportion with the national prosperity.
Their numbers had much increased as well as their
customers. Fresh agents arrived with every fresh
cargo. They had long quitted the stalls with which
they had been contented on their first settlement in
the island, and now were the dapper owners of neat
depôts in all parts of the kingdom where depôts
could find customers.

A few more centuries, and affairs began to change.
All that I have related as matter of fact, and which
certainly is not better authenticated than many other
things that happened two or three thousand years
ago, which, however, the most sceptical will not presume to maintain did not take place, was treated as
the most idle and ridiculous fable by the dealers in
pine-apples themselves. They said that they knew
nothing about a market-gardener; that they were, and
had always been, the subjects of the greatest prince
in the world, compared with whom all other crowned
heads ranked merely as subjects did with their immediate sovereigns. This prince, they said, lived in
the most delicious region in the world, and the fruit
which they imported could only be procured from his
private gardens, where it sprang from one of the trees
that had bloomed in the gardens of the Hesperides.
The Vraibleusians were at first a little surprised at
this information, but the old tradition of the market-
gardener was certainly an improbable one; and the
excellence of the fruit and the importance assumed by
those who supplied it were deemed exceedingly good
evidence of the truth of the present story. When the
dealers had repeated their new tale for a certain number of years, there was not an individual in the island
who in the slightest degree suspected its veracity.

One more century, and no person had ever heard that any suspicions had ever existed.

The immediate agents of the Prince of the World could, of course, be no common personages; and the servants of the gardener, who some centuries before had meekly disclaimed the proffered reverence of his delighted customers, now insisted upon constant adoration from every eater of pine-apples in the island. In spite, however, of the arrogance of the dealers, of their refusal to be responsible to the laws of the country in which they lived, and of the universal precedence which, on all occasions, was claimed even by the shop-boys, so decided was the taste which the Vraibleusians had acquired for pine-apples that there is little doubt that, had the dealers in this delicious fruit been contented with the respect and influence and profit which were the consequences of their vocation, the Vraibleusians would never have presumed to have grumbled at their arrogance or to have questioned their privileges. But the agents, wearied of the limited sphere to which their exertions were confined, and encouraged by the success which every new claim and pretence on their part invariably experienced, began to evince an inclination to interfere in other affairs besides those of fruit, and even expressed their willingness to undertake no less an office than the management of the Statue.

A century or two were solely occupied by conflicts occasioned by the unreasonable ambition of these dealers in pine-apples. Such great political effects could be produced by men apparently so unconnected with politics as market-gardeners! Ever supported by the lower ranks, whom they supplied with fruit of the most exquisite flavour without charge, they were, for a long time, often the successful opponents, always the formidable adversaries, of the Vraibleusian aristocracy, who were the objects of their envy and the victims of their rapaciousness. The Government at last, by a vigorous effort, triumphed. In spite of the wishes of the majority of the nation, the whole of the dealers were one day expelled the island, and the Managers of the Statue immediately took possession of their establishments.

By distributing the stock of fruit which was on hand liberally, the Government, for a short time, reconciled the people to the change; but as their warehouses became daily less furnished they were daily reminded that, unless some system were soon adopted, the islanders must be deprived of a luxury to which they had been so long accustomed that its indulgence had, in fact, become a second nature. No one of the managers had the hardihood to propose a recurrence to horse-chestnuts. Pride and fear alike forbade a return to their old purveyor. Other fruits there were which, in spite of the contract with the market-gardener, had at various times been secretly introduced into the island; but they had never greatly flourished, and the Statue was loth to recommend to the notice of his subjects productions an indulgence in which, through the instigation of the recently-expelled agents, it had so often denounced as detrimental to the health, and had so often discouraged by the severest punishments.

At this difficult and delicate crisis, when even expedients seemed exhausted and statesmen were at fault, the genius of an individual offered a substitute. An inventive mind discovered the power of propagating suckers. The expelled dealers had either been ignorant of this power, or had concealed their knowledge of it. They ever maintained that it was impossible for pine-apples to grow except in one spot, and that the whole earth must be supplied from the gardens of the palace of the Prince of the World. Now, the Vraibleusians were flattered with the patriotic fancy of eating pine-apples of a home-growth; and the blessed fortune of that nation, which did not depend for their supply of fruit upon a foreign country, was eagerly expatiated on. Secure from extortion and independent of caprice, the Vraibleusians were no longer to be insulted by the presence of foreigners; who, while they violated their laws with impunity, referred the Vraibleusians, when injured and complaining, to a foreign master.

No doubt this appeal to the patriotism, and the common sense, and the vanity of the nation would have been successful had not the produce of the suckers been both inferior in size and deficient in flavour. The Vraibleusians tasted and shook their heads. The supply, too, was as imperfect as the article; for the Government gardeners were but sorry horticulturists, and were ever making experiments and alterations in their modes of culture. The article was scarce, though the law had decreed it universal; and the Vraibleusians were obliged to feed upon fruit which they considered at the same time both poor and expensive. They protested as strongly against the present system as its promulgators had protested against the former one, and they revenged themselves for their grievances by breaking the shop-windows.

As any result was preferable, in the view of the Statue, to the re-introduction of foreign fruit and foreign agents, and as the Managers considered it highly important that an indissoluble connection should in future exist between the Government and so influential and profitable a branch of trade, they determined to adopt the most vigorous measures to infuse a taste for suckers in the discontented populace. But the eating of fruit being clearly a matter of taste, it is evidently a habit which should rather be encouraged by a plentiful supply of exquisite produce than enforced by the introduction of burning and bayonets. The consequences of the strong measures of the Government were universal discontent and partial rebellion. The islanders, foolishly ascribing the miseries which they endured, not so much to the folly of the Government as to the particular fruit through which the dissensions had originated, began to entertain a disgust for pine-apples altogether, and to sicken at the very mention of that production which had once occasioned them so much pleasure, and which had once commanded such decided admiration. They universally agreed that there were many other fruits in the world besides pine-apple which had been too long neglected. One dilated on the rich flavour of melon; another panegyrised pumpkin, and offered to make up by quantity for any slight deficiency in *goût;* cherries were not without their advocates; strawberries were not forgotten. One maintained that the fig had been pointed out for the established fruit of all countries; while another asked, with a reeling eye, whether they need go far to seek when a God had condescended to preside over the grape! In short, there was not a fruit which flourished that did not find its votaries. Strange to say, another foreign product, imported from a neighbouring coun-

try famous for its barrenness, counted the most; and
the fruit faction which chiefly frightened the Vraibleusian Government was an acid set, who crammed
themselves with crab-apples.

It was this party which first seriously and practi-
cally conceived the idea of utterly abolishing the ancient custom of eating pine-apples.   While they
themselves professed to devour no other fruit save
crabs, they at the same time preached the doctrine of
an universal fruit toleration, which they showed would
be the necessary and natural consequence of the destruction of the old monopoly.   Influenced by these
representations, the great body of the people openly
joined the crab-apple men in their open attacks.   The
minority, who still retained a taste for pines, did not
yield without an arduous though ineffectual struggle.
During the riots occasioned by this rebellion the hall of
audience was broken open, and the miraculous Statue,
which was reputed to have a great passion for pine-
apples, dashed to the ground.   The Managers were
either slain or disappeared.   The whole affairs of the
kingdom were conducted by a body called 'the Fruit
Committee;' and thus a total revolution of the Government of Vraibleusia was occasioned by the prohi-
bition of foreign pine-apples.   What an argument in
favour of free trade!

Every fruit, except that one which had so recently
been supported by the influence of authority and the
terrors of law, might now be seen and devoured in
the streets of Hubbabub.   In one corner men were
sucking oranges, as if they had lived their whole
lives on salt: in another, stuffing pumpkin, like can-
nibals at their first child.   Here one took in at a
mouthful a bunch of grapes, from which might have

been pressed a good quart. Another was lying on the ground from a surfeit of mulberries. The effect of this irrational excess will be conceived by the judicious reader. Calcutta itself never suffered from a cholera morbus half so fearful. Thousands were dying. Were I Thucydides or Boccaccio, I would write pages on this plague. The commonwealth itself must soon have yielded its ghost, for all order had ceased throughout the island ever since they had deserted pine-apples. There was no Government: anarchy alone was perfect. Of the Fruit Committee, many of the members were dead or dying, and the rest were robbing orchards.

At this moment of disorganisation and dismay a stout soldier, one of the crab-apple faction, who had possessed sufficient command over himself, in spite of the seeming voracity of his appetite, not to indulge to a dangerous excess, made his way one morning into the old hall of audience, and there, groping about, succeeded in finding the golden head of the Statue; which placing on the hilt of his sword, the point of which he had stuck in the pedestal, he announced to the city that he had discovered the secret of conversing with this wonderful piece of mechanism, and that in future he would take care of the health and fortune of the State.

There were some who thought it rather strange that the head-piece should possess the power of resuming its old functions, although deprived of the aid of the body which contained the greater portion of the machinery. As it was evidently well supported by the sword, they were not surprised that it should stand without the use of its legs. But the stout soldier was the only one in the island who enjoyed the blessing of health. He was fresh, vigourous, and vigilant; they, exhausted, weak, and careless of everything except cure. He soon took measures for the prevention of future mischief and for the cure of the present; and when his fellow-islanders had recovered, some were grateful, others fearful, and all obedient.

So long as the stout soldier lived no dissensions on the subject of fruit ever broke out. Although he himself never interfered in the sale of the article, and never attempted to create another monopoly, still, by his influence and authority, he prevented any excess being occasioned by the fruit toleration which was enjoyed. Indeed, the Vraibleusians themselves had suffered so severely from their late indiscretions that such excesses were not likely again to occur. People began to discover that it was not quite so easy a thing as they had imagined for every man to be his own fruiterer; and that gardening was a craft which, like others, required great study, long practice, and early experience. Unable to supply themselves, the majority became the victims of quack traders. They sickened of spongy apricots, and foxy pears, and withered plums, and blighted apples, and tasteless berries. They at length suspected that a nation might fare better if its race of fruiterers were overseen and supported by the State, if their skill and their market were alike secured. Although, no longer being tempted to suffer from a surfeit, the health of the islanders had consequently recovered, this was, after all, but a negative blessing, and they sadly missed a luxury once so reasonable and so refreshing. They sighed for an established fruit and a protected race of cultivators. But the stout soldier was so sworn an enemy to any Government fruit, and so decided an admirer of the least delightful, that the people, having no desire of being forced to eat crab-apples, only longed for more delicious food in silence.

At length the stout soldier died, and on the night of his death the sword which had so long supported the pretended Government snapped in twain. No arrangement existed for carrying on the administration of affairs. The master mind was gone, without having imparted the secret of conversing with the golden head to any successor. The people assembled in agitated crowds. Each knew his neighbour's thoughts without their being declared. All smacked their lips, and a cry for pine-apples rent the skies.

At this moment the Aboriginal Inhabitant appeared, and announced that in examining the old hall of audience, which had been long locked up, he had discovered in a corner, where they had been flung by the stout soldier when he stole away the head, the remaining portions of the Statue; that they were quite uninjured, and that on fixing the head once more upon them, and winding up the works, he was delighted to find that this great work of his ancestor, under whose superintendence the nation had so flourished, resumed all its ancient functions. The people were in a state of mind for a miracle, and they hailed the joyful wonder with shouts of triumph. The Statue was placed under the provisional care of the Aboriginal. All arrangements for its superintendence were left to his discretion, and its advice was instantly to be taken upon that subject which at present was nearest the people's hearts.

But that subject was encompassed with difficulties. Pine-apples could only be again procured by an application to the Prince of the World, whose connec-

tion they had rejected, and by an introduction into
the island of those foreign agents, who, now convinced that the Vraibleusians could not exist without
their presence, would be more arrogant and ambitious
and turbulent than ever.   Indeed, the Aboriginal feared
that the management of the Statue would be the *sine
quâ non* of negotiation with the prince.   If this were
granted, it was clear that Vraibleusia must in future
only rank as a dependent state of a foreign power,
since the direction of the whole island would actually
be at the will of the supplier of pine-apples.   Ah!
this mysterious taste for fruit!   In politics it has often
occasioned infinite embarrassment.

At this critical moment the Aboriginal received information that, although the eating of pine-apples had
been utterly abolished, and although it was generally
supposed that a specimen of this fruit had long ceased
to exist in the country, nevertheless a body of persons, chiefly consisting of the descendants of the
Government gardeners who had succeeded the foreign
agents, and who had never lost their taste for this pre-
eminent fruit, had long been in the habit of secretly
raising, for their private eating, pine-apples from the
produce of those suckers which had originally excited
such odium and occasioned such misfortunes.   Long
practice, they said, and infinite study, had so perfected them in this art that they now succeeded in
producing pine-apples which, both for size and flavour,
were not inferior to the boasted produce of a foreign
clime.   Their specimens verified their assertion, and
the whole nation were invited to an instant trial.
The long interval which had elapsed since any man
had enjoyed a treat so agreeable lent, perhaps, an
additional flavour to that which was really excellent;

and so enraptured and enthusiastic were the great
majority of the people that the propagators of suckers
would have had no difficulty, had they pushed the
point, in procuring as favourable and exclusive a contract as the market-gardener of ancient days.

But the Aboriginal and his advisers were wisely
mindful that the passions of a people are not argu-
ments for legislation; and they felt conscious that
when the first enthusiasm had subsided, and when
their appetites were somewhat satisfied, the discontented voices of many who had been long used to
other fruits would be recognised even amidst the
shouts of the majority. They therefore greatly quali-
fied the contract between the nation and the present
fruiterers. An universal toleration of fruit was allowed; but no man was to take office under Government, or enter the services, or in any way become
connected with the Court, who was not supplied from
the Government depôts.

Since this happy restoration pine-apple has remained the established fruit of the Island of Vraibleusia; and, it must be confessed, has been found
wonderfully conducive to the health and happiness of
the islanders. Some sectarians still remain obstinate,
or tasteless enough to prefer pumpkin, or gorge the
most acid apples, or chew the commonest pears; but
they form a slight minority, which will gradually
altogether disappear. The votaries of pine-apple pretend to observe the characteristic effect which such
food produces upon the feeders. They denounce
them as stupid, sour, and vulgar.

But while, notwithstanding an universal toleration,
such an unanimity of taste apparently prevails
throughout the island, as if fruit were a subject of

such peculiar nicety that difference of opinion must necessarily rise among men, great fruit factions even now prevail in Vraibleusia; and, what is more extraordinary, prevail even among the admirers of pine-apples themselves. Of these, the most important is a sect which professes to discover a natural deficiency not only in all other fruits, but even in the finest pine-apples. Fruit, they maintain, should never be eaten in the state in which Nature yields it to man; and they consequently are indefatigable in prevailing upon the less discriminating part of mankind to heighten the flavour of their pine-apples with ginger, or even with pepper. Although they profess to adopt these stimulants from the great admiration which they entertain for a high flavour, there are, nevertheless, some less ardent people who suspect that they rather have recourse to them from the weakness of their digestion.

CHAPTER XV.

A S HIS Excellency Prince Popanilla really could not think of being annoyed by the attentions of the mob during his visit to Blunderland, he travelled quite in a quiet way, under the name of the Chevalier de Fantaisie, and was accompanied only by Skindeep and two attendants. As Blunderland was one of the islands of the Vraibleusian Archipelago, they arrived there after the sail of a few hours.

The country was so beautiful that the Chevalier was almost reminded of Fantaisie. Green meadows and flourishing trees made him remember the railroads and canals of Vraibleusia without regret, or with disgust, which is much the same. The women were angelic, which is the highest praise; and the men the most light-hearted, merry, obliging, entertaining fellows that he had met with in the whole course of his life. Oh! it was delicious.

After an hour's dashing drive, he arrived at a city which, had he not seen Hubbabub, he should have imagined was one of the most considerable in the world; but compared with the Vraibleusian capital it was a street.

Shortly after his arrival, according to the custom of the place, Popanilla joined the public table of his hotel at dinner. He was rather surprised that, instead of knives and forks being laid for the convenience of the guests, the plates were flanked by daggers and pistols. As Popanilla now made a point of never asking a question of Skindeep, he addressed himself for information to his other neighbour, one of the civilest, most hospitable, and joyous rogues that ever set a table in a roar. On Popanilla enquiring the reason of their using these singular instruments, his neighbour, with an air of great astonishment, confessed his ignorance of any people ever using any other; and in his turn asked how they could possibly eat their dinner without. The Chevalier was puzzled, but he was now too well bred ever to pursue an enquiry.

Popanilla, being thirsty, helped himself to a goblet of water, which was at hand. It was the most delightful water that he ever tasted. In a few minutes he found that he was a little dizzy, and, supposing this megrim to be occasioned by the heat of the room, he took another draught of water to recover himself.

As his neighbour was telling him an excellent joke a man entered the room and shot the joker through the head. The opposite guest immediately charged his pistol with effect, and revenged the loss. A party of men, well armed, now rushed in, and a brisk conflict immediately ensued. Popanilla, who was very dizzy, was fortunately pushed under the table. When the firing and slashing had ceased, he ventured to crawl out. He found that the assailants had been beaten off, though unfortunately with the total loss of all the guests, who lay lifeless about the room. Even the prudent Skindeep, who had sought refuge in a closet, had lost his nose, which was a pity; because, although this gentleman had never been in Blunderland before, he had passed his whole life in maintaining that the accounts of the disturbances in that country were greatly exaggerated. Popanilla rang the bell, and the waiters, who were remarkably attentive, swept away the dead bodies, and brought him a roasted potato for supper.

The Chevalier soon retired to rest. He found at the side of his bed a blunderbuss, a cutlass, and a pike; and he was directed to secure the door of his chamber with a great chain and a massy iron bar. Feeling great confidence in his securities, although he was quite ignorant of the cause of alarm, and very much exhausted with the bustle of the day, he enjoyed sounder sleep than had refreshed him for many weeks. He was awakened in the middle of the night by a loud knocking at his door. He immediately seized his blunderbuss, but, recognising the voice of his own valet, he only took his pike. His valet told him to unbar without loss of time, for the house had been set on fire. Popanilla immediately made his escape, but found himself surrounded by the incendiaries. He gave himself up for lost, when a sudden charge of cavalry brought him off in triumph. He was convinced of the utility of light-horse.

The military had arrived with such despatch that the fire was the least effective that had wakened the house for the whole week. It was soon extinguished, and Popanilla again retired to his bedroom, not forgetting his bar and his chain.

In the morning Popanilla was roused by his landlord, who told him that a large party was about to partake of the pleasures of the chase, and most politely enquired whether he would like to join them. Popanilla assented, and after having eaten an excellent breakfast, and received a favourable bulletin of Skindeep's wound, he mounted his horse. The party was numerous and well armed. Popanilla enquired of a huntsman what sport they generally followed in Blunderland. According to the custom of this country, where they never give a direct answer, the huntsman said that he did not know that there was any other sport but one. Popanilla thought him a brute, and dug his spurs into his horse.

They went off at a fine rate, and the exercise was most exhilarating. In a short time, as they were cantering along a defile, they received a sharp fire from each side, which rather reduced their numbers; but they revenged themselves for this loss when they regained the plain, where they burnt two villages, slew two or three hundred head of women, and bagged children without number. On their return home to dinner they chased a small body of men over a heath for nearly two hours, which afforded good sport; but they did not succeed in running them down, as they themselves were in turn chased by another party. Altogether, the day was not deficient in interest, and Popanilla found in the evening his powers of digestion improved.

After passing his days in this manner for about a fortnight, Popanilla perfectly recovered from his dyspepsia; and Skindeep's wound having now healed, he retired with regret from this healthy climate. He took advantage of the leisure moment which was afforded during the sail to enquire the reason of the disturbed state of this interesting country. He was told that it was in consequence of the majority of the inhabitants persisting in importing their own pine-apples.

CHAPTER XVI.

A FINANCIAL PANIC.

N HIS return to Hubbabub, the Chevalier de Fantaisie found the city in the greatest confusion. The military were marshalled in all directions; the streets were lined with field-pieces; no one was abroad; all the shops were shut. Although not a single vehicle was visible, Popanilla's progress was slow, from the quantity of shells of all kinds which choked up the public way. When he arrived at his hotel he found that all the windows were broken. He entered, and his landlord immediately presented him with his bill. As the landlord was pressing, and as Popanilla wished for an opportunity of showing his confidence in Skindeep's friendship, he requested him to pay the amount. Skindeep sent a messenger immediately to his banker, deeming an ambassador almost as good security as a nation, which we all know to be the very best.

This little arrangement being concluded, the landlord resumed his usual civility. He informed the travellers that the whole island was in a state of the greatest commotion, and that martial law universally prevailed. He said that this disturbance was occasioned by the return of the expedition destined to the

Isle of Fantaisie. It appeared, from his account, that after sailing about from New Guinea to New Holland, the expedition had been utterly unable not only to reach their new customers, but even to obtain the slightest intelligence of their locality. No such place as Fantaisie was known at Ceylon. Sumatra gave information equally unsatisfactory. Java shook its head. Celebes conceived the enquirers were jesting. The Philippine Isles offered to accommodate them with spices, but could assist them in no other way. Had it not been too hot at Borneo, they would have fairly laughed outright. The Maldives and the Moluccas, the Luccadives and the Andamans, were nearly as impertinent. The five hundred ships and the judiciously-assorted cargo were therefore under the necessity of returning home.

No sooner, however, had they reached Vraibleusia than the markets were immediately glutted with the unsold goods. All the manufacturers, who had been working day and night in preparing for the next expedition, were instantly thrown out of employ. A run commenced on the Government Bank. That institution perceived too late that the issues of pink shells had been too unrestricted. As the Emperor of the East had all the gold, the Government Bank only protected itself from failure by bayoneting its creditors. The manufacturers, who were starving, consoled themselves for the absence of food by breaking all the windows in the country with the discarded shells. Every tradesman failed. The shipping interest advertised two or three fleets for firewood. Riots were universal. The Aboriginal was attacked on all sides, and made so stout a resistance, and broke so many cudgels on the backs of his assailants, that it was supposed he would be finally exhausted by his own exertions. The public funds sunk ten per cent. daily. All the millionaires crashed. In a word, dismay, disorganisation, despair, pervaded in all directions the wisest, the greatest, and the richest nation in the world. The master of the hotel added, with an air of becoming embarrassment, that, had not his Excellency been fortunately absent, he probably would not have had the pleasure of detailing to him this little narrative; that he had often been enquired for by the populace at his old balcony; and that a crowd had perpetually surrounded the house till within the last day, when a report had got about that his Excellency had turned into steam and disappeared. He added that caricatures of his Highness might be procured in any shop, and his account of his voyage obtained at less than half-price.

'Ah!' said Popanilla, in a tone of great anguish, 'and all this from losing a lock of hair!'

At this moment the messenger whom Skindeep had despatched returned, and informed him with great regret that his banker, to whom he had entrusted his whole fortune, had been so unlucky as to stop payment during his absence. It was expected, however, that when his stud was sold a respectable dividend might be realised. This was the personage of prepossessing appearance who had presented Popanilla with a perpetual ticket to his picture gallery. On examining the banker's accounts, it was discovered that his chief loss had been incurred by supporting that competition establishment where purses were bought full of crowns.

In spite of his own misfortune, Popanilla hastened to console his friend. He explained to him that things were not quite so bad as they appeared; that society consisted of two classes, those who laboured, and those who paid the labourers; that each class was equally useful, because, if there were none to pay, the labourers would not be remunerated, and if there were none to labour, the payers would not be accommodated; that Skindeep might still rank in one of these classes; that he might therefore still be a useful member of society; that, if he were useful, he must therefore be good; and that, if he were good, he must therefore be happy; because happiness is the consequence of assisting the beneficial development of the ameliorating principles of the social action.

As he was speaking, two gentlemen in blue, with red waistcoats, entered the chamber and seized Popanilla by the collar. The Vraibleusian Government, which is so famous for its interpretation of national law, had arrested the Ambassador for high treason.

CHAPTER XVII.

A Pleasant Prison.

PRISON conveyed the most lugubrious ideas to the mind of the unhappy plenipotentiary; and shut up in a hackney-coach, with a man on each side of him with a cocked pistol, he formed the most gloomy conceptions of dark dungeons, confined cells, overwhelming fetters, black bread, and green water. He arrived at the principal gaol in Hubbabub. He was ushered into an elegantly furnished apartment, with French sash windows and a piano. Its lofty walls were entirely hung with a fanciful paper, which represented a Tuscan vineyard; the ceiling was covered with sky and clouds; roses were in abundance; and the windows, though well secured, excited no jarring associations in the mind of the individual they illumined, protected, as they were, by polished bars of cut steel. This retreat had been fitted up by a poetical politician, who had recently been confined for declaring that the Statue was an old idol originally imported from the Sandwich Isles. Taking up a brilliantly bound volume which reposed upon a rosewood table, Popanilla recited aloud a sonnet to Liberty; but

the account given of the goddess by the bard was so
confused, and he seemed so little acquainted with his
subject, that the reader began to suspect it was an
effusion of the gaoler.

Next to being a plenipotentiary, Popanilla preferred
being a prisoner. His daily meals consisted of every
delicacy in season: a marble bath was ever at his
service; a billiard-room and dumb-bells always ready;
and his old friends, the most eminent physician and
the most celebrated practitioner in Hubbabub, called
upon him daily to feel his pulse and look at his
tongue. These attentions authorised a hope that he
might yet again be an Ambassador, that his native
land might still be discovered, and its resources still
be developed: but when his gaoler told him that the
rest of the prisoners were treated in a manner equally
indulgent, because the Vraibleusians are the most hu-
mane people in the world, Popanilla's spirits became
somewhat depressed.

He was greatly consoled, however, by a daily
visit from a body of the most beautiful, the most accomplished, and the most virtuous females in Hubbabub, who tasted his food to see that his cook did his
duty, recommended him a plentiful use of pine-apple
well peppered, and make him a present of a very
handsome shirt, with worked frills and ruffles, to be
hanged in. This enchanting committee generally con-
find their attentions to murderers and other victims
of the passions, who were deserted in their hour of
need by the rest of the society they had outraged;
but Popanilla, being a foreigner, a prince, and a
plenipotentiary, and not ill-looking, naturally attracted
a great deal of notice from those who desire the
amelioration of their species.

Popanilla was so pleased with his mode of life, and had acquired such a taste for poetry, pine-apples, and pepper since he had ceased to be an active member of society, that he applied to have his trial postponed, on the ground of the prejudice which had been excited against him by the public press. As his trial was at present inconvenient to the Government, the postponement was allowed on these grounds.

In the meantime, the public agitation was subsiding. The nation reconciled itself to the revolution in its fortunes. The *ci-devant* millionaires were busied with retrenchment; the Government engaged in sweeping in as many pink shells as were lying about the country; the mechanics contrived to live upon chalk and sea-weed; and as the Aboriginal would not give his corn away gratis, the Vraibleusians determined to give up bread. The intellectual part of the nation were intently interested in discovering the cause of the national distress. One of the philosophers said that it might all be traced to the effects of a war in which the Vraibleusians had engaged about a century before. Another showed that it was altogether clearly ascribable to the pernicious custom of issuing pink shells; but if, instead of this mode of representing wealth, they had had recourse to blue shells, the nation would now have advanced to a state of prosperity which it had never yet reached. A third demonstrated to the satisfaction of himself and his immediate circle that it was all owing to the Statue having recently been repaired with silver instead of iron. The public were unable to decide between these conflicting opinions; but they were still more desirous of finding out a remedy for the evil than the cause of it.

An eloquent and philosophical writer, who entertains consolatory opinions of human nature, has recently told us that 'it is in the nature of things that the intellectual wants of society should be supplied. Whenever the man is required invariably the man will appear.' So it happened in the present instance. A public instructor jumped up in the person of Mr. Flummery Flam, the least insinuating and the least plausible personage that ever performed the easy task of gulling a nation. His manners were vulgar, his voice was sharp, and his language almost unintelligible. Flummery Flam was a provisional optimist. He maintained that everything would be for the best, if the nation would only follow his advice. He told the Vraibleusians that the present universal and overwhelming distress was all and entirely and merely to be ascribed to 'a slight over-trading,' and that all that was required to set everything right again was 'a little time.' He showed that this over-trading and every other injudicious act that had ever been committed were entirely to be ascribed to the nation being imbued with erroneous and imperfect ideas of the nature of demand and supply. He proved to them that if a tradesman cannot find customers his goods will generally stay upon his own hands. He explained to the Aboriginal the meaning of *rent;* to the mechanics the nature of *wages;* to the manufacturers the signification of *profits*. He recommended that a large edition of his own work should be printed at the public expense and sold for his private profit. Finally, he explained how immediate, though temporary, relief would be afforded to the State by the encouragement of EMIGRATION.

The Vraibleusians began to recover their spirits.

The Government had the highest confidence in Flummery Flam, because Flummery Flam served to divert the public thoughts. By his direction lectures were instituted at the corner of every street, to instil the right principles of politics into the mind of the great body of the people. Every person, from the Managers of the Statue down to the chalk-chewing mechanics, attended lectures on Flummery-Flammism. The Vraibleusians suddenly discovered that it was the great object of a nation not to be the most powerful, or the richest, or the best, or the wisest, but to be the most Flummery-Flammistical.

CHAPTER XVIII.

Trial and Acquittal.

THE day fixed for Popanilla's trial was at hand. The prince was not unprepared for the meeting. For some weeks before the appointed day he had been deeply studying the published speeches of the greatest rhetorician that flourished at the Vraibleusian bar. He was so inflated with their style that he nearly blew down the gaoler every morning when he rehearsed a passage before him. Indeed, Popanilla looked forward to his trial with feelings of anticipated triumph. He determined boldly and fearlessly to state the principles upon which his public conduct had been founded, the sentiments he professed on most of the important subjects which interest mankind, and the views he entertained of the progress of society. He would then describe, in the most glowing language, the domestic happiness which he enjoyed in his native isle. He would paint, in harrowing sentences, the eternal misery and disgrace which his ignominious execution would entail upon the grey-headed father, who looked up to him as a prop for his old age; the affectionate mother, who perceived in him her husband again a youth; the devoted wife, who could never survive his loss; and the sixteen children, chiefly girls, whom his death would infallibly send upon the parish. This, with an eulogistic peroration on the moral qualities of the Vraibleusians, and the political importance of Vraibleusia, would, he had no doubt, not only save his neck, but even gain him a moderate pension.

The day arrived, the Court was crowded, and Popanilla had the satisfaction of observing in the newspapers that tickets for the best gallery to witness his execution were selling at a premium.

The indictment was read. He listened to it with intense attention. To his surprise, he found himself accused of stealing two hundred and nineteen camelopards. All was now explained. He perceived that he had been mistaken the whole of this time for another person. He could not contain himself. He burst into an exclamation. He told the judge, in a voice of mingled delight, humility, and triumph, that it was possible he might be guilty of high treason, because he was ignorant of what the crime consisted; but as for stealing two hundred and nineteen camelopards, he declared that such a larceny was a moral impossibility, because he had never seen one such animal in the whole course of his life.

The judge was kind and considerate. He told the prisoner that the charge of stealing camelopards was a fiction of law; that he had no doubt he had never seen one in the whole course of his life, nor in all probability had any one in the whole Court. He explained to Popanilla, that originally this animal greatly abounded in Vraibleusia; that the present Court, the highest and most ancient in the kingdom, had then been instituted for the punishment of all those who molested or injured that splendid animal. The species, his lordship continued, had been long extinct; but the Vraibleusians, duly reverencing the institutions of their ancestors, had never presumed to abrogate the authority of the Camelopard Court, or invest any other with equal privileges. Therefore, his lordship added, in order to try you in this Court for a modern offence of high treason, you must first be introduced by fiction of law as a stealer of camelopards, and then being *in præsenti regio*, in a manner, we proceed to business by a special power for the absolute offence. Popanilla was so confounded by the kindness of the judge and the clearness of his lordship's statement that he quite lost the thread of his peroration.

The trial proceeded. Everybody with whom Popanilla had conversed during his visit to Vraibleusia was subpœnaed against him, and the evidence was conclusive. Skindeep, who was brought up by a warrant from the King's Bench, proved the fact of Popanilla's landing; and that he had given himself out as a political exile, the victim of a tyrant, a corrupt aristocracy, and a misguided people. But, either from a secret feeling towards his former friend or from his aversion to answer questions, this evidence was on the whole not very satisfactory.

The bookseller proved the publication of that fatal volume whose deceptive and glowing statements were alone sufficient to ensure Popanilla's fate. It was in vain that the author avowed that he had never written a line of his own book. This only made his imposture more evident. The little philosopher with whom he had conversed at Lady Spirituelle's, and who, being a friend of Flummery Flam, had now obtained a place under Government, invented the most condemning evidence. The Marquess of Moustache sent in a state paper, desiring to be excused from giving evidence, on account of the delicate situation in which he had been placed with regard to the prisoner; but he referred them to his former private secretary, who, he had no doubt, would afford every information. Accordingly, the President of Fort Jobation, who had been brought over specially, finished the business.

The judge, although his family had suffered considerably by the late madness for speculation, summed up in the most impartial manner. He told the jury that, although the case was quite clear against the prisoner, they were bound to give him the advantage of every reasonable doubt. The foreman was about to deliver the verdict, when a trumpet sounded, and a Government messenger ran breathless into Court. Presenting a scroll to the presiding genius, he informed him that a remarkably able young man, recently appointed one of the Managers of the Statue, in consequence of the inconvenience which the public sustained from the innumerable quantity of edicts of the Statue at present in force, had last night consolidated them all into this single act, which, to render its operation still more simple, was gifted with a retrospective power for the last half century.

His lordship, looking over the scroll, passed a high eulogium upon the young consolidator, compared to whom, he said, Justinian was a country attorney. Observing, however, that the crime of high treason had been accidently omitted in the consolidated legislation of Vraibleusia, he directed the jury to find the prisoner 'not guilty.' As in Vraibleusia the law believes every man's character to be perfectly pure until a jury of twelve persons finds the reverse, Popanilla was kicked out of Court, amid the hootings of the mob, without a stain upon his reputation.

It was late in the evening when he left the Court. Exhausted both in mind and body, the mischief being now done, and being totally unemployed, according to custom, he began to moralise. 'I begin to perceive,' said he, 'that it is possible for a nation to exist in too artificial a state; that a people may both think too much and do too much. All here exists in a state of exaggeration. The nation itself professes to be in a situation in which it is impossible for any nation ever to be naturally placed. To maintain themselves in this false position, they necessarily have recourse to much destructive conduct and to many fictitious principles. And as the character of a people is modelled on that of their Government, in private life this system of exaggeration equally prevails, and equally produces a due quantity of ruinous actions and false sentiment! In the meantime, I am starving, and dare not show my face in the light of day!'

As he said this the house opposite was suddenly lit up, and the words 'EMIGRATION COMMITTEE' were distinctly visible on a transparent blind. A sudden resolution entered Popanilla's mind to make an application to this body. He entered the committee-room, and took his place at the end of a row of individuals, who were severally examined. When it was his turn to come forward he began to tell his story from the beginning, and would certainly have got to the lock of hair had not the president enjoined

silence.   Popanilla was informed that the last emigration squadron was about to sail in a few minutes; and
that, although the number was completed, his broad
shoulders and powerful frame had gained him a place.
He was presented with a spade, a blanket, and a hard
biscuit, and in a quarter of an hour was quitting the
port of Hubbabub.

Once more upon the waters, yet once more!

As the emigration squadron quitted the harbour
two large fleets hove in sight.   The first was the expedition which had been despatched against the decap-
itating King of the North, and which now returned
heavily laden with his rescued subjects.   The other
was the force which had flown to the preservation
of the body of the decapitated King of the South, and
which now brought back his Majesty embalmed, some
princes of the blood, and an emigrant aristocracy.

What became of the late Fantaisian Ambassador;
whether he were destined for Van Diemen's Land or
for Canada; what rare adventures he experienced in
Sydney, or Port Jackson, or Guelph City, or Goodrich
Town; and whether he discovered that man might
exist in too natural a state, as well as in too artificial
a one, will probably be discovered, if ever we obtain
Captain Popanilla's Second Voyage.